Days of the River Rider

Days of the River Rider

The Journals of John Bearman

A Novel by David L. Fleming

TCU PRESS
Fort Worth, Texas

Library of Congress Cataloging-in-Publication Data

Names: Fleming, David L., 1951- author
Title: Days of the river rider : the journals of John Bearman / a novel by David L. Fleming.
Description: Fort Worth, Texas : TCU Press, [2026] | Includes bibliographical references.
Identifiers: LCCN 2025049187 (print) | LCCN 2025049188 (ebook) | ISBN 9780875659480 paperback | ISBN 9780875659497 ebook
Subjects: LCSH: Border patrol agents--Rio Grande (Colo.-Mexico and Tex.)--Fiction | Cattle--Quarantine--Texas--Fiction | Foot-and-mouth disease--Texas--Prevention--Fiction | Ranch life--Texas--Fiction | Big Bend Region (Tex.)--Fiction | LCGFT: Diary fiction | Western fiction | Romance fiction | Novels
Classification: LCC PS3556.L437 D39 2026 (print) | LCC PS3556.L437 (ebook)
LC record available at https://lccn.loc.gov/2025049187
LC ebook record available at https://lccn.loc.gov/2025049188

Cover photograph by Solomon Butcher. Courtesy of the Nebraska State Historical Society

TCU PRESS

TCU Box 298300
Fort Worth, Texas 76129
www.tcupress.com

For Gail

Contents

Acknowledgements

Robert Fleming for introducing his younger brothers to the beauties and mysteries of the Big Bend. Mike and Daryl Fleming for their suggestions in matters of plot. Dan Williams for giving me another run at the rapids of regional fiction. My wife Gail Fleming, who gave me the best compliment with this story that I ever got from her. She did not live to see the manuscript as a book, but it has her name on it. My daughters Bethany and Rebekah for sharing Big Bend adventures, both on the river and in the desert, and for being incredible women. Gail's uncle Butch for making me believe I had another book in me. Bethany's husband Mike Baker for graphics. Rebekah's husband Aaron Cook for shared memories of the Rio Grande. And thanks to Paige Gulley, my copy editor, who made the crooked places straight with her skill and insight.

Prologue

On the gravel ridge above the floodplain approximately 748 river miles from the mouth of the Rio Grande are the ruins of a River Rider's hut. Because of its elevation, the ruins are easily seen for several miles across the Flats along the river. Were it not for the twisting of the river and the thick growth of cane and salt cedar along its banks, anyone at the hut could see and be seen from many more miles distant.

The hut was built in 1943 to house a River Rider whose chief duty it was to patrol the Rio Grande and enforce the quarantine on South American cattle in an effort to stop the epidemic of foot-and-mouth disease *aftosa,* as it was called in Spanish. The quarantine was a joint effort by the American Inspection and Quarantine Division, Bureau of Animal Industry, Department of Agriculture, and the states of South America, where the epidemic started, flourished, and did much damage to American herds of the Southwest, beginning in the late 1920s. Teams of inspectors and veterinarians started a campaign to inform the population, destroy animals that were sick, or vaccinate healthy but exposed ones. If cattle were found to be infected, they were summarily shot and the carcasses were covered with quicklime and buried. In Mexico, the process was less efficient, while in Texas, a backhoe and bulldozer were kept just off the road north of Maravillas Canyon, and a trunk line had been run from the Stillwell Store to a point near Maravillas Canyon. The telephone was to be used for quick contact with county and federal officers under the supervision of Earl Fallis, Chief Patrol Inspector, Alpine, Texas, in case of an incident involving infected cattle on the Texas side of the river.

The River Rider was a man named John Bearman, about whom very little is known other than that he came to fill a need, did it well, and moved on. He was instructed to allow no cattle to cross the Rio Grande into Texas and mingle with Texas herds or to be moved across the border to be sold without first being inspected at government crossings. The quarantine was a serious financial matter to ranchers in Mexico and Texas alike. Along the Rio Grande in Mexico, unscrupulous cattlemen sometimes sought a quick market by moving infected cattle, and more than once, rifle fire exploded from the salt cedars as Mr. Bearman hazed Mexican cattle back into the river. Their message was clear: Leave our cattle alone. His message was equally clear: Your cattle are sick and not fit for human consumption. Keep them in Mexico.

The quarantine officially lasted from 1943 to 1956.

In 1976, a group of canoeists, exploring the ruins of the River Rider's hut, found a niche in the west wall just above ground level, hidden by a half-inch thick piece of flagstone cemented on edge. Weather or geology had caused the cement to crack and the flagstone to slip. In the niche was a metal box of the type used by machinists for drill bits. The box contained three silver certificate one-dollar bills, three Indian Head nickels, Bearman's pocket journal, several random sheets of notepaper tucked between the leaves, and two small rocks shaped like valentine hearts.

There are missing pages in the journal and the unexplained writing on the notepaper to consider, but the following is an extrapolation of facts to make a story out of the significant days of the River Rider.

The dollar bills and nickels remain a mystery, as do the heart-shaped rocks.

I

Near Persimmon Gap, April 1945

```
4/19/1945 Bucks Springs near P. Gap.
Moon, half, waning.
Garrisons doing well. On way to
Marathon.
Mules fine. No movement at Maravillas.
Mild, windy.
```

J. Bearman

The day John Bearman heard that Annie Tinsley was dying, he had arrived in Marathon, Texas, aboard his freight wagon, planning to file his report via telegram and stock up on food supplements for his animals, canned goods, coffee, and tobacco for himself. The report he sent to Cap'n Fallis in Alpine was mostly in code or shorthand to save expense and concerned movement of cattle along the Rio Grande, as well as the illegal crossings of nonresidents. For his own purpose, he kept a copy of his report in a bound pocket ledger, using the form of a diary and often including the date, moon phase, and weather.

He had spent the previous night at the Garrison ranch outside of Persimmon Gap, a rough halfway point in his fifty-six-mile trip to town, and helped Josh Garrison splash a mixture of Cooper-Tox on a serious but not infected wound in a young bull's left flank caused by, according to Josh, "The Great and Evil Who Knows What?"

"This stuff is for hoof thrush in horses," Bearman had reminded Josh. "It's a good pesticide. Let him have his head."

"You could just splash it on him, don't you think?"

"Swabbing is better. Let him have his head."

"It's not a horse, Josh."

Garrison was a patient man, older than Bearman by a score of years, and tolerated the dance the bull led them on before they could begin to doctor the cut and prevent screwworms from taking hold. Bearman, holding the rope around the bull's neck, wanted to snub the bull to a stout post or hog-tie it, but Garrison had his way, claiming the bull was a pet and that snubbing it would "wilden" the creature, making it harder to catch next time. It was Garrison's bull, after all. So, for a while, they followed the bull in tight circles in the dusty pen. Bearman, in the meantime, was amazed and amused by the tendency in some people to do things in the hardest way possible. Supper had been on the table half an hour before the two of them came in the house, dusty, smelling of hot bull and spilled Cooper-Tox.

At the table, Elvie Garrison, a short, stout woman who talked well and often, with a pleasing Southern accent, entertained Bearman with a story of their twelve-year-old's adventures trying to catch and tame kangaroo rats that seemed to have the ability to pass through walls at will, taking bait with them. Bearman knew she had probably told the story before. Until the news about Annie Tinsley and all that followed, there were not often new stories in that part of the Big Bend, where even the wind seemed a lonely thing.

They all agreed that perhaps eliminating the pests would be better than trying to tame the little varmints. When she finished, with a gentle laugh at her son's expense, Bearman, who was feeling the day's ride in his shoulders, forearms, and fists, remembered that when he first moved to his station on the Rio Grande almost three years before, he had observed that he might be too far out to be bothered by rats.

"They'll find you, John," Elvie had predicted, clearing the table.

"Probably," he had answered, but Elvie had been proven right.

Out on the covered porch before true nightfall, Bearman showed the boy, Arvin, how to make and set a Paiute deadfall mousetrap. Together they gathered the pieces, Bearman fashioning the sticks while Arvin found the necessary flat stones. The boy took the pieces into the house to show Elvie and then to the storeroom to set the trap with the rind of bacon she had given him. It took him several tries.

The two men smoked in silence for a while, then Josh, touched by his boy's enthusiasm over such a small thing, said, "Hope he gets one."

"He will," Bearman assured his friend, looking off into the darkness of the flat.

"How'd you come to know such a trap?"

"I've been hungry."

"Not while you worked for me."

"No. Elvie took care of that, bless her heart."

"How's the job going?"

"It's a lot of river to watch."

"Get lonesome out there? I've heard you're all the way down by Big Canyon."

"Bullets from across the river keep me company."

"So, beyond the fireworks, much trouble with that big ranch across the river?" Josh asked quietly.

Bearman tapped the dottle out of his pipe, then he said, "I may have to kill a man."

He made his cot on the porch after Josh had gone inside, and he watched the moon come up, two cycles from full. The dark, seemingly stove-in part reminded him briefly of fouled pumpkins in a patch of ground too wet back in the garden behind the house where he was raised. The house was now, like his parents, long gone. His family had farmed in East Texas, a land of trees and shade and close horizons. He preferred the vistas of the West, where a man could see from a distance what was coming his way. Sometimes.

The moonlit ranch was alive with animal movements, both from the corral and through and around creosote bushes beyond the yard on the flat where the spring was, and Bearman could track the course of a number of coyotes by their sporadic yips and howls—close, then farther away to the east. *Been at the spring*, he thought. He almost said the words out loud to his horse, Dollar-Five, which, neither tethered nor corralled, more like a faithful canine, had wandered close to the house, but Bearman was conscious his hosts might hear him through open windows and kept his musings to himself.

For a while yet, as the moon lost its color rising above the arid flat and making ghostly humps of the near and distant hills, he tried to think consecutively about what he had chosen for his life, his thoughts sometimes distracted by the nearby flurry of a bat or random images that broke into mental plans and wonderings, which eventually led him to think of Annie Tinsley, about whom he had not yet heard. He knew her baby was due anytime, had been for several weeks. He wondered about that, but could not imagine a likely order of events. She'd either had it, or she hadn't. She'd had it and she and the baby were well or they weren't. She'd either had it at the ranch or Tinsley took her to Alpine, but Bearman could not believe that a man even as inept as Morton Tinsley could subject his pregnant wife to a trip over that long rocky track up and down hills and through creek bottoms. It seemed to him that every time he traveled that road out from the river basin, he saw pieces of Tinsley's old Dodge amid the roadside rubble. When he had passed the Tinsley place at a distance on his way out, there seemed to be no one about.

He listened for the coyotes a while longer, then fell asleep.

II

Outlaw Flats, March 1943

```
3/16/1943 Arrived site middle of
afternoon. Weather sharp at night.
Moon 3 days past full. Comforts and
foodstuffs remain in wagons. Unloaded
block forms for adobe bricks.
Site level and well-chosen. Brothers
entertaining.
Can't help thinking about– [scratched
out] – train station in Marathon.
```

J Bearman

Looking back, the day John Bearman crossed the old Reagan Brothers ranchland to what would be his home and station, possibly for the next several years, was a significant day in his life and history. To most of the homesteaders in the Big Bend and residents of Marathon, John Bearman would become a mystery. Ostensibly, he had left the employ of Josh Garrison where he was a lonely fence rider to take on the equally lonely job of government River Rider, a minor official hired by the Department of Agriculture to patrol the Rio Grande basin. Bearman's secondary duties were to uphold the statutes and regulations of the State of Texas and to report infractions. No stranger to the Big Bend country, Bearman was a relative newcomer to the basin of the Rio Grande.

He had appeared along the river road that March day in 1943 with two county parolees from Alpine, brothers, and two wagons—one belonging to Bearman, wider than most and with rubber tires; the other a fifteen-foot spring wagon belonging to the brothers, Steve and Phineas, who preferred to be called Brother. The wagons were loaded between them with building supplies, a small wood heater and two-burner kerosene stove, minimal furniture, some books, and foodstuffs, mostly Heinz baked beans, flour, and lard. Bearman's guns included a .45 Colt's revolver and a treasured Model '92 Winchester his father had given him for his twenty-first birthday nine years before. It was the last gift he would ever receive from either parent, and he prized it among his possessions.

Using the topographical map provided, the three located the ridge the government had picked for its view south, almost as far as Maravillas Canyon, a long, narrow valley now called *La Vega de Los Ladrones* or Outlaw Flats by the locals. It was the only stretch of river not bounded on either side by canyons for a hundred miles either upriver or downriver and was a frequent crossing for Mexican ranchers who drove their cattle across the river to graze on precious Texas grass; smugglers avoiding the excise tax on bootleg whiskey now that Prohibition had been lifted, or the Mexican tax on wax made from candelilla plants; and, of course, outlaws from both nations, from whom the area got its name and reputation. The *Sierritas de Guadalupe*, the dominant mountain chain, well back from the riparian desert in Mexico, had an easily accessed pass. Though sparsely settled along the river in 1943, trespasses were frequent and serious. Outliers tended to keep a loaded rifle in a corner of every room in the ranch house.

For John Bearman, the location and job were an easy fit. Loyal to his country and to his commitment, he was determined to keep his assigned territory free of Mexican cattle in general and smuggled cattle showing signs of the disease in particular. Foot-and-mouth disease is highly contagious and would sweep through a herd in short order, rendering the meat unfit for human consumption. It was not uncommon to destroy an entire herd to keep the infection from spreading.

With the help of the brothers, both gifted stone layers, Bearman was to build a one-room hut, about ten by fourteen feet, from adobe bricks and native stone, of which there was an abundance for the picking. The adobe bricks they would make themselves. Due to the possibility of high winds, rafters would be cemented to the top of the rock walls and covered with metal. They were to frame in a door and one window opposite the door, facing the river. Finally, they would build a fire circle for cooking outdoors and a bench close by with piled rocks and flagstones on top. It was intended to be little other than a line camp, but it began to look like more than that. The county road grader had cleared a space for the hut and left a number of cement bags. Native materials were as close at hand as the toe of a boot.

When they had unloaded Bearman's simple furnishings from his wagon, the brothers joked about his Victrola and his box of books, which, although not great in number, were weighty and included Volume 28 of *Gammel's Laws of Texas, The Complete Works of Shakespeare* in one volume, *The Lincoln Library of Essential Knowledge*, several books of poetry, and the Bible.

"You going to read to the coyotes, Mr. Bearman?" Steve, the older brother, asked.

"The tarantulas," Phineas suggested.

"Maybe the mules."

"Hand me that box," Bearman said. "Reading to you two would be the same, whatever critter you picked."

"Reading," Steve said and rolled his eyes.

But the men were impressed and silenced the second night when Bearman cranked up his Victrola and played arias from *La Bohème* after supper when the evening sky had faded to a dark shroud lit with clouds of stars. It was a dreaming time, a remembering time, a time of thoughts and moods easily reflected in the light of the fire. Sitting out on the hillside on their cots in the cooling darkness smoking, Bearman told them the story of the poor poet and the ailing seamstress in Paris a hundred years ago.

At first the brothers listened in silence, but as the plot thickened and the plight of the lovers got more desperate, the brothers interjected heatedly with options anyone would choose in order to save his true love and "get themselves out of the danged mess they was in."

"Goshdarnit, don't you think so, Mr. Bearman?" Steve asked. "Goshdarn poets anyway—useless sons of bitches."

After that, they listened in silence, Bearman's horse close by, listening, too, and Bearman saw the younger brother wipe his eyes more than once. At one point in the recording, Steve flipped his cigarette into the fire with a spray of sparks and asked Bearman softly if he knew what the lady was saying, since the aria, *D'onde lieta uscì*, was in Italian.

"Does it matter?"

"Guess not. Poor girl."

"How does the story end?" the younger brother asked when Bearman lifted the needle from the record.

Bearman didn't have the heart to give them the details due to their naivete and his own experience with Annie Tinsley at the train station in Marathon four days earlier. Instead, he quoted Shakespeare. "A sad tale's best for winter."

"What the heck?"

"It ends badly."

"Then why do you like it so much to bring that Victrola all the way out here and listen to it over and over?" Brother asked.

"Why does a man live?" Bearman answered.

Steve cautioned Brother, "Don't answer that, and don't ask him nothing more."

Directly down the slope at the river's edge was a warm spring, which Bearman and his helpers walled in with rocks and cement. It was a patch job at best, and Bearman thought a windmill would be appropriate at the hut, with a water tank. When he shared his idea with the brothers, they laughed, as was their nature. They told Bearman there was small chance that anyone not under compulsion would be willing to haul pipe and mill and tank all the way out there for seven days of beans, jerky, and an occasional catfish. Having only begun their freighting business since their release from the jail at Alpine where they were briefly incarcerated for petit larceny, they accused Bearman of misleading them as to how far they would have to go to reach the building site.

"Where did you two grow up?" he asked them, ignoring their complaint.

"We was born in Alpine," Steve answered, setting aside an empty bean can and reaching for his tobacco after a healthy belch.

"But we lived on ranches wherever Pa could get a job," Brother said. "He was a farrier."

"Then you should know that there is no such thing as a short trip in this country."

Steve shook his head. "You win. Shuffle the cards."

Past the middle of the afternoon on the fifth day, they were sitting in the shade on the east side of the hut, resting. Once that wall was head high, it had already become a habit with them. Sometimes they napped. Sometimes they set trotlines. Sometimes they shot bean cans with their pistols, or, more accurately, Bearman did while the brothers shot rocks close to the cans.

"Close," Steve said once.

"Not even," Brother jeered.

"What did y'all do to be put in jail, anyway? If you don't mind my asking."

"How did you know about that, Mr. Bearman?"

"Man at the livery stable when I was waiting for you to show up."

"That old gossip," Steve said.

"We stole a wheelbarrow," Brother said.

"You didn't have to tell him that," Steve huffed.

"*That* wheelbarrow?" Bearman gestured toward the front of the hut.

"No, not that particular one," Steve said.

Brother said, "We'd been in town and had a good time, but a good time is the same thing as *too much* good time, if you know what I mean. It was cold as toes, and my brother was too drunk to walk home and too heavy to carry."

"Shut up."

"The hardware store was close by, so I broke in the back and got a wheelbarrow. It was dark as the inside of a rock, and I must have made enough noise to wake the old guy that owned the store. He lived upstairs. Hadn't gone fifty feet before the old guy came runnin' after us. He thought we was Indians."

"Mexicans," his brother said.

"No. I surely heard him calling us filthy Indians before we run into that ditch where the skunk was."

"What's the difference, Brother?" Steve wanted to know.

"Between what?"

"Mexicans or Indians."

"Well, a thing is either a thing or it's not."

"He thought we was Mexicans."

Bearman tried to picture their escapade, then said, "Let's get back to work. Don't make me have to pick up any more roofing nails out of the dirt."

"I don't think them nails like the roof," Brother said. "But that danged hammer sure likes my thumb."

"I seen Mexicans across the river when I was on the roof," Steve said.

Brother nodded. "Me too."

"Doing what?" Bearman asked, surprised they had only just then said anything. He had also seen horsemen and cattle across and upriver, not close but sometimes close enough to make out their curious faces. Back in the catclaw and huisache were crude brush huts, and Bearman had already seen the smoke of wax camps during the day and the faint wavering light of campfires in the distant night.

"I guess they was doing their business, but this one guy was some mighty curious."

That March, the Rio Grande flowed clear and deep in the pool below the hut, and each evening, the men would strip, wash their clothes, and bathe. The action of floating in the water was a tonic to overheated skin and sore muscles.

"How long can you hold your breath?" Brother asked on the seventh day.

"I don't know," Bearman said, shaving. He paused the straight razor under his chin. He was standing in the river up to his chest, moving slightly against the current, the pale skin of his body luminous in the water.

"Yo!" Steve said from the edge of the deep water. "Some little fish is trying to eat my peedinker."

"Come on, Mr. Bearman. Every kid tries to figure that out sooner or later."

"Been a long time since I was a kid."

"But you remember."

"About a minute."

"Steve there thinks he can breathe through his eyeballs." Brother laughed.

"Fact," Steve said, swimming closer. "A man's breathing apparatus is all connected in the head—mouth, nose, ears, and eyes. I figured out how to hold my eyes just right to breathe around them."

"Ever try it?" Bearman waded toward the ledge where they left their clothes on the hot rocks to dry.

"Once. I lasted two and a half hours."

"Then what happened?"

"I don't know. I drowned after a minute and a half."

Bearman smiled and shook his head while the brothers hooted and laughed at having set up Bearman with the joke.

"Check the trotline, otherwise it's beans again tonight," Bearman said. He finished shaving and climbed out of the river, the brothers following him.

Their laughter abruptly died at the thought of having beans again.

At the end of ten days, the two helpers left with the big wagon and four mules. Bearman made them promise they would return in about a fortnight with a load of hay, horse feed, four ten-foot pieces of one-inch galvanized pipe, fittings, a hand pump, and wire for a corral for the mules, which Bearman would hobble until then. Bearman was left with his own wagon, mercifully equipped with springs, the two mules, and Dollar-Five, whom he'd named in memory of a bet he had made with Annie Tinsley before he had left Marathon the same day he met the brothers. He had seen her standing in the shade of the train station platform in Marathon, and some hint of the woman she was reached out to him.

Aware that his horse had come to stand behind him, Bearman called after them, "Plan to stay a while when you come back."

"Oh sure," Steve said and laughed.

Brother began singing in a comic voice, *"Beans, beans, are good for your heart . . ."*

Bearman heard the song for at least a mile and a half, sung to the accompaniment of the rattling of the mostly empty wagon. Then it was *"O solo mio . . ."* until they topped the high hill and were gone, even as the dust of their passage. Satisfied she and the man were not going anywhere, Dollar-Five shook her mane and began to browse toward the river.

"*Goshdarnit.*"

III

Near the Mouth of Big Canyon, March 1943

```
3/28/1943 Sunday Afternoon. Half Moon
late. Men and cattle moving across
the river.
Cloudy, cold wind. Just
staring—remembering.
```

J Bearman

The day the pair left, Bearman felt the depth of his isolation, but it was not a new experience. As a boy, his mother had pitied him in a silent, watchful way because she could see already that he would be lonely as a man. She could not or did not pinpoint the origin of his inherent separation from others; she just saw that around other people, her son remained not aloof but alone. He was a reader and took joy in reading of strange times and strange lands. He could easily lose himself for an afternoon dwelling on some perplexity from another century. When approached, he always engaged, and peers, few as there were, tended to try to draw him out and enjoyed his company, but there was that something—maybe a "difference," maybe a uniqueness—that found him alone when the sun went down. There had been a girl about his age when he was ten with whom he was good friends, but she had died.

God had created them male and female, had made a helper, a perfect fit for man, but none for John Bearman, it seemed. Whatever it was that made him a man alone, had she been able to, she certainly would have cast it out.

Now, for a day and a half, he did very little except tend to his animals, arrange the inside of the hut, and find and pocket stray roofing nails that had caromed off the metal roof due to a misaimed hammer blow. Tired of homestead confinement due to necessary chores, he would leave his hillside and watch across the river, but the Mexican interest in his activities seemed to have died down.

After the first two days of that more or less idle acclimatization on the ridge above the river, John Bearman saddled Dollar-Five and explored his immediate territory. The first time he rode, he followed the incline of the ridge to the relatively flat top of a hill, almost a mesa. From that vantage point, he could indeed see, here and there, the upriver course of the Rio Grande for perhaps twenty miles and any disturbance of dust that rose across the Flats. He decided the top of the mesa-that-was-not-a-mesa would be a profitable observation point when cattle moved toward the river in the morning and trailed to familiar ground for the night.

Downriver marked the entrance of a spectacular canyon out of Texas, known unimaginatively but accurately as "Big Canyon." The walls of the canyon opposed equally high walls across the river, and the floodplain was reduced to ledges and boulders that acted as a barrier to further ingress along the water by foraging cattle. Only men would consider a crossing in the turbulent rapids. Bearman's riding would follow the southwestern trend of the river channel. Yet above him, the land rose into low mountains of solid rock and benches deceptively greened by creosote bushes.

The ridge had been established for two weeks before he had any real idea of what he had taken on as a defender of Texas land and law. Riding along the river, he was both cooled by its waters and cooked by the reflection of the sun off its sandy beaches where floods had scoured the bank free of river cane. He found random shade in the abundant but low-hanging pinnate leaves of catclaw, mesquite, and huisache, which in the spring was fragrant with golden blossoms that attracted bees and wasps alike. Twice he had hazed Mexican cattle free of symptoms across the river upstream from his rock hut. The first time there were three in a bunch, moving up from the water to graze on Texas grass. Dollar-Five quickly disabused them of that intention as Bearman rode halfway across the river to check for brands and signs of infection, which were absent, and to make certain the cattle did not come back.

Following the graded road on the way back to his camp, Bearman came upon a Mexican where the road dropped down across a deep cut before rising again on the other side. The man was effectively hidden from anyone not on either lip of the arroyo. He was standing beside two burros, their legs and bellies still wet. At Bearman's approach, the man took off his hat, and the burros shifted at Dollar-Five's aggressive movements. Bundles of raw wax were tied on the burros.

"*Hola, Señor,*" the man said.

Bearman nodded, then said, "*¿Cómo se llama?*"

The man said his name was Umberto Diaz; the Anglos called him Berto. He was waiting for a man coming in a truck to whom he would sell his wax.

"I see you many times when you build your *casita.* It is a good house, no?"

"You live across the river from me?"

"*Sí, y mi familia.* We make the wax."

"You pay the Mexican export tax?" There was no import tax.

"The tax?"

"The tax."

"*El jefe* give it."

"Who is your *jefe?*"

The man shrugged, and Bearman said, "Sorry, mister. You're going to have to wait on your side of the river."

"*No le hace,*" the man said, turning his burros. "*Adiós.*"

Bearman watched him cross the river, then rode back to his camp.

In lieu of the corral he had yet to build, Bearman hobbled his mules and appreciated their resignation, although in truth, they had little reason to wander. There was an abundance of grass along the hillside up from the river. Their temperament was unequalled in his experience for their disinterest in human beings. He had found horses and mules generally either to like human beings or to fear and dislike them, but the mules regarded him and any other man or woman with the same attention and deference as they would a fence post. Or maybe even less, due to the fact that a fence post of any real substance was rare in that country and might attract more than casual interest even from a mule. In short, the mules were neither friendly nor aggressive, but obedient and easily led, which made them worthy of their job, and Bearman, in turn, could neither like nor dislike them. In any case, they made for poor company.

Dollar-Five, on the other hand, needed no hobbles, for she was seldom out of eyesight or call. Even when Bearman went somewhere in the wagon, Dollar-Five would follow untethered or walk beside the mules as if evaluating their performance. She was an unusually intelligent and affectionate animal, and the bond between the man and the horse was so strong and so mutual that to describe it fully bordered on the sentimental, like something from a romanticized story. In the warmer weather, Bearman left the door to his hut open, and the horse would often stand halfway in, listening to the Victrola or to Bearman talk to himself, often asking the horse's opinion.

Dollar-Five's attention to Bearman was such that she seemed to strain toward understanding his words, sometimes tossing her head irritably and nickering as if to encourage Bearman to repeat himself. The word *rope* was a favorite of hers, and Bearman would play a game with the mare in which he would hide the rope, then call for it and send Dollar-Five in search of it. Somehow, she always knew where the rope was, so hiding it to avoid the game was no use. The game was after the manner of a trick, which Bearman disapproved of as demeaning to horses, but a man as much alone as he was yearned to be answered now and then, even if it was by a horse, although he never called for a rope in the presence of anyone else. At least not until the day he met Annie Tinsley.

But the mare's favorite and frequent moment was when, in a story or just for emphasis, Bearman would shout something that sounded like "Sho now!" but was, in reality, a barked and shortened form of the words "sure enough," which meant that whatever it was had reached the point of being enough. Bearman had learned the usefulness of explosive language when dealing with cattle and men. To Dollar-Five, it meant action was forthcoming, and the mare would stomp her right front hoof and snort and neigh.

As part of his job, Bearman had sought for and found the registered brands of ranchers along the river in order to identify them against the cattle from Mexican ranches. His own brand, a dollar sign over a five, more a memorial to an interlude at the railroad station in Marathon than a practical identifier, attracted the curious, of which there are always some. They discovered that the Dollar-Five brand was sure enough recently registered in Bearman's name, although he owned no cattle, not even sheep, just his horse. The two mules and the wagon were provided by the government as long as he needed them. One rancher mused, "I sure would like to see what kind of brandin' iron that guy uses to make a mark like that on a critter."

Within six months of his arrival in the Flats, Bearman had become known as "that guy." Men would talk about what they felt was his lack of real employment, even though they appreciated the need to contain Mexican cattle to the other side of the river. There was some debate among the idle skeptics about where he had come from and whether he was doing the job he was paid for, or if something else was going on instead. He would be seen coming or going around Marathon on his business, and people would say, "There's that guy," or, "That guy used to ride fence for Garrison," or, "I heard that guy was talking to Annie Tinsley."

Homer Hobart at the telegraph office would explain, "Just like always: once a month, every month, he comes to visit his Uncle Sam. Uh-huh." Sometimes, due to his reticence, which could lead others to consider him brusque, men would say, "Who does that guy think he is?"

To the few outlying ranchers, like the Garrisons, McKinneys, Rooneys, and Tinsleys who had watched the dust of his incoming caravan of supplies and had, in the years that followed, visited him on the ridge above the river, John Bearman appeared to be just a taciturn loner, capable and friendly without being intimate, and certainly the last person in the world who would kidnap a dying woman.

IV

Marathon, March 1943

```
3/15/1943 Monday. Weather fine. Moon 2
days from full, bright. Filed report.
Picked up wagons.
Met AT and [scratched out] long trip.
```

J Bearman

The day John Bearman first set eyes on Annie Tinsley, he had ridden his horse into Marathon to pick up his loaded wagon and rendezvous with the two brothers with their own wagon. The loaded wagon was at the livery, but the brothers, new to the freighting business, were absent, and double-checking the supplies in the two wagons against the bills of lading did not fill in the time.

"Ever heard of these people before?" Bearman asked the blacksmith.

"Been in business a few months. Used to be stone masons before they began hauling. Tried to name their outfit *Chianti* after the mountains down around Fort Davis, but they couldn't spell it. Their wagon has *Sheyantee* painted on the side. They tell people it's the name of an Irish selkie who fell in love with a fisherman who was a relative of theirs. Danged if I know what a selkie is."

"It's a mythological creature that can shift shapes from a seal to a beautiful woman."

"Then what happens?"

"You would have to ask them, Mr. Oliver."

"The women?"

"No, the brothers."

"They would most likely make something up. I heard they was in jail a few months ago. Don't know why."

Time passed. Bearman considered the road ahead and the amount of daylight left. His horse drowsed in the shade of the west-facing side of the livery, as it was still shy of noon, but she would occasionally shake her mane and look at him. Where the horse stood, ground hitched, she could see all kinds and lengths of rope, and she apparently had her own idea as to how to pass the time.

When Bearman heard the train pulling to a stop at the Marathon station, he told the blacksmith he would be back and called the mare whose name then was simply "Horse," and the two of them went up the street to see who got off. Rounding the station, he saw a young woman standing apart in the shade of the station platform, a carpetbag held with both gloved hands, wearing a brown corduroy split skirt, a white blouse topped with a red scarf or bandana, a short wool jacket, and an old-fashioned straw boater that made her seem like a figure from a Whistler painting, standing on a rocky point of the New England coast, looking out to sea, waiting for someone. He had never seen a Whistler painting like that, did not know where the comparison came from, but was sure that if there were such a painting, it would look like this woman, and Whistler would have painted it.

There were others on the platform; tradesmen, porters, drummers, the engineer, and the conductor, each going about his separate business, but Bearman had no eyes for them after a quick glance. The woman turned and looked at him as if he might be the person meeting her, since the waiting room was empty. It was clear to each that the other was neither known nor expected. Bearman was a little abashed by the curious force of her gaze, at the same time subtly encouraged by the way she held his own. The two of them realized a seemingly false sense of recognition. He rode past the platform in the fill between the building and the train, secretly urging the mare to prance, and disappeared around the far end.

When the woman had made sure she did not know this man, part of her felt vaguely disappointed by that fact. She moved closer to the elevated edge of the platform. Stirred and questioning himself, Bearman rode again into her sight. The attention she gave to his person and horse, and his handlings of the reins as he sat the double-cinched saddle caused him to stop. Face to face with her, he still believed she was a picture. He dropped the reins and dismounted, considering it rude to look down at her from horseback. Standing on the ground in front of her, they were nearly eye-to-eye.

"Hello, ma'am," he said awkwardly, as if speaking over a telephone. Something about her made *howdy* seem too artificial, although that was his usual form of greeting. He took off his hat. "Or should I have said miss?"

The woman tilted her head to one side, and the light fell on her smooth face and kindled a glow in her piercing brown eyes. Her expression was neutral, but there was the ghost of a smile on her lips, a challenge, a one-up.

"Maybe you should not have said anything at all."

Looking at her, completely seeing who she was and who she might be, Bearman felt an emotional ease and excitement he had never before experienced with a woman. He dropped his eyes to his hat and nodded. "A fool speaks many words while the wise remain silent."

"Is that my cue to stop talking?"

"I was spanking myself just then. Didn't you hear my mother's voice?"

"Did it sound huffy, as in compressed air escaping brakes?"

"No, ma'am or miss. Many things but never huffy. Does the choice of that word apply to the offence of my presence in your day?"

She again ignored his probe for information. Instead, she decided to put him on the defensive. Since it was obvious how proud he was of his horse, she decided to deny the obvious. She said, "I shouldn't think but what that is too much horse for you. She does not look sufficiently trained."

Bearman dusted off his hat and smiled. Beside him, the mare flicked her ears forward. Bearman had no idea what he was doing or saying. It was as if he were listening to one of his opera recordings and just following along.

"You being a judge of horses and men," he said.

"Some horses and some men."

"Present company excepted?"

She shrugged. "You know the tree by the fruit."

Bearman pretended to turn to his horse with a surprised look. He gathered the reins and looped the ends twice around the saddle horn. "Excuse me, ma'am or miss, but I left my rope at the livery."

"Better go get it," the woman said indifferently.

"No need. My horse will get it."

Bearman turned to his horse and said, "Rope!" The horse wheeled and trotted away toward town.

"Oh my," the woman said. "I believe you just lost that pretty mare."

"She's getting a rope. She'll be right back."

"I would be greatly surprised," the woman said, willing to back up her earlier assertion that she was a judge of horses and men, although now more than a little doubtful.

"Care to bet?"

"I'm not a betting person, thank you."

"You most certainly are."

She blushed. It was a dare, but so what? For the moment, she was far away from city streets, their implied neighborhoods, institutions, and imposed decorum. She reached in the pocket of her skirt and withdrew a wrinkled bill and a coin. "All I have with me is a dollar and five cents in change from lunch in Sanderson."

"Done."

"And what are you betting, sir?"

"I bet a ride on my horse against your dollar five."

"That sounds rather one-sided to me."

"Which side?"

Bearman heard a shout from down the street. They both looked in that direction. The woman half-hoped her ride, since he was already late, would be delayed just a bit longer.

"I believe someone is chasing your horse. She probably stopped in someone's yard and trampled the roses."

"Roses?"

"Those are flowers."

"Out here?"

They heard another shout, closer, and Bearman's horse walked up beside him and tossed her head, a length of coiled rope in her mouth, one end dragging in the dirt. The blacksmith was next, panting and frowning. "Your blasted horse stole one of my ropes."

The mare snorted and released the rope into Bearman's hand, who passed it to the blacksmith.

"She's not a blasted horse, and where would she go, with me here and the wagon down the street?"

"Well . . ."

"Find one and jump in it," Bearman suggested ungraciously and turned back to the woman, who had moved away, her cheeks reddened.

The blacksmith looked at the woman, then looked at Bearman and grinned. "So that's how it is," he said to himself and turned back to the stables. "Blasted horse, anyway."

Bearman had nothing against the man at that point in their dealings, but he resented the old gossip's knowing attitude and how it had embarrassed the woman. "Even a calm day can have a random gust in it," he said to her after the smithy was gone. "You owe me a dollar five."

The woman again took the money from her pocket and tendered it to Bearman. He did not want to take it, nor did he know why he asked for it. He did not want to continue the game they were playing, either, but already feeling stupid, he did not know how to stop the play.

She surprised him. "Good day, sir." She started toward the west end of the platform that faced the street.

"Wait."

She turned, her chin a little uptilted, her eyebrows raised.

"I don't really want your money."

"I am not a welsher."

"I don't believe I've ever heard a woman use that word before."

"Nevertheless," she said, suppressing a smile. Seeing the street empty except for the departing blacksmith, she stepped back into the shade.

Bearman felt as wanted as ditchwater to someone with a full canteen. "Staying in Marathon?" he asked.

"As if you had a right to ask such a personal question."

"Is that a yes?"

"No."

"Alpine?"

"Why would I leave the train here?"

Bearman tried one more time. "Close by?"

She paused and looked at the uninteresting side of a Pullman car. "I have a place along the river. *We* have a place on the river."

"That river?" Bearman asked, nodding toward the south. He chose to pretend he did not hear the plural pronoun. It could mean anything.

"Is there another hereabouts?"

Bearman whistled softly. "Pardon me for saying so, but you don't seem the Western type," Bearman observed, fishing for more information.

"I do not believe you know me well enough to say that, nor I you, to answer it," the woman said in a level voice that, with rising color on her cheeks, betrayed real offense. She took a step toward him as if she wanted to strike him.

Bearman liked that. "It is true I do not know you, having never seen you before, except maybe once in a sunset on an October evening when I was seventeen, but I do know one thing about you for certain."

"What could it be? Let me count the ways. Hmm . . . nothing."

"You still want to ride my horse."

"I lost the bet, remember?"

"I tricked you."

"Then give me back my dollar and five cents, cheater."

"Tricky, maybe, but I am not a cheater. And I'm keeping your dollar five, because I like the sound of it."

"There is no sound to a paper bill and a single coin."

"I like the sound of the words."

"You must be easily pleased."

"You must not be."

Again, there was that slight movement toward him. Bearman smiled. It was a disarming smile, and it disarmed her.

"How about it, ma'am or miss?"

The woman hesitated, now both wishing her ride would come and wanting him to be delayed yet a bit longer. She was aware that she and this audacious man were playing a game, and she wanted to see how it ended. She felt a concession would put her behind.

"You know you want to."

She did, but still hesitated. "What's her name? You do name your animals, do you not?"

"I've been calling her Horse, but I think from now on, I'll call her Dollar-Five."

"Smug. Presumptuous."

"No, ma'am or miss, but because of the memory of a bright spot in a dull morning."

He unloosed the reins from the saddle horn and held them toward her.

"Will she take me away from annoying people?"

Bearman looked up and down the platform. "I don't see any of those."

"I have a mirror in my bag."

"You will never need it."

"I am expecting to be met."

"My name is John Bearman, and I am glad to meet you."

"Will you hold my bag?"

"No. But I'll watch it for you."

Bearman stepped to the edge of the platform where the mare waited, and when the woman followed, he took her carpetbag and set it down beside him. He gave her the reins, and the mare looked at him.

"You'll wrinkle your skirts, I'm afraid. I didn't think of that."

"I have others," she said over her shoulder.

The woman led the mare along the platform until it was abreast the planking, then she stepped into the nearer stirrup and swung a long leg over the saddle. The mare trembled a little at the feel of a new and tentative rider, but Bearman calmed both horse and rider with a word, and off they cantered along the platform and around the end of the building out of sight. Bearman was fascinated both by the woman's nerve and her posture in the saddle. *Maybe not a Whistler*, he thought. *Maybe a Russell.* Whichever or whoever, she would be worthy of the paint. The other men on the platform, away from the waiting room, might have agreed. They, too, stopped and watched the woman in the old-fashioned boater ride the bay mare.

After she had gone, Bearman had a brief interval in which to consider what he was doing, but no clear conclusion came to him except that this was a woman unlike any he had ever known and that her presence charged him with happiness.

When she returned, she brought the mare to a stop with a light rein and dismounted before Bearman had a chance to help her. Standing in the gravel, she gathered the reins and stepped to the edge of the platform with her right hand raised. Bearman took it and lifted her onto the platform. He thought later that no hand he had ever taken had felt like hers. She handed him the reins reluctantly and smiled. Her boater was slightly askew and feathers of brown hair fell in soft wings along her cheeks. Her face was flushed with the knowledge of her own daring and the exercise of the ride. She had seen no sign of anyone approaching the station in an automobile.

She said, "I have never done anything like that before in my life, Mr. Bearman."

"You ride well, though."

"I wasn't referring to the ride. I have ridden horses all my life. I meant . . ." She broke off and looked away. "You must think I am a very forward woman."

"Would that be so terrible?"

Bearman took the reins, then dropped them and put his hand along the mare's jaw. He knew then that the game they had been playing was over.

The woman looked at him seriously for a moment. "Not for you, I think. I think you would understand it."

She continued looking at him while he stood earnestly watching the changes in her face. She dropped her eyes, then looked to the side, toward the end of the station house. At the same time, they both reached downward for her carpetbag. Bearman held the handle until they stood face to face again. The woman seemed embarrassed now, almost ashamed of herself. It made Bearman uncomfortable. When a couple from town rounded the corner and stepped up on the platform on their way to receive or send a telegram, the woman started and stepped away.

Bearman felt a slight dismay. He could tell the woman regretted talking to him.

"Change your mind about the horse?" he asked lightly, trying to help them both.

She followed his gaze. "Yes. She loves you. She's like a pet but more than that—like a human soul trapped in the body of a horse." She stopped. Her voice was constricted by an emotion Bearman could sense but could not name.

There was a pause. She looked down and shook her carpetbag for emphasis.

"I really must—" she started. She looked at Bearman, a brief glance. "I'm afraid I must go. I must ask someone. My . . . ride should have been here before now."

"I don't loaf around train stations waiting to pick up pretty girls," Bearman said quietly. "I was waiting on a couple of men to help me haul supplies out to my place by the river. They were late, and I was getting bored, so when I heard the train pull in, I came to see who got off. It's a part of what I get paid for."

The woman fidgeted with the handle of her carpetbag, and Bearman stopped. Then when she looked up, he said, "When I saw you, I guess I was putting on a show. You bested me, though. I don't mind saying that."

She shook her head. "I'm not like this, either."

"Well, don't regret it."

"I don't want to. Only, it feels strange. I don't know you."

"You know more about me than I know about you."

"I suppose so. My name is Annie Tinsley. If you live along the river, we may be neighbors, if such a thing is possible in this part of the country. We have a ranch near Maravillas Canyon." She blushed and dropped her eyes. "My husband is Morton Tinsley. Do you know him?"

Bearman called "come here" to the mare with a snick and caught up the reins. He looked at the saddle she had sat upon and marveled again at her poise and balance.

"I know him," Bearman said, nodding over his shoulder. "He just pulled up."

A porter had taken Annie's trunk from the train and now approached her with a receipt. His name was Jebby, and Bearman had known him since his days of working for Josh Garrison. "Your trunk over there Miz Tinsley, whenever you ready to claim it. Be sure say hello to Mister Morton for me if we have to go on."

"I will, Jebby," she said, reaching in a pocket of her skirt, but the dollar bill and the nickel were gone.

"Allow me," Bearman said and tipped Jebby a silver dollar.

"Most gracious, Mister John!" Jebby said. He touched his cap and walked away down the platform, humming "Someone's In The Kitchen With Dinah."

With a murmur of slight protest, Annie Tinsley turned to look for her husband, who had stopped their Dodge too far from the station and was climbing back in to move it closer. His lack of depth perception was familiar to all who knew him and made him a terrible driver and a poor hunter. When she turned back to Bearman, she saw that he had mounted Dollar-Five and was already starting forward.

She spoke a word softly, knowing or hoping he would not hear her.

As he passed her, he touched the brim of his hat without looking at her. He rode back to the livery stable where two Black Irish brothers were playing horseshoes in the dust, and he did not again look back up the street.

"Ma'am."

V

Outlaw Flats, October 1943

```
10/13/1943 Mon., Hunter's moon.
Afternoon. Rode south. Mexican herd
of 28, counting calves. Scrub cattle
Brand Omega.
Killed rabid bull. Zebu. Met Mexican
rider for Rancho Ornelos. Marcos
Pulaski. Armed. Took away old Iver
Johnson pistol. Cattle drifted back
across river. Burned bull. Pulaski
friendly?
```

The day the hostilities with the Emilio Ornelos ranch began, John Bearman saddled Dollar-Five with the intention to investigate the unoccupied Taylor farm, which had comprised roughly one hundred and sixty acres of bunch grass, lechuguilla, mesquite, and low banks along the river where Rueben Taylor had planted corn, beans, and chili peppers, which he sold along both sides of the river until old age and near blindness caused him, his wife, and his oldest daughter to pack up and move to Del Rio.

This was before Bearman had come to the river, but Bearman had heard about them from Josh Garrison. They were well-liked and respected. Taylor had never had a single ear of corn stolen out of his field in all the years he farmed in that hungry country. The wild animals, including feral donkeys, were not so respectful.

Presently, the inhabitants along the river in the business of rendering wax from candelilla plants got their few supplies from a village store located on the flat across the river from Bearman's camp. Either that or they made the long trip to La Linda upriver, where the price for raw wax was higher.

The walls of the Taylor adobe were still standing, but the roof had caved in, and pieces of seventeen-foot metal roofing had either been blown away in a windstorm or were salvaged for the roof of a cowshed by someone living up or down the river. There was a spring of warm water there, across the river from the old homestead that Bearman wanted to investigate, and it was a perfect fall day in the Big Bend country along the river where the ash and mesquite were losing their foliage, and the river cane was topped by golden tassels a foot and a half long. It was mildly hot in the sun and cool in the shade. The mixed fragrance of the season was in the air.

The day made Bearman want to sing, but he talked instead.

"Tell you what, Dollar-Five, if I was a young man, I'd try to get the deed to some of this beautiful worthless country and settle down."

Dollar-Five switched her ears around and shook her head. She was still getting used to her new name.

"I know. I have a place and a purpose, but that hut isn't exactly a home in which a man can walk from one room to another with windows and such in each one. And Elvie Garrison was right. The mice have found me, but they have yet to gnaw inside my food locker. Had to string a wire for my clothes or pieces of them would be in every nest this side of the river.

"Well, don't act so bored. How would you like those little critters gnawing on all your tack?"

Dollar-Five responded to the question mark with a shake of her mane.

"Let's climb this hill and see what we can see."

What he saw was a small bunch of rangy cows, some with calves, grazing on a bench covered in Bermuda grass. Though they were in various colors and sizes, they looked stunted and inbred. He figured the average weight of the cows was less than nine hundred pounds, although they appeared full grown. He had seen cows of this type across the river, but up close they looked worse. Dollar-Five was restless in the face of that many cows, as if every riparian acre on the Texas side of the river belonged solely to her and her master. She tossed her head as if in disgust. The cows regarded them through dull eyes, still chewing, and continued grazing. Bearman could see their brands were all the same: the Greek letter omega. It was a Mexican brand.

"Steady, Dollar," Bearman cautioned. "Something's not right. Mexico cattle. A man on a horse usually means roundup. These aren't a bit afraid of us. That means a man on a horse is a herdsman, leading them to green pastures. Don't act like you don't know what that is. Let's get a count and see if we can convince these interlopers to go home."

Dollar-Five tossed her head again, and Bearman used a saddle movement to indicate she was to go forward. As he urged the mare among the cows, he pulled his journal from his breast pocket and noted the place and date. He then counted the cows, including the stunted yearlings. On a whim, he dismounted to judge the reaction of the cattle to a man on foot. The cattle became skittish, drifting more directly toward the river. *Herded, but not close*, he concluded.

He had just finished and was moving away from the cows to better head them to the river when a Zebu bull crashed through the brush and cane and snorted to a stop at the edge of the clearing with its forehooves spread and its jaws dripping strings of saliva. Imported from Brazil and generally believed to be the cause of the foot-and-mouth epidemic, the bull towered above the scrubs. Startled, the cows trotted a few feet, then stopped and looked at the bull, which began to toss its head, throwing strings of saliva across its hump and pawing definite grooves in the sandy soil. Bearman was surprised that an unprovoked bull would act in such an aggressive manner, especially if it were, as he suspected, used to being herded, unless it was sick or hurt. But this was no victim of foot-and-mouth, despite the similar symptoms.

Bearman knew the bull was about to charge him and his horse, but he did not remount. He wanted to know if the bull was blind. Taking in his hand the loops of his lariat from the saddle horn, he left Dollar-Five and ran at the bull. Having never been attacked by a man afoot, the bull hesitated. Bearman shouted something that sounded like "*Sho now*!" and turned without slowing to do so. Dollar-Five was waiting, not even trembling, and leaped to Bearman as the bull charged them both. Bearman threw himself in the saddle, said, "Go on!" and Dollar-Five carried him out of the clearing into the brush with the bull rocking his fury behind them, the dust of horse and bull a cloud in the still air.

Bearman had discovered that bulls, like bees, would often chase a man just so far, usually to the edge of their territory, then quit, but as he rose with the landscape, the bull was still following, threateningly close. Bearman drew his pistol and turned in the saddle to see the bull coming at him like an earthmover breaking new ground. He fired at the bull's forelegs, trying not to hit the maddened bull. He fired again to no avail. Making the elevation, he turned Dollar-Five across a flat. They outpaced the bull, and as the distance between them increased to about eighty yards, the bull slowed down, trotted in a circle sniffing the air, and finally stopped. Dollar-Five was having a good time, but the bull was spent. It stood unsteadily, its great dirty white flanks expanding and shrinking with each rasping breath, gobs of ropey saliva flecking its jaws and dripping wherever it turned its head. It roared again and pawed the earth while the dust they had raised settled on the brush and grass, brown from the seasonal drought that followed the rains of July and August.

"That bull's sick and half blind," Bearman said. "Let's go look."

Bearman rode in a wide circle. The bull now seemed to be only barely aware of the horse and rider. It stood heaving there in that landscape made for passing through. As he moved to the bull's left, Bearman saw the angry gash in the bull's side and underbelly. It was crawling with infection. The screwworms had found the wound, but Bearman did not think this accounted for the rage, fearlessness, blindness, and drooling. The bull watched him without seeming to comprehend him. It extended its neck to roar again then seemed to choke.

Rabies, Bearman thought and drew his Winchester from the saddle scabbard with every intention of putting the bull down then and there. He backed Dollar-Five, who had scented the disease of the bull and wanted to get farther away. When they were in front of the bull, which was now looking back toward the river, Bearman levered a cartridge into the chamber and put a bullet between the bull's horns. It staggered. The 38-40 round was small for a crazed bull. He slid the rifle back in the saddle scabbard without ejecting the spent shell and rode close enough to use his .45 Colt's. It took two rounds. The bull dropped.

A horseman, secretly watching, suddenly rode out of the brush upriver and topped the rise where Bearman sat his horse. Bearman tensed in surprise. It was a settled fact in Bearman's mind that anyone he encountered on his patrol was a threat. He holstered his pistol, unwilling to provoke the man from that distance, and waited to see what the man would do. For a minute or two of mutual appraisal, they faced each other silently across that landscape. The bull's carcass lay between them.

The stranger nudged his horse closer. Bearman could see that he wore a revolver on his right hip, but he held the reins in his right hand, his left resting open on his thigh. Dollar-Five pointed her ears forward and stamped her right hoof.

The man studied the bull, its nervous system slowly burning itself out, then turned his attention to Bearman. "*Hola,*" he said. "*¿Cómo está?* You have killed the dangerous bull."

Bearman did not respond or move. Dollar-Five stood poised for action against this strange human on his ugly gelding. Bearman waited.

"I was looking for that bull, *Señor,*" the man said.

"Your bull was sick to the point of death. He had rabies."

"Rabies? What, he is a dog to get rabies?"

"He had a wound on his flank. He fought something that was sick. But that's not the problem. The problem is that your sick animal was on this side of the river."

"The river?"

Bearman eased Dollar-Five closer to the man, passing the dead bull. He had dealt with this man's kind of behavior before. It was an act of innocence and incomprehension.

"What are you doing here?"

"I look for the bull," the man nodded toward the clearing they had left.

"Whose ranch?" Bearman demanded.

"*¿Cómo*?"

"Whose cows? Yours?"

"The cows?"

"Move, Dollar-Five," Bearman said as he touched his heels to the horse's withers and in a heartbeat crossed the intervening space beside the other horse, stirrup to stirrup with the Mexican. Crowding the man further, Bearman drew his Colt's and pushed it into the man's side. The move was swift and so perfectly executed that the Mexican was not only surprised but also impressed.

"Hand over that pistol," Bearman ordered, nodding at the Mexican's hip. Up close, Bearman could smell woodsmoke and sweat on the man's clothes. Taking the pistol from the stranger, he put it in his own holster, and still holding his Colt's on the Mexican, he said, "I asked you a question. You got a straight answer, make it. I don't favor being played with."

"*¿Quién es, usted*?" the man asked, the false cheerfulness gone from his voice.

"I'll tell you who I am," Bearman said, still crowding the man, who muttered, "*¡Cuidado, hombre*!" and tightened his grip on the reins. Bearman grabbed the bridle of the other man's horse to hold him close while Dollar-Five maintained the contact by sidestepping.

"I'm the man sent down here by the United States government to ride this river and keep infected skunk cattle like those back yonder on the other side. I need to know whose cattle they are right now or I'll confiscate them, telegraph the sheriff in Alpine to send a trailer to haul them away, and you or your boss can go to Alpine and pay the fine and the fee, or the scrubs will be inspected and auctioned off and the money kept. Either that, or I exercise a court order to shoot them. You *comprende*, or are you going to play the dumb Mexican, which won't work anymore, not since Villa attacked Columbus, New Mexico, twenty-seven years ago. My only uncle died in that raid."

The Mexican considered him. He had watched the building of this man's hut from across the river and wondered about his character. On still nights, he heard the music and stepped away from his companions to pause on the river's edge to listen, moonlight on the water. He had wondered at the kind of man the newcomer was. Meeting Bearman for the first time, he felt a kinship with a man who could have such music in such a distant place. He did not, however, like how fast or blunt he was. Even so, he admitted the *gringo* had bested him.

"Talk, Mister. These your cows or someone else's?"

"Not mine."

"They're not mine either, but that doesn't tell me anything I want to know. Are you alone?"

"*Sí.*"

"I don't walk past liars."

"No, *Señor*, I am not lying. The cows belong to the Ornelos Rancho."

"Brand like the letter omega?"

"The what?"

With the barrel of his Colt's, Bearman traced an upside-down horseshoe with curled ends. "Like that?"

"*Sí.*"

Bearman let go of the bridle and moved Dollar-Five back a step. "Where is that?"

"Across the river and over the pass in the *Sierritas de Guadalupe*. I am sometimes a herdsman to watch the cows."

"Which means you bring them over and take them back."

"*Sí.*"

Bearman briefly considered the cows he had seen. "How can you ranch with such sorry-looking stock?"

"There is always a market for anything. The *vacas* are poor, but sometimes nature is not kind, and geography is a curse. Where will nature not find you, and where is the place of security?"

Bearman shook his head at the speech and demanded, "What is your name?"

"My name is Marcos Pulaski."

"Pulaski? True?"

"*Sí*. My mother is Mexican. In the revolution which you speak of, not to our credit, things got mixed up as between men and women. My father was Anglo."

"Why did you pretend to be stupid?"

"Frustration can wear down the resolve of an enemy."

"And you ride for a big ranch across the river?"

"*Sí*."

"I've got a count for my report. You can take your stock back across the river and keep them there. Any cattle out of Mexico fall under the quarantine. Does this bunch show any sign of the foot-and-mouth?"

"Not this bunch."

"True?"

"*Señor*, you keep questioning my honor. If you do not believe me, give back my pistol, and we'll see who is truthful. No sickness in this bunch. The cows will wander in such a dry place as this desert. It is natural."

"A river has two sides. Keep them on yours. *Adiós*."

"Wait, *Señor*. What about my bull? There is reparation? That *hombre* was no scrub. The *jefe* will not be happy to lose that one."

"The bull was trespassing, like you are. He could infect every cow in that bunch. In fact, there may be others right now sick from this bull."

"How are you called?" the man asked, again stopping Bearman, his tone different, confidential.

"John Bearman."

The man nodded. "Then I tell you something, *Señor* Bearman. It is very, very secret. I, too, work for the government, the government of Mexico. They send me to watch the Ornelos Rancho. *Señor* Ornelos try to make money moving infected herds to Texas with no inspection. I am trying to stop him while I work for him."

"A spy," Bearman said with disapproval.

"*Señor*, put dishonor out of your thinking. This man sent infected cattle to my village over the mountain. The men do not know. They milk the cows, butcher others. The children get the *aftosa*, very sick. Their mothers cry. The men stand together in the dark smoking. What can they do? The evil has already happened."

Bearman took a long breath. He knew how deep the wound of a lost loved one was, but he did not ask Pulaski for any details.

"If I run into trouble with Mr. Ornelos, where would you stand?"

Pulaski nodded his head at the possibility. "I am bound by my mission and the cries of my children. I will help you, but I cannot be caught."

Bearman gave Pulaski a long slow look. He noted every detail of the man's face and posture. Pulaski was of medium height, slender, with an intelligent face and piercing eyes. Bearman decided to believe him. "If you speak the truth, we want the same thing," Bearman said, then he added, "I had no way of knowing you were an agent, Mr. Pulaski."

"*No le hace*. But tell me: the music you have. What is it called?"

"I have arias from *La Bohème,* an Italian opera."

"It is very beautiful but very sad. I sometimes come to the river to listen with my daughter, and I hear the voice of another woman inside the singing. Is it so for you?"

"It is music."

"How can you stand it? No. Do not answer that question. You do not have to. Thank you for bringing it to this place of conflict."

Bearman touched his hat in farewell. "You know that bull had to be put down."

"*Seguro*. I was searching for it to put it down. But what about my pistol, eh?"

"I'm keeping it for a while."

"I could have need of it."

"Not today. Looks better if I keep it. Come by my hut sometime when I am riding. It'll be on a shelf just inside the door."

"Then some other day. *Adiós*."

"*Adiós*," Bearman said and watched Marcos Pulaski turn back down through the brush to the clearing. From a higher spot, he could see the river and the cows being hazed across, moving quickly as if the water were cold on their legs. Then Bearman saw another man on horseback ride to the river's edge and confer with Pulaski. The new man could see Bearman on his hill. The new man drew a revolver and fired into the air. Bearman saw the ghost of smoke and a heartbeat later heard the report. Whether it was a threat or a signal, Bearman did not know, but he could guess.

Bearman turned Dollar-Five back toward the dead bull. He spent the rest of the day burning the carcass with all the dry wood he could find, dragging some up from the tangle along the river and breaking off the limbs of any standing trees above the floodplain. In between foraging trips, he and Dollar-Five rested in sparse shade upwind from the smoke. Both were hungry, but Dollar-Five was the more readily satisfied. Bearman's jerky made him thirsty. Eventually, Bearman took out Pulaski's pistol and thought about the man. He knew the patrol of the river was a joint undertaking between the two nations. He just hoped Pulaski was who he said he was. It would make his job easier if Ornelos were convinced to behave himself.

He inspected Pulaski's Iver Johnson for a while, ejecting the cartridges, spinning the cylinder, dry-firing it, and looking down the barrel. He called Dollar-Five and took cleaning supplies from his saddlebag—a small can of gun oil and a rag, which he carried against the chance of one of his weapons being submerged in the river while he was afield. Pulaski's pistol was old and well used, but dirty. Bearman also discovered that the cylinder stop was so worn that it was possible for a round to be slightly off-center in the barrel, if not seated manually by gently rolling the cylinder back and forth. *Dangerous.* Nevertheless, he cleaned the pistol and reloaded it.

It was a long afternoon.

Later, as the sun went down, he banked the coals and ashes on the carcass with a branch of salt cedar, called Dollar-Five from the river clearing where she had wandered, and rode back to his hut in the glow of the desert twilight.

"Another woman's voice."

VI

Near Maravillas Canyon, November 1944

```
11/29/1944 Wed. Full moon. Cattle
being driven south to M. canyon.
Recent signs, no cattle. Moved across
river again. Why? Helped AT catch
horse. [scratched out] and she is so
[scratched out]
```

The day John Bearman found Annie Tinsley afoot in the tangled land away from the river, he had been following tracks in the sandy gravel on benches and flats where the presence of cow flop gave him an idea of the amount of stock being moved and its general health, for diarrhea seemed common. Even when he lost the tracks themselves, the trail was obvious. There being no outbound roads across the river in the Flats, it seemed to Bearman that a goodly number of cattle were being pushed upriver toward Maravillas Canyon where a semimaintained road on the Texas side led out to the main road at Black Gap. The trail he was following passed within three miles of the Tinsley ranch house.

It had been over a year since he had met Annie Tinsley at the train station in Marathon. He had sometimes stopped by the Tinsley place either as a matter of duty or a matter of courtesy. In all that time, he had only seen Annie Tinsley twice: once as she passed an open outer doorway, going from one room to another, and once briefly at a window. She had neither watched him nor spoken to him either time but had merely appeared in a place where he happened to be able to see her.

That day back in 1943, Annie Tinsley had been returning home from an extended stay in San Antonio, nursing her mother, who inevitably and tragically died of tuberculosis. Bearman had not known who she was when he had shown off in front of the station for her benefit. He was soon to be a neighbor of Morton Tinsley along the Rio Grande; Bearman only knew him through attending cattlemen's meetings at the Gage Hotel in Marathon but gave no thought as to whether he was married or not. Ten years Annie's senior, Morton was a harried man who, though well-intentioned, would always be diminished in ability by the number and persistence of the strange maladies and misfortunes that afflicted him. There were also times when his experience deserted him completely, like the week he spent trying to remove a nut from a piece of machinery that had reverse threads on the bolt.

Annie Tinsley herself was only a moderately strong woman when it came to the rigor and isolation of desert living. She had been tested her whole life in feminine fields, for which she often seemed to have no natural aptitude, thus denying her somewhat unusual nature the chance for expression and exercise. She was, at heart and in private, adventurous and impulsive in a time and place that put a premium on female decorum and submissiveness. The abandon of the jazz age, even in a mild form, had yet to reach the Big Bend country, if it ever would.

John Bearman, intuitive through his own silent nature, had instantly drawn from her the personality, perspective, and voice that defined her as an individual in the world, and the rare validation he gave her, even in the first fifteen minutes of what had been their sporadic acquaintance, so invigorated her that Morton, that night at table, thought she had found alcohol and drunk it, particularly after the months of care for her dying mother. At one point, she blushed and professed her feelings were indeed due to being released from sickroom duties (bless her mother's heart) and in being home again. But in moments of fluttering introspection, she knew her feelings were caused by memory of the attention of the young man in Marathon.

Bearman, whether invited in or not, had never crossed the threshold of the adobe-and-frame house. He had never stopped by with the intention of meeting Annie Tinsley, but after each visit, even after the two times he had seen her, he had ridden from the ranch with a feeling of loss and emptiness that sometimes took hours to overcome. When he did not see her, he thought about her. When he saw her, he saw her completely, even to the point of perceiving through posture, intent, and speed of movement what her thoughts and awareness might have been at that moment. It was a strange and complicated way of seeing. He did not like to think about why he should have it, and he had no idea what to do about it.

On this day, he was riding nearly five and a half miles from his place when he saw the saddled horse standing, reins trailing, under a lightning-struck mesquite on a bench twenty sloping feet above the river. He knew the horse to be one of Tinsley's and the saddle likewise, and thinking he was disturbing a resting rider or Annie Tinsley herself, he moved away from the river, turning up a gravel slope between creosote bushes, ocotillo, and lechuguilla.

The shod hooves of Dollar-Five made a racket in the loose rock, but silence was not his purpose, it being all right with him if in such a manner he could alert the hidden rider that another rider was near but moving away. A white-winged dove called resonantly from somewhere before him, and high above him, a falcon screamed and wheeled. Bearman noticed these familiar things but felt strangely tense. He knew his caution was not a reaction to perceived danger but to something more disturbing.

He turned at the top of the slope toward a draw that opened to the road that would take him back to his hut, and then he knew what he had already unconsciously known. A hundred yards up the draw, he saw Annie Tinsley. She was sitting under the twisted limbs of a huisache tree for what little shade it afforded, on the edge of a flat boulder. Her hat was pushed back, and her face was red and set in tight horizontal lines.

She was furious.

Bearman rode slowly up to her. Dollar-Five seemed to remember her and nickered.

"I saw your horse back yonder," he said without a greeting. "Are you waiting for him, or is he waiting for you?"

She turned away from him, swatted a noisome fly away from her face with her hand, then looked at him.

"Do I know you?" she asked.

"We've met."

He pulled Dollar-Five around and rode back the way he had come. In a few minutes, he returned, leading her horse. Annie Tinsley had been on her feet watching him since he had turned back down into the draw. She had told herself she really had no intention of ever meeting or speaking to this man again after that interlude at the station in Marathon, yet here he was, and here she was, in his debt. Her face was a deeper red than before, and Bearman noticed, when he was near, that her skin seemed dry.

"Can you saddle up?" he said. "We're not far from the river. You need some water."

"Of course, I can ride. And I have a canteen" she answered, mounting the sidestepping horse with some difficulty.

"You need more than a hot canteen. Come on."

In the saddle, she was dizzy. Bearman rode close at her side, unobtrusively ready to catch either her or the reins, whichever should fall first, but she rode steadily beside him, except once when, in spite of herself, she swayed closer to him as if to avoid the pinnate leaves and thorns of a mesquite. Their shoulders touched, and she caught his scent. She leaned away again, reprimanding herself. This man had a tendency to bring out actions and words from her that she could not predict, explain, or justify. They picked up the cattle trail and followed it down through the break in the cane growing thick along the bank.

At the river, they rode out into the shallows, the main channel being along the Mexico bank. Bearman swung down. He felt the water cold against his boots, then cool as he kicked around Dollar-Five to where Annie Tinsley sat her horse. He did not then reach up to help her from the saddle but stood close, catching the reins from her hand as she got down. An unseen rock rolled under her right boot, and she lurched against him, this time by accident. He did not reach then, either, to catch her, but braced himself so that she could steady herself against him.

"Easy now," he said.

She stepped away from him, caught a handful of stirrup leather, and pulled the red bandana from her throat. Holding on to the leather with her left hand, she bent and dipped it in the river. She bathed her face and neck while the horses drank and Bearman watched her.

Annie Tinsley bent again, wet her temples and neck, then straightened with droplets of water falling on her shoulders and the front of the khaki blouse she wore. Her riding skirt hung down from her hips to just above the tops of her boots, and she had avoided wetting it. She wore a gun belt with a tooled holster, holding a pistol with wood grips. It looked to Bearman like a short-barreled .38 revolver. He approved of the thought, if not the gun.

Bearman handed her his canteen, watched her drink, then took it, stoppered it, and tied it back on his saddle. He stepped downriver and caught Dollar-Five's reins to lead both horses back onto the bank. The Tinsley horse was now compliant enough, but Dollar-Five liked the water. Bearman looked at the mare a certain way, snicked, and she followed him without further resistance.

When Annie Tinsley joined him in the shade of a salt cedar, he asked, "Have an accident?"

She sat abruptly on a log of gray driftwood, so that he looked down upon the soft felt of her hat. The afternoon wind found them in the rustle of a diminished breeze.

"No," she said, her tone sarcastic. "I got tired of riding and got down to walk." Again, she immediately regretted surrendering to what this man inspired in her. Had they known each other before in some other distant time and place? Had he been the boy who sat behind her in grade school and pulled her pigtails? In a more natural voice, she said, "I dropped the reins to pick up a rock that caught my eye."

"What were you doing riding around out here by yourself?"

"Is that any of your business?" she snapped evasively.

"It wasn't, but since I found you in distress, my interest makes it my business."

"I don't like the word *distress,* as in *damsel in distress.*"

"Then don't get in it."

"Do you plan all your disasters ahead of time?"

She looked at him then, and Bearman smiled. "You win. Shuffle the cards."

"Are we gambling again?"

"One of us is. What kind of rock was it, if I'm not being too nosey?"

"Have you used that word since you learned to shave?"

"Never had to."

She pulled from her pocket a smooth black rock with a thin white streak of quartz in it, about the size of a silver dollar. The rock was roughly shaped like a valentine heart, and being black, Bearman knew it had probably stood out against the limestone gravel. She handed it to him reluctantly lest he laugh at her foolishness.

Bearman turned it over in his hand and rubbed the smooth surface with his thumb. He nodded. "I missed this one," he murmured, then quickly added, "Volcanic. Were you prospecting, by any chance?"

"Hardly." He gave it back, and she put the rock away.

"What spooked your horse?"

"I assume he saw something I didn't. At any rate, he seemed to blame me for whatever it was and wouldn't let me close."

"You tried."

"I tried for at least a mile, and it was not even in the direction of home. And up and down in gravel and that horrible lechuguilla."

Dollar-Five seemed to give Tyler, Annie Tinsley's horse, a reproachful shake of her head.

"Must have been some ordeal," Bearman sympathized.

She turned away and seemed to meditate, as if trying to put random thoughts in their place. Then she looked up at him. "Of course, I remember you. And your horse."

"You acted like you didn't."

"I apologize. That was rude. I wanted to quirt somebody or something, and there you were."

"Ever obliging."

"Did you really name her Dollar-Five?"

The mare's ears turned forward. Bearman laughed softly and nodded. "It's my brand now."

He was glad to hear her say she remembered him, but then there seemed nothing else to say. He took off his hat, ran his fingers through his hair, then put his hat back on. He looked at her. He wished she would take her hat off so he could see her hair.

"I'd take my hat off to you," she said, "but I look a fright when my hair tumbles down."

"I doubt that," Bearman said after a pause, during which he swallowed his surprise at her seemingly telepathic comment.

She looked up at him. Her face was flushed now, her eyes dark and large. She dropped her eyes and watched the ripples of the river's current. A young gar splashed the surface near the edge of the shallows.

"You said something like that once before. I don't remember what it was exactly. You seem to have a way of coming in the back door, if you know what I mean."

"I said you would never need a mirror."

She nodded, not looking at him. "That was rather bold of you then, and twice so now that you know who I am."

"Still true."

She shook her head. Bearman wished she would look up.

"I'm afraid that if I look at you, I'll start to believe you," she said.

Again, Bearman felt she had read his mind.

They became aware at the same time that there was a rider across the river watching them. It was Marcos Pulaski, the Mexican from the Ornelos ranch. He shouted, "Why you no marry the *señorita, pendejo*?"

"¡*Cállate*!" Bearman shouted back.

Pulaski laughed and made his horse rear like a stunt rider in a small-town rodeo, then he turned and disappeared in the brush. Another rider appeared from the brush and threw a look across the river. It was then that Bearman knew Pulaski was playing his part.

An awkward silence settled over them. Even the eyes of a stranger reflected the sunlight. Annie Tinsley started to stand then sat back down with a slight "oh."

"Just one of my friends across the river, saying hello," Bearman offered in the silence.

"I speak Spanish," she rebuked him.

"Yes, ma'am."

She looked down at the bandana in her hand. She folded it, still wet, and set it aside on the log.

"Guess you got settled in all right," Bearman said after another pause, when it became clear to him that he would have to continue a conversation or ride away. Their silences were awkward and painful.

"Yes."

"All you hoped it would be—living out here?"

She still did not look at him. "Is anything all we ever hoped it would be?"

"Sometimes even more."

"You think so?"

"I do."

"In your little rock house. Yes," she said at his murmur of surprise, "I've seen it. I rode over that way last Christmas looking for Morton. You did not seem to be at home."

"Next time stop in and make sure," he suggested.

"You know," she said, "I thought in the West, I would have the chance to, the freedom to—" She broke off and seemed to be searching for the right words. "Do things," she finished vaguely and looked up at him. He appeared so tall and solid against the afternoon sky. Like her, he was dressed in khaki but with a blue bandana around his neck, as opposed to her red patterned one. His .45 sagged a little on his right hip, and a hunting knife hung on his left. His unadorned chaps fit his form the way well-used leather gloves mold to the shape of the hands that use them.

"Do things," he prompted.

She nodded. "I've always wanted to do . . . things."

"Does that include being left afoot in the desert?"

"I knew where the river was. And home."

Bearman shifted his feet and focused on the difference in the feel of the two sets of reins he held. He looked up at the sky above the catclaw. He thought, *What would have happened if she had been hurt and no one knew?*

"I wasn't helpless, if that's what you're thinking," she added in his silence, with an edge to her voice.

"No, ma'am. I didn't think that. A year out here is long enough to get to know where things are. I was just imagining . . ." He did not finish.

There was a pause, longer than before.

"Well," she said. "I guess I should be getting back now. Thank you for catching my horse."

Annie Tinsley got to her feet. She smoothed her skirt down above her wet boots, then lifted her hat and set it back straight on her hair.

"Before you go," Bearman said, shifting his posture. "Could I ask you, what things you wanted to do?"

She looked at him and smiled. The color in her face deepened, but it was due neither to the heat nor embarrassment. No woman had ever looked at Bearman that way before. He handed her the reins to her horse. She took them below his grasp, the two of them close together.

"I don't know how to say them, now that I've been asked," she said with a shrug and a shake of her head. "Things. Like an adventure."

Bearman felt closer to her then, but uncomfortable, too, at the feeling. The smile was gone from her face, but the serious look that replaced it was neither troubled nor closed. Her vision seemed to have turned inward for a moment.

"I suppose that if you don't elaborate on your thoughts, I don't have to elaborate on mine," she said. Then she added, after noticing his expression, "You didn't tell me what you were imagining."

"Nope."

She held his gaze a moment longer and knew then what he had been imagining. It caused her color to further deepen. Bearman almost spoke again, but she turned to her horse, put one boot in the stirrup, and mounted. Bearman made no move to help her.

"Good day, Mr. Bearman," she said, not unpleasantly.

"Good day, ma'am." He touched his hat and watched her walk her horse away from the river until the cane hid her from his view, and then he listened until the sound of the horse diminished and was gone.

He walked down to the river, Dollar-Five beside him, searching across it and then above it to the mountains in Mexico. He wondered if Pulaski was looking for him, and if he knew about the cattle being moved nearby. All was quiet except the river and the wind in the cane behind him. The sun at his back was turning the mountains across the river into vivid, rocky ramparts. He knew he would lose daylight if he did not hurry along the trail he had thus far followed.

As he turned away, he saw the wet bandana on the log where Annie Tinsley had been sitting. He picked it up and squeezed the excess water out of it, then shook it straight, holding it by two corners. The white paisley design within the red was typical of bandanas, and it seemed to him to be the same one she had worn when they met for the first time. He wondered how long it would take for Annie Tinsley to miss it. He knew he would miss one of his. He would not have forgotten it in the first place. He took it with him to his saddle, then pocketed it as he rode northeast to a trail that curved around and ended again at the river's edge. He sat Dollar-Five and watched and listened.

After a few minutes, he left the river's edge and rode east back to his "little rock house."

All the things I could have said.

VII

Near Big Canyon, November 1944

```
11/30/1944 Wed. Full moon, bright.
Clear. Cold. Fish jump in river when
beavers pass. Y came by, discovered
plan to smuggle sick Omega cattle to
unknown point from M. Canyon road.
Have new plan.
```

J Bearman

The day Walter Yoakum wandered out of the desert that stretched in Texas for a hundred miles beyond the river valley, he found John Bearman sitting in the shade of the ramada that was attached to his hut and roofed with river cane. Bearman had taken his one chair out of the hut to rest in and faced the upriver stretch of the Rio Grande. He was smoking a straight-stem briar pipe and squinting across the heat haze in search of telltale dust. He saw none; nor did he see any disturbance of bird or animal, or a sudden clouding of the water due to a muddy disturbance of upriver cattle crossing. But he knew cattle had crossed and been trailed toward Maravillas Canyon, then apparently pushed back across the river again. Why, and where were they now?

It was the middle of the afternoon, the drowsy time of the day, warm before the chill of night, and Bearman was replaying in his mind his meeting with Annie Tinsley the day before. Around his neck, he wore the red bandana, almost a scarf, that she had left on the log at their parting. He told himself he wore it as a gentle taunt, if he ever met her again, implying she was not as conscious of the whims of the desert as she claimed to be. The reality was that the bandana was hers and held some of her fragrance, despite the wetting in the river. The bandana was now his most prized possession, equal even to the rifle his father had given him. He had no intention of giving the bandana back.

The one thing that stood out in his recollection of their meeting was that Annie Tinsley seemed to have read his mind. His face burned a little at the possibility that she was actually able to do so, yet, thinking about her, he himself had a sense of her presence, as if at that moment he knew exactly where she was and what she was doing. She had accused him of being bold, which he was, but wasn't she bold also? And now, wasn't he figuratively trespassing? What had gotten into him?

It was a relief to hear the clatter of Yoakum's sorry-looking but sturdy mare come over the ridge. Bearman exhaled the last puff of a dying bowl and set his pipe on the upended wooden box beside him, one of several that he used for furniture. His hat was pushed back on his head, and the brim was out of his way when he leaned forward with his elbows on his knees to watch Yoakum ride up to the makeshift corral and slide off with a slight bounce when his boots hit the ground. How the man could manage to bounce on that hard ground, Bearman could not begin to guess. Maybe he did not actually bounce but instead landed on his toes then rocked back on his heels. It looked like the bounce one made from the ground to the stirrup: a sort of hop.

It was the kind of afternoon best suited for idle musings.

Dollar-Five came up from below to see this new arrival, stuck her head into the shade of the lean-to, seemingly checking on Bearman, snorted, then wandered back down toward the river where a thicket of desert willows kept her cool when the first November cold fronts played out and daytime heat returned. At any rate, Yoakum's mount was apparently not worth noticing.

"Hey, old timer," Yoakum said, walking into the shade.

"Hey, yourself, young man."

Though Yoakum was twice Bearman's age, his ironic greeting never varied.

"You stink," Bearman said as Yoakum leaned next to him against the rock wall. He had brown smears of dung on his pant legs.

Yoakum laughed. "The river is my next stop. Been a long march. I try to take a bath every few weeks, whether I need it or not."

"There's soap next to the washstand."

"I've got my own, thank you. Well, Watchman, what of the night?"

"Hot and dusty, getting hotter and dustier."

"The whole state is from what I hear. Any Alamo hijinks going on around here? Strange lights, weird noises? Thousands of Mexicans crossing the river, shouting '*¡Adelante*! *¡Adelante*!'?"

"Not that I know of."

"You would," Yoakum said. "Well, river first, then a good chew, a little talk, and then supper. By the way, what's for supper?"

"Surprise."

"Does it come out of a can?"

"You'll find out soon enough. Go water that horse and get cleaned up. Or better yet, get rid of that plug and get cleaned up."

"Don't you insult Rosie that way. She ain't old, and she's a goat on the mountain trails. I'd like to see that spoiled brat of yours take some of those ledges."

After a pause of concession, Bearman said, "You win. Shuffle the cards."

Without offering to help, Bearman watched Yoakum hang a stirrup on the saddle horn, loosen the cinches, and lead his horse into the corral. The horse found the water trough quickly enough as the indolent mules watched from the shade of their own ramada, built with mismatched tree limbs for uprights and roofed with cane stalks and leaves. Yoakum untied his saddlebags and slung them over his shoulder. After he closed the gate to the corral, he followed the footpath down toward the river.

His voice came from around the hut: "If I'm not back by suppertime, eat it in my memory."

Yoakum said something else, followed by a laugh, but Bearman did not understand it. He sat back and looked upriver at the sinuous ribbon reflecting the blue of the Texas sky. He was glad for a reason to think of someone else for a while. Wally Yoakum was just the man to distract him from thoughts and memories of Annie Tinsley. Bearman was starting to get disgusted with his preoccupation and mooning. He reached up to draw the bandana from his neck, but let his hand fall before he had done so. Maybe he wasn't that disgusted after all.

Most of what Bearman knew about Yoakum was that the man lived by himself downriver, somewhere back in the canyons of the Rio Grande where he oversaw a business that Bearman thought was either bootlegging or wax smuggling. Bootlegging and smuggling both involved water and transportation. The water issue was handled by the river. Any kind of transportation out of the maze of canyons and rocky creek bottoms was seemingly out of the question. He might even have been hopelessly prospecting. There were other stories about the man and a now-deceased wife that sounded more like legend and myth than fact. Those who preceded Bearman alluded to Yoakum as a range detective or a veterinarian working with the Mexican authorities.

But, in truth, Bearman did not really care what Yoakum was doing back in those canyons. He had always enjoyed the man's company, since the days when Yoakum would stop by the Garrison ranch on his way to what he called "the outside." Elvie Garrison used to frown at Yoakum's eccentric ways, especially when he pestered Elvie to run away with him, but Josh Garrison and Bearman got a kick out of him. Friendly company was rare in that part of the world, and in the cases of employment or point of origin, it was considered rude to pry beyond what was offered.

After a while, Bearman heard Yoakum's boots on the gravel in front of the hut, and Yoakum stepped into the shade again. He was wringing wet except for his hat and his boots. He dropped his saddlebags and shook himself.

"Son, I want to tell you that that river is a true gift to this country. Feels like mercy when you're in it, but get out of it in wet clothes on a hot day, and you'll shiver your teeth out, both upper and lower."

"You'd better hope those clothes dry before dark. What'd you do, anyway, fall in?"

"Nope. Wash day."

"Still stink."

"It's the soap in my saddlebags. *Eau de Paris*."

"Paris, Texas?"

"Lord have mercy. Ever been there?"

"Not on purpose."

"Well, get used to the fragrance of grace. *Ooh là là*; I may smell like this all night."

"I hope not. Your box is inside the door to the left."

"Know where it is. Has the peaches girl label on one end. I never know whether to sit on her or put her in the dirt."

"Not much difference, being as how it's you, but if you sit on her, wet as you are, she'll be gone when you get up. Maybe she'll be on your pants. People will start calling you *Peaches* behind your back, whatever you smell like."

"That's enough," Yoakum said, and ducked in the door for the box that had held a case of canned peaches. He came out with the label end down. "I'll put her in the dirt this time, poor thing," he said, doing so. When he was settled, he leaned over and said, "You all right, honey?"

Bearman smiled.

For a time, neither of the men spoke. The humming silence of the desert fell upon them. Bearman filled and smoked his pipe again. Yoakum shivered now and then and chewed his tobacco. They fell into that easy silence between two people that indicates amiability.

Something whanged off the upriver side of the hut and whistled away into the hillside. After a couple of beats, they heard the rifle report and echo.

"Great God Almighty!" Yoakum exclaimed.

Bearman smoked. "Target practice from across the river. So far, they've missed the window. I think they have some old Springfield rifles left from the revolution."

"I dang near swallowed my chew."

"Good for stomach ailments."

"Let's get 'em. Impolite not to answer an invitation to a shindig." Yoakum drew his Colt's and edged to the corner.

"Right now," Bearman said calmly, "there are two men across the river. One you see and one you don't. While you're thinking of potting the one you see, the other is getting ready to pot you. It's not just the shade that puts me on this side of the hut."

"What about your horse?"

"They don't mess with the mare. They think she's a spirit animal."

Yoakum returned to his box. After a while, he muttered, "Dadgum. Glad I kept my clothes on while I was in the river."

"So are they, probably."

"That happens frequent, does it?"

"Often enough, but as long as they spare the window and the roof, I don't mind. Besides, I think I have a friend across the river who kind of keeps those activities under control."

"How long you say you been out here?" It was not a real question.

"Long enough."

"What kind of friend?"

"The kind who's an agent for the *federales* to help end this outbreak of foot-and-mouth by maintaining the quarantine. The children can't even drink the milk of infected cows."

"So, in Texas, we have Mr. Bearman. In Mexico, they have *Señor Bearmano*."

"Serious stuff, Wally."

"I know it is. Didn't mean to be disrespectful. I get silly after I've had a bath."

"All right."

They settled back into their silence. The sun rippled the air over the Flats and put a blue haze over the westerly mountains. Yoakum followed the flight of two buzzards circling with fixed wings above the nearer hills. He gestured at them. "Seems sometimes we got the same job they got. Just two buzzards floating around, looking," he said and spit.

"Better to be a buzzard than the buzzard's supper."

Yoakum was keenly aware of the gestures of his young friend and saw him clinch his jaw and slightly shake his head. When Bearman did not speak, Yoakum asked, "Something on your mind, John?"

"I was once told that if there was no solution, then there was no problem."

"Did you give that fella money?"

"Do you believe that every problem has a solution? I'm not talking about just blowing everything up and walking away from the fire. I'm talking about a sane, righteous solution that doesn't hurt anybody but solves the problem, world without end, amen."

"How many questions was that?" Yoakum asked leisurely.

"Let's start with yours."

"Which one?"

"The first one."

Pause.

"The buzzards?"

"No."

Pause.

"The buzzards' supper?"

"Get a dictionary and look up the word *obtuse*."

"You got one?"

"Can you read?"

"I used to could read and write, both. Now I just draw pictures in the dirt and spit on them."

Bearman let it slide. The buzzards were still riding the thermal air currents, but farther away, which was good. The sight of circling buzzards was, in that country, about as welcome as plumes of smoke in brush country.

Yoakum spit. "Say I was a detective," he said.

"If anybody asks," Bearman said, surprised at the admission.

"Say I was a detective," Yoakum, not easily diverted, said again.

"All right," Bearman said and waited.

"I come over here and find you sitting in the shade in the late afternoon on a fine day. Not doing nothing, just sitting. The mules doing nothing. Your horse down by the river talking to mermaids, excuse me, *beavers*, otherwise doing nothing."

Bearman tapped out the dottle from his pipe against the heel of his hand. He did not look at Yoakum.

"Do things."

"Right away, you haul up a piece of moth-eaten philosophy apropos of nothing obvious except for one small item."

The silence stretched.

"Which is?"

"Ho ho. Got your attention, didn't I?"

"Don't waste it, Santa Claus."

"You're wearing a female's scarf around your neck. Appropriate, ain't it? The placement, I mean."

Bearman picked up his pipe and put it down again.

"And that's the problem, and the 'no solution' is because she ain't for you," Yoakum concluded with a laugh as he noted the blush spread across Bearman's tanned cheek. "It's the way of the world, son: want the best; make do with the rest."

"You think you're smart, but I think you got everything you know from the funny papers."

"Huh. Nope. If I'm smart, it's because I don't waste a perfect afternoon sitting in the shade, thinking. People that think all the time get tangled up in their own lariat. They're like that Shelley poet who wrote, 'I fall on the thorns of life and bleed.' Only an idiot who thinks too much would write something like that." He paused and spit. "His front name was Percy," he added.

"Shelley?"

"He wrote it."

"You're quoting Shelley?"

"I get feeble-minded now and then. Comes from living alone. Besides, I don't know Shakespeare like you do."

"How about this from Shakespeare: 'He thinks too much; such men are dangerous.'"

"Cassius was. Shelley wasn't. He was just a fool. Can you imagine him stumbling around in this country, falling on every form of cactus known to man? It would be: *Leave that alone, Percy. Don't sit there, Percy. Quit walking backwards, Percy. That's not fur, Percy.*"

"You staying for supper or not?"

"Depends on what we're having. No, I take that back. It doesn't matter what we're having. I'm staying, might stay all night."

"What's the play?"

Yoakum spit. "I've a story to tell to the nations."

They had beans and salt pork, warmed-over biscuits from breakfast, and coffee.

"About a week ago, I had a dream that set me roaming," Yoakum said in the twilight as the two men once again sat under the ramada next to the hut. It was quiet and still. Dollar-Five stayed close, as if she wanted to hear the story too.

"In the dream, a voice was telling me to go upriver. It woke me up, and I looked around, and there was nothing going on. So, I thought, huh, and went back to sleep. Then again, same dream voice, telling me, 'Arise and go upriver.' So, same thing. I looked around. There was just me. I tried to go back to sleep, but I kept thinking about that voice and all the stories I've heard about lost gold mines."

"How long have you been out here?"

"Don't laugh. You ever been up on Dead Horse Mountain and seen those ghost lights chasing each other across the flat there?"

"No."

"Well, I'll tell you, it's plenty curious."

"All right."

"Back to the dream: I felt like Samuel in the Bible. I finally go back to sleep, and the voice tells me a third time, just one word: 'Upriver.'"

"When was this?"

"Two days ago. So next day, I can't do anything but remember that dream. Couldn't even lace my boots. The laces broke."

"Maybe the dream was telling you to buy new laces."

"John, John, John," Yoakum shook his head. "Yesterday I rode upriver as far as Maravillas Canyon. When it got on toward dark, I started hearing thirsty cows bawling. Now, I knew the only man that had cattle over there was Morton Tinsley, and he runs his cattle plumb away from Maravillas, over toward Bourland Canyon, so there's very little chance of them mixing with infected stuff out of Mexico."

"How do you know where and what Tinsley runs?"

"Listen to what I'm saying. Just listen. There's no girl in this story, and I hate being interrupted.

"Now, I knew those cows weren't Tinsley's, so I cut away from the Canyon and followed the sound until I found a corral in a hollow back from the river. There's a wide draw there, but too good a place for lookouts. The corral held thirty or forty head."

Bearman was paying attention now. "I followed the trail of cattle out that way yesterday, but it turned back to the river, sure as day."

"I saw you, but you missed a trick. They double-herded you; took a sick bunch and mixed up the tracks with another bunch, probably also sick but not showing. They just took those back across the river, pretty as you please, and hid them over there for next time. You had other things on your mind, I guess, and missed the switch."

"Skip that part."

"When they split the two bunches, they turned the sick critters up into the rocks. That first bunch were sure enough sick, John—drooling and mincing with the foot-and-mouth. And they were being watched. I had to crawl a hundred yards through the brush and cow flop before the moon rose, and then it was so bright, I thought I would never be able to get away. I'm fairly sure one guy saw me but turned his back.

"It was a temporary corral, and I believe whoever penned those scrubs was waiting for trucks to haul them out the back door to someplace between here and El Paso. The meat of those cows is poison."

"Could you make out any brands?"

"If they had any, I couldn't read them, but they looked slick to me. There are different zones in Mexico where the quarantine is more severe. They don't mark their cattle in those zones if there's a chance of smuggling for a profit. And that includes goats and hogs."

Bearman thought about it. "Tough," he said. Then he added, "The trail I followed showed cattle with the squirts."

"That was them before the split. Why do you think I smelled so bad?"

Bearman put his pipe down. "What about the part of your dream with gold in it?"

"Oh, I've heard those stories about the Reagan brothers and their search for a mystery canyon with a gold mine in it. And, by the way, they claim the guy that found the first chunk had been across the river near Maravillas Canyon. But I'll tell you the truth, finding those cattle was gold to me."

"How so? They're worse than worthless to anybody."

"Say I was a veterinarian."

"You're a veterinarian?"

Yoakum nodded. "Texas A&M University, class of '27."

"I thought you claimed to be a detective."

Yoakum nodded again. "Cattlemen's Association of Brewster County. Four years. All one and the same."

"You old sidewinder. And all this time, I thought you were a bootlegger and a smuggler, living back in the canyon at a wax camp."

"I do live thereabouts."

"How?"

"There's trails and secret ways all back in the mountains and canyons. You think primitive people just stood on the edge of a cliff looking down at the river wishing there was a way to get to it? Mister, they found a way. Then I found it. I come and go as I please."

Bearman took up his pipe again. He filled and lit it and sat smoking without talking. Then, he said, "And you heard a voice telling you three times to go upriver?"

"I might have made that part up."

"What do you want to do?"

"I want to make sure those poor beasts stay where they are until they're dead, covered with quicklime, and buried. If they are being moved tonight, we can catch the men, and confiscate their truck or trucks. Between the two of us, I think we have the authority to do that. But everything those cows came in contact with has the virus. Every cloven foot that crosses their path is in danger. This whole mess just goes on and on."

"The people in the valley across the river . . ."

"That's right. I care about those people. Smugglers have to bring those cattle in over the pass in the *Sierritas* and herd them through the valley."

"We rode over it on the Texas side yesterday."

"We did, but you know horses ain't affected."

"I know that, but why didn't you tell me all this other stuff earlier?"

"My clothes were wet, and I wanted supper. Also, I didn't want to give you time to think about it."

"Think about supper?"

Yoakum shook his head. "No. That was hardly worth thinking about. I didn't want you thinking about the trouble we're going to run into out there in the dark. I ain't never hunted coyotes with you before."

"*Sho now*," Bearman said softly to Dollar-Five, and the mare tossed her head, stomped, and neighed.

VIII

Maravillas Canyon, November 1944

```
11/30/1944-12/1/1944 Full moon,
around midnight. With Y. Located
corral. Maravillas. MP aided
```

J Bearman

The day Yoakum arrived at Bearman's hut did not end with the setting of the sun; now they sat their horses halfway up a slope on a road, little more than twin ruts, so they could not be seen silhouetted against a starry sky, and the low sound of their voices would not carry in the windless, cold dark. It was just after eleven o'clock that night, and they were close enough to Maravillas Canyon to use caution.

"Moon's coming up," Bearman said quietly, nodding at a faint glow on the ridge of the lower mountain to the southwest. Directly ahead of them, the immediate desert stretched in hidden undulations of flats and draws. To the south, the rising walls of Maravillas Canyon were dim and black. The roadway through that broken country snaked and rose and fell again, following a path of least resistance. The two men were still too far away to hear any penned, thirsty cattle, and Bearman wondered if Annie Tinsley could hear them in the still of the night. It was a passing thought of professional interest only, he told himself.

"It'll be a while before it clears Bourland Canyon," Yoakum said and spit. On his hip, he wore a .45 Colt's identical to the one Bearman wore, and his Marlin .30-.30 was in his saddle scabbard as Bearman's Winchester Model '92 was in his. They had several boxes of ammunition in their saddlebags as well as plenty of pigging strings. Bearman hoped it would not be a shooting affair.

"They'll drive without headlights, anyway," Yoakum continued. "Headlights show a long way in the desert and always draw attention."

"Yep."

"*Amigo*," a voice sounded to their right, beyond the berm of the roadway where rocks and dead creosote brush had been pushed to the side by the county maintainer.

Yoakum immediately jumped his horse to the left into the living brush and drew his pistol, neck reining the horse to face the voice head-on.

"Wait," Bearman said. "I know that voice." Then he called, "Pulaski?"

"*Sí, Señor* Bearman," the man answered and stepped onto the whiter rocks of the roadway. He was afoot and held his hands away from his sides. The butt of an automatic showed in the pocket of his khaki pants.

Bearman turned to Yoakum in the dark and said, "Hold up, Wally. This man is the agent for the Mexican government I told you about."

Yoakum came back onto the road. "Dang near was the ex-agent," he growled, still holding his pistol. "Where's his horse?"

The other two did not answer. Dollar-Five snorted. She knew exactly where Pulaski had tied his horse.

Bearman swung down and dropped the reins. He ducked under Dollar-Five's neck to face Pulaski. The mare pretended to nip his shoulder as he went by. The two men shook hands.

"When I saw you yesterday with the Señora Tinsley, I thought you would be coming this way this night, *amigo*, but I was afraid you might not come because of the trick they played."

"I fell for it. I did find it strange you were so far upriver."

"It is an old trick of Señor Ornelos to follow the sick cows with healthy cows. If there is a problem with a roaming inspector, there is always *mordida* in the jefe's pockets, the *cabrón*. A little monies, and Señor Inspector looks at the sky to see if it rains soon. The cows go on by. *Escuchame*, I have waited for you because the work that must be done tonight, must be done by you, and now your friend. I cannot be a part of it."

"Why not? Surely your job will be finished tonight. Why be secret still?"

"Because it ain't done," Yoakum said, dismounting and joining the other two. "It will be years before this epidemic is wiped out. Yoakum is my name, Mister. Glad to meet you."

"*Yo también*. I saw you yesterday. I was afraid the others would do you harm. You are the mystery man from the canyons, eh? Many stories about you and *la Mujer del Rio*."

"What?" Bearman asked.

"Wait off on that," Yoakum growled.

Bearman searched the farther darkness for sound, then said, "What is your mission now, Marcos?"

"It is the same. Ornelos has no brand on the sick cows. The trucks will be hired by a man who does not exist, but this night, Ornelos will be there to carry the monies."

"Proof," Bearman said.

"*Creo que sí. Pero*, there is more. There is a—how do you call it? —a pipeline from Zacatecas moving the sick cows to Ornelos, who brings them over the pass in the *Sierritas* to get rid of in Texas. This must be stopped. With luck, I will go with the other riders to this place. I cannot know when that may be—this month, next, next year—but what happens at the place of the sick cows will break that pipeline. The quarantine will be complete. *Oye*, if I go, I will be gone a long time, *para siempre*."

"Don't let that happen," Bearman said. "Tell me what is going on here tonight. The moon will be above the mountains soon, and we don't want that light."

"*Seguro*. A mile and a half from here, *más o menos*, a draw comes up from the river and turns into two draws."

"I found that one yesterday," Yoakum interrupted.

"*Perdón*, but you rode in the back door, Señor. The place of which I speak is farther to the east and wide."

"You have a way of coming in the back door."

"Leave the road and follow the draw on the right. You will find the cows. Ornelos is shipping thirty-one tonight. Those too sick to load will be turned loose. He will not use this *pinche* corral again."

"How many riders?" Yoakum asked.

"*Seis*, counting me."

Yoakum's horse nickered. Yoakum said, "Rosie found Mr. Pulaski's horse."

They listened in silence for a minute. The single cry of a lone coyote came from the north. Bearman looked at Yoakum, then turned to Pulaski.

"How are the riders placed?" Bearman wanted to know.

"Four at the corral or near it. The horses do not like the smell of the sick cows, so the riders drift upwind, but close. One *hombre* goes south to watch the road. I am to the north. When the trucks come, we return to the corral to help the loading."

"How many trucks?"

"More than one, surely."

"What do you think?"

"Probably two at the most. Ornelos has no trucks this side of the river, and they have to travel the state road for a while before they find the private road where the cattle are processed. *Caravanas* would draw the eye."

"Do you know where they process the meat?"

"No, *amigo*. Nor have I heard it spoken of."

"Look yonder," Yoakum said quietly.

The other two turned to the southeast, where a white glow was highlighting the serrated crest of Bourland Canyon while the lesser tailings across the river were already alight.

"I go now," Pulaski said and shook their hands. "*Vaya con Dios*," he said, turning away.

"*Y tu*," both men said.

"Do not shoot me by mistake," Pulaski added with a laugh.

"I see you have an automatic now," Bearman said. It was a question.

"Poker game. I gave my old one to Manuel. Thanks for cleaning it, but I did not trust it. You did me *mucho* favor."

He laughed again and was gone from sight. Bearman heard the clatter of loose rocks and the scrape of dead brush against the chaps Pulaski wore, then the clack of shod hooves on the rocks away into the desert night.

"Seems like a good guy," Yoakum said, climbing back into the saddle.

For a minute, Bearman listened, standing in front of Dollar-Five, now holding the reins. He turned to the mare, face to face, and said, "Did you try to bite me a while ago?" He clicked his teeth for emphasis. Dollar-Five looked away, then stepped against Bearman and snorted.

"I'll leave you two alone now," Yoakum said.

Bearman swung up into the saddle and held Dollar-Five still while he said, "I'm ready to ride. And on the way you can tell me all about *la Mujer del Rio*."

"Want the best; follow the quest."

They had no means to soften or mute the sound of the horses' hooves on the rocky desert road other than to ride slowly, but after three-quarters of a mile farther, the sound they made did not really matter, for they could hear in the distance the grind, rattle, and chug of more than one large truck coming up from Maravillas Canyon without lights.

"How many galoots you figure riding in those trucks?" Yoakum wondered.

Bearman was focused on finding a draw leading away from the river and wide enough for a cattle truck to travel in and maneuver to come back out again. He had ridden this far several times on patrol and driven his wagon down this rough road countless times on trips to Marathon, but the dark misled him more than once. He was fooled by shadows and similarities.

"Maybe two or three. Loading sick, thirsty cows can't be an easy job in the dark, even with the moon."

"Say there's three in each truck. We don't count your friend, although he'll have to act mean to keep on being a spy. He said there were five men out here already, so make that twelve against two."

"Eleven and a half against two. Other than bravado, we don't have to expect danger from Pulaski—that's the draw up ahead. The trucks will turn there. Let's get off the road."

They swung off to the left, hunting low ground. They found it and dismounted, standing close against their saddles.

"So that makes it five and three-quarters against one," Yoakum said quietly and spit.

Bearman was listening for the trucks while he tried to follow Yoakum's arithmetic. One minute they sounded close, the next they could hardly be heard at all due to the ups and downs of the road. He knew once they arrived at or close to the corral, the men would come in to help and their hands would be filled with reins and ropes, their eyes with dust. But one or two might remain behind to guard the way while the others loaded.

"Are you worried about it, Wally?" Bearman looked over at his friend.

"Let me ask you a question, John. When you were a kid, did you ever play with that infernal toy called a jack-in-the-box?"

"I knew a little girl who had one," Bearman answered after a pause, as if he had to think about it, or perhaps was reluctant to talk about it.

"My folks gave me one for Christmas when I was about seven. Thought I would like it. I liked it about as much as watching someone blow up a balloon until it pops and scares a year off your life. No matter how many times I cranked that piece of tin, the clown that popped out always caught me by surprise. The anticipation got on my nerves—fool thing to give a kid. Right now, I keep thinking there's a surprise out there somewhere, and it will pop out when we least expect it."

"I thought you tried not to think," Bearman said.

"Using a man's words against him is a female habit, John. I'm ashamed of you. What a man says is for that moment only and cannot be used against him later."

"Trucks," Bearman said, nodding toward them as they came into view.

Bearman saw the vague form of a rider pull up at the mouth of the draw and wait for the trucks. The trucks were close enough now that he could see the reflection of the moon off the hood and windshield of the first one. He was glad they were not using headlights, as the grills of each truck were pointed directly at him and Yoakum for the space of two minutes before they turned into the draw about fifty yards away.

The shadows were deep in the draw, and the drivers were having trouble navigating around half-buried boulders and leaning brush. After several yards of doubtful stop-and-go, the lights of the first truck came on, yellow because of a weak alternator or battery or both, and Bearman saw movement behind the second truck when it followed the first into the draw. They were both big cattle trucks with high sideboards.

"Now?" Yoakum asked.

"What do you think?"

"You won't catch me in that trap. I'll say this, though: a detective ain't necessarily a gunfighter. I feel more like a vet right now."

"Let's hope it won't come to gunplay. Our job is to overcome, subdue, and confiscate. No one wants to die over thirty sick cows. I hope."

"I can do what needs to be done, but waiting to do it makes me loco."

Bearman, watching the draw, saw a bend take the lights, the shadows deep once more, but he was sure there was a man lingering in the draw. He said, "There's a man in the draw following the trucks, probably the scout to the south. I'm going in on foot with Dollar-Five. If you hear gunfire, come on. If you don't hear guns after five minutes, still come on, but on horseback and ready to make some noise. I want to get to the corral before they turn those cattle loose. You'll know what to do when you get there."

"How am I supposed to tell when five minutes are up?"

"Count to three hundred slowly."

"You going to tell me goodbye?"

Bearman laughed and looped the reins loosely around the saddle horn. Dollar-Five felt the difference and watched Bearman closely. "I tried telling you goodbye once before and you stayed two weeks. So what's the point? Do your job, and you can stay for breakfast."

"You don't have to threaten me."

Yoakum mounted while Bearman led the mare across the road and into the mouth of the draw. As the shadows took Bearman, Yoakum softly sang,

A penny for a spool of thread
A penny for a needle,
That's the way the money goes,
Pop! goes the weasel!

IX

Maravillas Canyon, December 1944

12/1/1944 Full moon. Orion bright.
With Y. Located corral.
Maravillas. MP aided. Gunplay. Man
killed. Accident. Captured two cattle
trucks. Ornelos ranch hands escaped
or detained.

When Bearman faded into the draw with Dollar-Five at his shoulder, he felt a chill wind that he had not felt before, and he clearly heard what had been smothered before: the bawling of sick and thirsty cattle. To most people, cattle were just big, dumb or picturesque animals, but Bearman had carried a lost newborn across his saddle more than once and tended to many cows whose large brown eyes had looked on him with something he imagined was close to human comprehension.

A good portion of the country around him near the dry riverbed of Maravillas Canyon was still in the shadow of Bourland Mountain, but up ahead of him in the distance, the desert was getting lighter. He drew his rifle from the saddle scabbard and quietly levered a cartridge into the chamber.

He whispered, "Slow."

The mare twitched her ears and moved up the draw at a walk while Bearman followed close at her flank to blend his form with the mare's. When they had caught up close to the rider, who had paused to light a cigarette, Bearman moved up to the mare's head and softly commanded, "Rope!" Dollar-Five used whatever secret knowledge she had that enabled her to find the nearest rope, and she leapt ahead, threw her neck across the startled man's lap, and snatched the rope away from the saddle horn where it lay coiled. The man's horse squealed and reared in fright, but the *vaquero* was a good one and held on rodeo-style while it spun and bucked.

"Good girl," Bearman praised Dollar-Five, taking the rope from her mouth and sliding the rifle back into its scabbard. He then ran to the rider's side and pulled him out of the saddle. At first, the man continued to hold the reins, but the horse jumped away toward the mouth of the draw, and the reins slid through his gloved hand. Bearman searched him quickly for weapons and found a pistol and a knife. The pistol he tossed to the side, but the man tried to use the knife before Bearman could pull it from its sheath. Bearman leaped away and returned again. As the man rolled in the gravel to get on his knees, Bearman struck the man's face with the stiff loops of the coiled rope several times until he was able to kick the knife from the man's hand. Then he dropped the rope and rolled the man over onto his stomach.

"*¿Quién es?*" the man sputtered.

"*Cállate.*"

Bearman pulled the man's hands behind his back and tied them, then removed the man's boots and tied his ankles. Up ahead, around a bend, the trucks were being turned to face the way they had come. Lights flashed across the draw.

"If you make a sound, I will kill you," Bearman said harshly.

"No *comprende*," the man wheezed.

"You *comprende* this?" Bearman put the muzzle of his .45 against the man's left eye.

"*Sí, Señor.*"

"*Cállate.*"

Bearman stood up and holstered his Colt's. He collected the man's boots, knife, and pistol and carried them to Dollar-Five. He dropped the weapons in the nearer saddlebag but threw the boots away into the desert. He went back to the man and dragged him over to the steep side of the draw, out of the way.

From up by the corral, he heard voices, cattle bawling, and the sound of wood sliding on metal. In the absence of a chute, they were unloading board ramps. Then two horses came up the draw, and Bearman pulled his pistol and stood beside Dollar-Five. The riders were too close for him to do anything else but wait.

It was Yoakum and Pulaski.

"I see you got one," Yoakum said. "Empty horse ran by us like you promised to feed it."

"Watch him. Don't talk," Bearman cautioned and holstered his pistol. He left the mare ground-hitched and caught the bridle of Pulaski's horse, pulling horse and rider back toward the mouth of the draw. Moonlight lay along the western reaches of the draw.

"Listen," he said when they were well away from the bound man. "Tell me what you want to do. That man has seen you, probably recognized you. How can I help you?"

Pulaski did not hesitate. "You must treat me as you have treated Mario. Take my weapons and my boots and tie me loosely. Together, we will escape back to the river and cross. I do not speak for any of the others. Mario is young. He will be a better man when this is over."

"What about your boots?"

"Maybe, perhaps, they will not be hard to find, and where I find one, there will be the other."

"I don't want the horses."

"They will find their way. I am sorry you have to do this thing with the cows, but thank you very much for your help."

"Get down."

Pulaski dismounted, and Bearman did as he asked. Pulaski handed over the automatic with a laugh. "Same shelf?"

After Bearman tied him up, he gripped Pulaski's shoulder and dragged him out of the trucks' path. He shooed the horse and ran back to Dollar-Five, who had turned and was looking for him. He put the weapons in the saddlebag and mounted. He drew close to Yoakum, who was alternately working his chew and spitting on the bound smuggler as he tried to wriggle out of reach, muttering, "*Cochino*" each time he was hit.

"We have to get up this draw," Bearman said.

"Dadgum."

"This has to be taken care of sooner or later, so it might as well be now. Which side do you want—moonlight or shadow?"

"Let the old man have the shadow, what there is of it."

"Good luck. Go, go."

There was no longer any need for stealth, and they rode up the draw in unison, pistols drawn. At the corral, Bearman saw that the trucks had not been loaded. The ramps had to be adjusted. There was a man by the first truck. Bearman rushed him and had his pistol on the man before the other knew what was happening.

"*Manos arribas*," he said tersely, admitting no resistance. "*¡Deme su pistola ahora mismo!*"

The man hesitated. He was wearing a bandana over the lower part of his face, more for dust and odor than secrecy, and his hat covered his eyes. His shoulders were hunched under an old wool coat. He decided to use his pistol and jerked it from his pants. Bearman shot him off his horse.

That was all it took. Noise and pandemonium and movement and shouts and gunfire broke out in and around the draw. So many things happened at once that Bearman could not later recall events in their proper sequence without Yoakum's help: *"That was when that guy rolled down the ramp, bouncing on the cleats."*

Bearman heard Yoakum shouting, "*¡Manos arribas!*" from the other side of the truck, then three shots, and Yoakum charging closer to the corral, shouting, "Put those hands up or so help me, I'll blow you to kingdom come! Put 'em up! ¡*Arribas*!" Another gunshot, different caliber. "Try it, eh? Why, I'll cut your heart out and send it to Cincinnati! Your *mamacita* will roam the desert with tears in her eyes looking for your unmarked grave! I'll water them thirsty cows with your blood! I'll weave your greasy hair into a lanyard to hang toilet paper on! Look out!" More gunfire, from a .45 Colt's this time, moving toward the back of the second truck in line.

The truck beside him rumbled into gear as if to leave, but Bearman turned Dollar-Five against the door, stood in the stirrups, and put his pistol at the driver's window. "Turn it off," he said, and was about to say it again in Spanish, but to his surprise, the driver was Anglo, and another Anglo man sat beside him. That was all he could determine about them in the gloom of the cab. To his further surprise, the driver said, "Mr. Bearman? It's me and Brother. You remember us?"

It was the two brothers who had helped him build his hut. "Steve?"

"That's right. Don't shoot us. We didn't know anything was wrong when we took this job."

"This is your truck?"

"Yes sir. We traded our wagon for it, plus some other stuff." When Bearman did not reply, he added, "It was just a job. Man offered us fifty bucks to move a bunch of cows to another ranch."

"All right. Turn the truck off and put the key in your pocket. You and Brother get down on the floorboard and stay there till I come back. Do not leave the truck. I've got a crazy man for a partner. He would shoot your eyes out and later be sorry and try to put them back in."

"Can he do that?"

"Stay in the truck."

"Yes, sir." The truck went silent except for the slight ticking of a cooling motor.

Bearman had been in the shadow of the truck when two riders jumped the ramp from the second truck in line and powered up the side of the draw toward the open desert. They were plainly visible in the moonlight, and their horses had not yet reached their full speed after pawing up the slope. One of them turned to look at Bearman and taunted him with an obscene gesture. The man was dressed in better clothes than any of the Mexicans he had seen so far, and the bandana had fallen from his face. Riding beside him was an Anglo Bearman recognized. He still held his pistol and raised it now, but he had already shot one man in self-defense, how badly he did not know, and he was sure he had nothing to fear from the two racing away. They would be across the river in half an hour.

Bearman urged Dollar-Five toward the second truck in line, which was running, its deep, throaty sound uniting all the other sounds of the fight, for a fight it had surely become. The cab was empty, and again Bearman stood in the stirrups to reach in and shut down the engine.

Yoakum was still cursing his adversaries instead of calling for help, so Bearman knew, despite Yoakum's earlier jitters, that he was hell on wheels in a fight and holding his own. It was also clear that the Mexicans had been there as workers more than defense. They were probably only prepared for a local rancher, curious at hearing the cows, who would prevent them from covering their tracks.

But Bearman's musing ended when a man in the bed of the first truck swung out above him, holding on to the truck rail with his right hand and holding a pistol with the other, aimed directly at Bearman's chest. Startled by the sudden appearance of the man above her rather than on the ground, Dollar-Five shied away, but not before the gun went off six feet from the mare's face, and Bearman slumped in the saddle, dropping the reins and leaning on the pommel.

Three horsemen came around the end of the truck closest to the corral, as had the other two. Yoakum pulled hard on the reins and dodged the two trucks like a barrel racer to head off the trio that had given him so much trouble. He was just passing when a man swung out from the bed of the first truck with a pistol in his hand, aimed at something on the other side of the truck.

Before Yoakum could shoot, the man fired, and the pistol exploded in his hand. He then fell and rolled down the cattle ramp, bouncing slightly on the cleats. Yoakum's horse jumped the ramp, and Yoakum saw Dollar-Five falter, then lift her head. Bearman's hat was gone, lying in the gravel behind him. He raised his head in the moonlight, and Yoakum saw the black smear of blood on his left temple. Dollar-Five, likewise, was bleeding from a cut high on her forehead, almost dead center between her ears.

Yoakum rode over, the escaping trio forgotten. "Look at me, John."

Bearman looked at him. "I'm all right. Dollar-Five . . ."

"We'll talk when I get back. This ain't finished yet. I've hog-tied a couple of drivers and one Mexican rider, but I need to make sure the others are gone."

"Go."

Without another word, Yoakum rode away in the shadow of the trucks toward the corral. The cattle were milling and bawling and pressing ineffectually against the barrier that held them. A third of their number were on the ground, too sick and dehydrated to stand.

Yoakum checked the bindings of those men who had yielded or had no weapons to begin with. He knew he was presenting himself as a target, but he also knew that any man left to interfere with him had to be aware he would be facing greater courage and greater fire power. The cattle were not worth it. When Yoakum had satisfied himself that his prisoners were secure, he rode a circle around the area, the moon high and clear above him. Without seeing anyone, he returned to Bearman. His friend's condition was his only worry now.

After Yoakum rode away, Bearman slid from the saddle, took the three steps to the front of the mare, and caught the bridle to pull her head down, eye to eye with him. Dollar-Five sniffed him, smelled the blood, nickered softly, then huffed her breath in his face. He did the same.

"I'm sorry, Dollar-Five," he said. "That man jumped us both, but he was using Pulaski's old pistol. When he pulled the hammer back, the cylinder went past the stop, and the gun blew up when he pulled the trigger.

We only got a piece or two of lead. We're all right, but I thought sure you were gone, and that took the wind out of me just when I needed it most. *Sho now*, right?"

Bearman released the bridle. Dollar-Five looked to the left and to the right, then took a step forward and draped her neck over Bearman's shoulder. They were standing like that when Yoakum returned.

"Ain't that a picture," Yoakum said, resting both arms on the pommel of his saddle, his hat pushed back.

"Save it for me."

Bearman rubbed the mare's jawline, then walked to the cab of the first truck and knocked on the door.

"Who is it?" Steve said.

"Steve, do you have a flashlight in there?"

"Yes, sir." There was a pause.

"Could I have it, please?"

"Just a minute." There was some talk and some knocking around, and then the door squeaked open, and Steve passed down a flashlight. "Is the shootin' over?" he asked.

Bearman turned away as soon as he got the flashlight and went back to Dollar-Five. Although she shied a little when he put the light in her face, she let him raise her forelock to find a shallow one-inch cut that had already stopped bleeding.

"Why don't you use that fancy bandana to wipe the blood off *your* face? You look worse than Marfa on a Sunday," Yoakum said, watching his young friend. They were both letting the adrenaline burn itself out.

Bearman shook his head. "Got another bandana in my back pocket."

"Always carry two?"

"One to wear and one to use."

"Functional accessories. What's next?" Yoakum shook his head and bit off a fresh chew from the plug he carried in his shirt pocket.

Bearman went past the truck and shined the light on the man he had shot out of the saddle. The man squinted against the light and moaned.

Looking closer, Bearman could find no blood. It wasn't until daylight and after finding the man's pistol that Bearman realized he had instinctively fired low at the movement of the man pulling his pistol from his waist. His bullet hit the Mexican's pistol above the grip and ricocheted into the man's silver buckle. The buckle saved the man's life, but he would hurt for many days.

"*Levántate,*" Bearman said. "Get up."

"No *puedo,*" the man moaned. "I can't."

Bearman drew his pistol and fired a round into the sand by the man's head. The sound of the shot startled men and animals alike.

"*Levántate,*" Bearman said again, and the man rolled over onto his side and stood up, his arms wrapped around his belly, moaning and calling on the Virgin Mary.

Yoakum had dismounted and was standing ready with two pigging strings. He led the man to where the other prisoners were tied and separated, and he tied the complaining and praying man securely.

"Next time, raise your hands when you're told to," Yoakum told him.

"*¿Qué?*"

"Oh, shut up and be still."

When Yoakum returned, he found Bearman wearing his hat again, but tipped back, his face wiped clean. Two men were standing with him. "Wally," he said, "this is Steve and his brother, Brother. They helped me build my hut."

Yoakum shook Steve's hand and said, "Yoakum."

Brother said, "They call me Brother."

Yoakum snorted. "Ain't you got a front name?"

Steve said, "It's Phineas."

"Why'd you tell him that?"

"It's your name. He asked."

Yoakum laughed. "Phineas."

Brother said, "What do you do when you work two mules?"

Steve said, "Yoke 'em," and laughed.

Yoakum said, "You win. Shuffle the cards," and shook their hands again.

Bearman said, "You guys can decide later who is escorting whom to the dance. Right now, we have to clean up this mess, notify the authorities, and get the heavy machinery and quicklime out here to put these sick animals in the ground."

"We figured twelve hombres and only lost the one whose gun blew up. Eight got away. These two babies are still here. I've got three tied up by the corral. That makes thirteen. We figured pretty close," Yoakum concluded.

"We figured closer than close. There was a weasel in the can we didn't expect."

"Who?"

"The night guard at Black Gap: Lenny Carmichael."

"Dadgum."

X

Near Big Canyon, December 1944

```
12/1/1944 Sent S with Y to inform
station. Waited for heavy machinery.
Killed cattle. Quicklime. Captured
one C truck. Other truck released.
Unexpected visitors.
```

J Bearman

Yoakum shook his head. "Lenny Carmichael is a weasel all right. It's no secret he has a *señorita* in Mexico he visits regularly. He's also connected to the lie that eating meat from vaccinated cattle causes sterility, and you know the Church has to have them babies. Carmichael offers to buy the stock for nothing and then sells it again, sick or not. He's supposed to have a herd over around Dead Horse Mountain, but nobody ever found it."

Bearman frowned. "Did anybody ever look?"

"In Mexico? When I rode with some so-called authorities, they used paperwork to start fires."

Bearman turned to the brothers. "Steve, who was there at the Black Gap turnoff when you passed? And why didn't they stop you?"

"We didn't see nobody, just the tents and the machinery."

"No cars or trucks?"

"No, sir."

Yoakum said, "Carmichael and his friend *Señor Mordida* had a hand in that. Bet you Carmichael was making his last run in a split with Ornelos."

"We didn't run into anybody named *Mordida*," Steve said. "I'm sure of that. A man on horseback told us to keep driving."

"*Mordida* is Spanish for *bribe*. This little enterprise cost Ornelos."

"What about the fifty bucks me and Brother was supposed to get?"

Bearman turned and faced the east. The river flowed mostly north at that point, so east was Mexico. "I reckon it's over there somewhere," he said.

"Doggonit, Steve," Brother said.

Yoakum said, "These two boys ain't exactly clear of suspicious misdeeds, as far as I'm concerned."

"Then we'll give them a chance to redeem themselves," Bearman replied.

"We just thought it was a job. The man in Alpine was white. He seemed a good fella. Said he had a ranch down here," Steve added quickly.

"A ranch? What was his name?" Yoakum asked.

"Said he was Eugene Rhodes. We could call him Gene."

Bearman laughed. "Eugene Rhodes is the name of a western writer out of New Mexico. He died in June."

"How we supposed to know that?"

"You aren't. Listen, Steve, I want you to go back to the camp at the Black Gap turnoff and take Mr. Yoakum with you. He'll vouch for you and Brother on my say-so. Find out where everybody is. There's a trunk line there from Stillwell's store. Cap'n Fallis in Alpine will need to know about this. Wally, get on that phone and get some people out here. We'll need the backhoe and the bulldozer and enough quicklime to cover the carcasses. You decide how much or they will. We'll also need an officer and a coroner for the deceased. Steve, be careful about being stopped along the way out or being followed. Wally?"

Yoakum nodded.

"Get a move on. I don't look forward to standing around in the moonlight with angry smugglers just across the river while we watch a bunch of sick cows."

Yoakum nodded and spit. "Come on, Steve. Let's see what this big boy can do. Brother, you take care of my horse while I'm gone, but don't try to ride her. She's worse than Bearman's fancy pants when it comes to a stranger on her saddle."

"Is that true, Mr. Bearman?" Brother asked.

"No."

"That's all right," Yoakum laughed. "I can tell that same story an hour from now, and they'll still ask you if it's true."

They lifted the ramp attached to the brothers' truck, slid it into the bed, and closed the gate. The noise of the big engine turning over was disturbingly loud after the desert silence of the fight. Bearman was glad to see it go. The cows started bawling again, and that sound got on Bearman's nerves.

He said to Brother, "Let's take a look at who we've got hog-tied."

They walked past the second truck, and Bearman told Brother to check for the key. Brother climbed up and opened the cab door. The dash was in shadow, so he felt around and found the key. "It's here," he said, backing out of the cab.

"Let me have it."

When Brother gave Bearman the key, he asked, "Whose truck is this now?"

"The state or county gets it for now. Likely a search of the title will show it's registered to a ranching conglomerate in New Jersey that does not exist. Who knows?"

"Shame," Brother said. "It's almost brand new."

Bearman surveyed the big COE truck. "I've never seen one like it," he said. "Of course, I wouldn't have."

The prisoners were the truck drivers hired for the job. They were clearly brought out of Mexico only for that purpose and had never heard of the Ornelos ranch or the quarantine. They had been picked up from the village of La Linda, upriver from the Black Gap, where a mine for fluorspar operated. They were then given a ride to where the big trucks were parked. A man the others called *jefe* had ridden with them. Other than that, they were told nothing and had nothing else to tell.

"Just like me and Steve," Brother said, when Bearman translated.

"The poor and the innocent are always pawns in the game of misdeeds."

"Is that from one of your records?"

"It might as well be."

Before the equipment and men arrived, Bearman scouted a place for the kill zone. There was level ground above the draw, but the limestone ledges revealed by erosion in the draw suggested the same above and would require more than the D7 bulldozer could manage that night. He went back to the draw, which obviously had not carried water for many years, and decided they could kill the cattle in the corral and, once covered with quicklime, push in the walls of the draw. The slope could be figured so that the left hand of the forked draw could carry any doubtful runoff. The other advantage to leaving the cattle there was that if they tried to move them, the sick and thirsty animals were sure to stampede for the river. The cattle would be killed where they were.

"I don't want to see that." Brother shook his head.

"It's not a pretty sight," Bearman agreed.

Bearman and Brother took the horses and led them away from the draw to find a place to tie them upwind of the work that was left to be done. They untied the ankles and wrists of the prisoners and got them to help load the ramp into the bed of the remaining truck. Bearman and Brother put the prisoners in the truck too, retied their ankles and wrists, and closed the rear gate. The prisoner with the bruised belly complained and prayed the whole time. Bearman climbed up into the cab and lumbered it out of the draw and clear of the anticipated equipment. He was troubled about why no one had been seen at the Black Gap turnoff.

The moon went into the west.

Almost three hours later, the brothers' truck appeared on the road, with a backhoe about a mile behind it and a truck pulling a lowboy trailer loaded with the D7 Caterpillar behind the backhoe. When the truck hauling the bulldozer rounded a bend, Bearman saw two official vehicles trailing behind it in the dust. As they all got closer to the draw, Bearman felt the ground vibrate.

When the vehicles were parked, the men gathered in the draw. Bearman was surprised to see Cap'n Fallis, the senior patrol officer for the district, among the arrivals.

"I was in Marathon," Fallis said. He ruefully explained that the men at Black Gap had been taken by surprise about bedtime and tied and left in the fuel tent. Yoakum winked at the story. Or Bearman thought he did.

"What have we got, Mr. Bearman?"

They walked the draw, and Bearman placed the events in the story of the fight. The bulldozer operator agreed with Bearman's decision to leave the cattle where they were, and he walked back to the truck. Two men whom he had brought with him began to unload sacks of quicklime into the front bucket of the backhoe. The lights of the vehicles threw a carnival pattern across the desert.

Bearman was not part of the slaughter. He and Cap'n Fallis sat in the inspector's car with a flashlight between them while he told his story again and worked through the details of the fight and the death of the one man whose gun exploded. He showed Fallis the ruined gun. He asked the agent if there would be an inquest, and the agent said he would let Bearman know. Bearman tore a sheet from his notebook with a tally of the cattle and gave it to Fallis. He described Pulaski and told of his help and suspicion about what he called a "pipeline." He explained about the brothers and vouched for them. Although the doors were closed and the windows rolled up in the Plymouth, they could hear the work of the .30-.30's. There was a long break of silence while the quicklime was spread, then the bulldozer started up.

Finally, Bearman was ready to leave. Fallis thanked him for his work and mumbled something about "blasted border country." Bearman went to round up the others and invite them for breakfast and coffee at his place. Off to his right, a man from the state had discovered a relatively small yearling that had escaped the bars of the corral. It looked up at the agent, and the agent shot it.

Bearman found his friends squatting in the dark near the horses. Looking back at the draw, Bearman reflected that the activity looked like the birth of a small town in the middle of the night.

"Is it over, Mr. Bearman?" Brother asked.

"Yes. Steve, do you think that monstrosity of yours can make it over to my place?"

"Mr. Bearman, that truck has got a low gear so low that it could pull the moon out of the sky, if you could ever lasso it."

Bearman turned to Yoakum, who asked, "What are you proposing?"

"Let's all go over to my place for breakfast and coffee. Right now, I'd give a pretty penny for my pipe."

Yoakum looked at Steve. "Forget low gear. Put her in high and let's get out of here before the first can of beans is opened."

They all laughed, burning away more tension as they left the slaughter behind them.

Back at the hut, Bearman fired up his kerosene stove and filled the coffeepot while the brothers built a fire in the circle of rocks near the door where Bearman cooked everything that needed an oven, Dutch or otherwise, such as biscuits. The night was chilly enough to make the fire feel good, and Yoakum found his box, while the brothers used the flagstone bench that they had made during their first trip out there. The one chair in the camp was Bearman's chair.

Yoakum still needed to talk, but none of them wanted to talk about the night's work.

"Boys," Yoakum said, spitting in the fire, "while John is in his little hut figuring the best way to poison us, I want to ask you two a question."

Steve and Brother looked at him.

"Have either of you dark-haired sons of Erin ever heard of *la Mujer del Rio*?"

The coffee was boiling when Bearman came outside, carrying the Dutch oven. He set it down in the coals of mesquite and salt cedar and century plant stalks and used his long-handled shovel to put more coals on the lid. He said to the brothers, "I know you're about to hear a story, so if at any time you want to interrupt Mr. Yoakum, think carefully before you do. Wally, you are not allowed to shoot either one or both of them."

"Give a gun to Steve. He likes to shoot stuff," Brother piped up.

"You do, too," Steve retorted.

"But not like you. You like the noise."

"What's wrong with that?"

"See what you done, John," Yoakum said. "Once started, these boys can chase more rabbits than any twenty other people on a good day with ten dollars in their pockets."

"We saw some rabbits on the road last night," Brother said.

"It's still last night," Steve told him.

"After midnight, it becomes a new day."

"It's not a new day until the sun comes up."

Bearman went back to his cooking, and Yoakum went back to his story, his voice a little louder, more insistent.

"When I first came out here, the quarantine had just started, and I knew I would have to walk both sides of the river. That meant making myself plenty unpopular with Mexican ranchers and Texas ranchers alike, thinking to make a dirty dollar off smuggled cattle."

"Like them tonight."

"Son, don't interrupt me with statements of the obvious. This story is best told in the dark, and it won't be dark much longer."

"The fire makes it light," Brother said.

Yoakum raised his voice a little. "John?"

Through the open door of the hut, they heard Bearman say, "No."

Yoakum sighed. "Let me start over. Have either of you ever heard of *la Mujer del Rio*?"

"What's a *mujer*?" Brother asked.

"It's a woman."

"I know *rio* means river."

"And there is no wonder why Ireland is an island." Yoakum shook his head and spit.

"Tell us about the woman," Steve said. "We like stories about women. Maybe she was a selkie."

"*La Mujer del Rio* was thought to be a legend about a ghost woman all in white who had supernatural healing powers," Yoakum persisted.

Brother interjected, "What did she look like?"

"I bet she was old and ugly, all wrinkled up and scary," Steve said.

"That's the kind of woman you like," Brother sniggered.

"No, it's not."

"What about that woman at the lumberyard?"

"What woman?" Steve said and pushed Brother's shoulder.

Yoakum called again, "John?"

"Still no" came the reply.

Yoakum forged on. "Being an enemy, so to speak, of the unscrupulous ranchers in the Big Bend, I needed to find a hideout. It had to be close to the river and high enough to scout movement. John has a good place here for scoutin', but terrible for defense. Mexicans shoot across the river all the time."

"We saw them shootin' when we was buildin' Mr. Bearman's hut," Brother said.

"No doubt."

"Didn't we, Steve, and us up on the roof in plain sight."

"Well," Yoakum forged on, "I went farther down the river into Big Canyon, where only a fool would think of living due to the high walls of the canyon that were sheer from base to the top. But I could see evidence of primitive people up there, and I figured that if they could live in that canyon like eagles on a nest, so could I.

"So me and Rosie began to study wildlife until we found a very old trail that followed the Texas side of the river from top to bottom."

"Who the heck is Rosie? Is she the *mujer*?"

Yoakum drew his pistol and fired a round close to where the brothers sat, shattering a piece of limestone. The brothers tumbled backward off the bench.

Bearman came outside and Yoakum said, "I didn't shoot 'em, but I'll be John Brown if I try to tell them another story."

Bearman said, "Steve, get that hay hook by the door and lift the lid on the Dutch. See if the biscuits are done."

"Yes, sir." He did, and they were.

"I've got gravy in the frying pan and hominy in the little Dutch, plates and forks. Use those empty cans for coffee cups."

"Good gracious," Yoakum said, forgetting his peeve. "No beans?"

After they had eaten and the brothers had cleaned the dishes,

Bearman told them privately, “Mr. Yoakum was married once. Her grave is in that canyon.”

XI

Marathon, April 1945

```
4/19/1945 Bad day. Trouble at
Maravillas. AT dying.
Heading home with rough thoughts.
How could . . .?
```

J. Bearman

The day John Bearman heard that Annie Tinsley was dying, he had arrived in Marathon, Texas, in his wagon, planning to file his report via telegram and stock up on food supplements for his animals and for himself. As was typical of that time of year, particularly April but also August, there was an uncomfortable humidity in the atmosphere and the resulting useless "clouds without water" as Jude so well described them in his short letter to the Brethren. But humidity was rare in the Big Bend and tended to aggravate short tempers and dampen restraint. Though a proven ingredient in quarrels and hard words, weather was a poor excuse for the way Bearman felt. There seemed to be more than humidity in the air.

After he filled out the telegram blank, he watched impatiently as Homer Hobart, the operator, fumbled between his key and a chunk of cornbread that showered crumbs whenever touched, which was often.

"That good cornbread, Homer?" he asked mildly.

"The best." Hobart paused and started to elaborate.

Bearman cut him off. "Is there a telegraph operator in this town?" Still mild.

"I'm the operator," Hobart said, confused.

"Then why in the name of all that's good and beautiful don't you leave the blasted cornbread alone and send my message and give me my receipt?"

"No need to get huffy, Mr. Bearman."

"Homer, you've never seen huffy." It was the second time he had heard that word at the station, and he fought off the memory of the first instance.

Eventually, he left the station, looking neither left nor right, refusing to encounter visual reminders of his first meeting with Annie Tinsley. Honey was sweet, he reasoned, but too much honey at once would choke a man.

He stepped down from the platform, folding the receipt into his shirt pocket beside a letter from the department, and proceeded to the general store, which Dollar-Five both liked because of the smells and did not like because Bearman always unlooped the reins from the saddle horn and tied the mare. She tended to annoy any other horse when she was free to move about while the other horse was hitched, which in turn tended to annoy the owner of the horse.

Bearman gave the storekeeper his list and wandered the aisles, looking at all the things he did not need. Despite the appealing merchandise, he found himself repeatedly at the front windows as if expecting to see someone. Each time he looked out, Dollar-Five saw him and stamped her right hoof. When the store began to fill with customers, he told the proprietor to stack his stuff by the side door; he was going to get some lunch and would return with the wagon.

At the hitching rail, he told Dollar-Five he was going to get something to eat, and she could either stay there or go down the street with him to the livery stable, but either way, he had to tie her. Familiar with Bearman's routine, she looked down the street and snorted, so that's how they went.

At the livery stable, he removed Dollar-Five's saddle and blanket and put them on a sawhorse by the rail. She both liked that and didn't. She felt better physically but knew it meant she would be left out. Bearman told the blacksmith, who seemed preoccupied, to put them somewhere to dry out, and he walked another block to the only restaurant in Marathon.

It was after noon, but not yet one o'clock, and the single large dining room was crowded. The high pressed-tin ceiling was supported by two rows of ten-inch square posts on which were mounted the heads of mule deer and antelope, their horns obscured by the clustered hats of patrons, who were mostly men. Bearman ignored the racks and made his way without notice or acknowledgement between the tables until he saw with complete surprise the familiar face of a man who had known Bearman's family when they lived near Bryan in East Texas. His nickname was Butch, but everybody who knew him called him Cuz. He was that kind of man.

"Amazing what you can see when you don't have a gun, ain't it?" he said, standing up to shake Bearman's hand.

Bearman said, "Hello, Cuz. Are they ever going to build a jail that will hold your sorry boots?"

"Haven't yet. How's tricks?"

Bearman took off his hat and put it crown down on the table in front of an empty setting. A waitress stopped at the table to see if Cuz wanted more coffee, and Bearman ordered a steak with potatoes, green beans, and a chunk of homemade bread. He explained briefly what he was doing, then he asked, "The real news is what you're up to this far from shade trees?"

"Scoutin'," Cuz said. "Heard the livestock had eaten all the good stuff, and folks were movin' on with goats and such like. Mohair. Sheep. It's a buyer's market, and I'm a buyer."

"Cattlemen from this part of the country are having a problem moving their surplus stock, which includes sheep and goats. Bad press. People are afraid to take a chance. It would only take one infected animal to poison a herd."

"Faint heart never won fair hand. I have faith in inspectors and men like you. I'll take what I can get."

"Uh-huh. Traveling alone?"

"No. Mama's shoppin', and I wanted some coffee. We're off to Alpine when the train gets steam up, so to speak. In fact, there's Mama now. It's a day for miracles. Every time she wanders off, I'm afraid I'll never see her again," he added with a laugh.

Bearman stood and gave the woman a hug. Taking after Wally Yoakum, he said, "Why don't you leave this old mossback and run away with me, Julie?"

"You have a house?"

"Sort of."

"How many rooms does it have?"

"Just the one."

"Forget it, then. When I leave Butch, it'll be to trade upward, not backward. You remember that little shotgun house we lived in when your folks were still alive?"

The train horn blew.

"We better go, Mama." Cuz retrieved his hat off the nearest post. "You behave yourself, young man," Cuz said, and they shook hands again.

"Come home sometime," Julie added, and Bearman thought, *To what?*

When they were gone, Bearman sat down again and marveled at the coincidence of seeing old home folks on the one day in weeks he had come to town. Only later did it occur to him that the meeting was an omen of tragedy to come.

The waitress appeared with his order, and Bearman was putting pepper on his steak when he heard from the next table the only name he knew that could cause his heart to either speed up or slow down.

The table was occupied by several men he recognized, one of them a doctor, the only real surgeon in the Big Bend. The doctor had returned that morning from a visit to Mrs. Tinsley, he said, who had survived a difficult labor after a debilitating pregnancy but would probably not survive the next week. A girl child had been born eleven days before, healthy, although underweight, and was in the care of a Mexican wet nurse. While there were no physiological problems or complications, Mrs. Tinsley had evidently lost her heart in the ordeal and would respond to nothing, either from her husband or from the doctor's black bag. As there was not anything else he could do, he had returned to town. His only other responsibility was to notify the coroner of Annie Tinsley's imminent death.

"That Tinsley woman ain't thirty yet," one of the other men at the table said.

"Nevertheless," said the doctor, waving a clean, pale hand, "the depression into which she has fallen is beyond the power of drugs to bring her back. In fact, drugs would make it worse. I suggested moving her to the hospital in my car, but Mr. Tinsley thought it better if she died at home."

"Morton Tinsley's an idiot," said another.

"But if she ain't hurt?" the first man persisted.

"The mind, the heart, the soul, the spirit—whatever you want to call it—has been seriously hurt. What should be a time of joy for that family has become one of tragedy."

"But . . ."

"I'll tell you the truth," the doctor added. "I have put *broken heart* as the cause on more than one death certificate in my life."

Bearman looked at the fork in his rough hand, then put it carefully down beside the heavy crockery platter. For a full minute, he stared at the opposite wall, seeing not it but the woman he had met at the train station two years before. Something about her had led to a sparring match between them, one dare after another. He almost smiled at the memory. Instead, he remembered briefly the day he had found her afoot. That memory did not make him want to smile. It made him catch his breath.

The men at the next table concluded it was a shame and went on to talk of other local events in which Bearman had no interest. His forearms resting on the table, he blinked and looked down. An urge to move, to be away, prodded at him. He pushed back from the table and stood up, having eaten very little of his food. He dropped the chunk of homemade bread into his left coat pocket. He lifted his hat from the table and let it rest on his head. From his shirt pocket, he took the telegram receipt and a letter, but the folded dollar bill he sought was in his other pocket.

"*A dollar, five is all I have left from lunch at Sanderson.*"

He placed the dollar bill under the edge of the plate and turned away. He did not look at the men at the next table as he went by them. He did not, in fact, look at anyone or anything with the intent or ability to see. The memory of the way out guided him through the tables.

One of the men at the doctor's table said, "Hey, ain't that the guy who caught some Mexicans trying to smuggle sick cows last fall?"

They all turned to watch Bearman walk away stiffly between the tables.

"That guy?"

"He looks like he's on his way to round up some more."

"Glad I'm not one."

After a pause, "Huh. I heard Jessie got a repossessed car."

"What kind?"

"Repossessed."

Bearman left the restaurant, carrying a growing emptiness inside of him as he walked to the livery stable where his little party of horse and mules and wagon waited for him. He kept revolving in his mind the contradiction that an unhurt person, free of disease, could be so near death. If it was not physical, then it had to be mental. He remembered when his parents had been murdered. He had felt a sense of loss so deep that he could not eat and only slept, exhausted. But birthing a healthy baby was surely not a loss.

Dollar-Five nickered when she saw Bearman approach. It was obvious from ten feet away that she had not been cared for. The hair on her back was matted with dried sweat, and there was no water set out for her. The mules and the wagon stood in the sun where Bearman had originally left them while there was ample shade in the wagonyard close by.

The blacksmith was sitting by the anvil on a stool made from a cut length of cottonwood stump, talking to another man and shaking his head.

"Oliver!" Bearman called. "Why hasn't my horse been groomed and watered, and why in the name of common sense are the saddle and blanket in the dirt? Get up from there and do your job before I burn the place down."

"Your horse must have kicked over the sawhorse," Oliver said.

"Now, hold on, Mr. Bearman," Gray Dyer, the local pastor, said. "Sam has a sick boy, high fever."

"The doctor is over at the restaurant. Tell him that. I've got fifty miles ahead of me, and I wanted to make Garrison's before dark. Why are my mules standing in the sun?"

The other man stood up. He said, "You obviously don't understand—"

"Shut up, Gray," Bearman snapped.

He untied Dollar-Five and told her to find water. When she ambled over to the trough in what Bearman called her "haughty walk," he almost smiled. Then he turned his glare on the two men still at the anvil and went past them to the mules, which he led to the shade of the wagonyard and the water trough there. He went back to Dollar-Five, picked up her blanket and saddle, carried them to the wagon, and dropped them in. He heard Annie Tinsley's voice say, "*I'm not like this.*" He went into the stable and came out again with a currycomb, then curried Dollar-Five in long strokes. She swished her tail in approval.

The blacksmith got up and came over. "I'm sorry, Mr. Bearman," he quavered. "I didn't think you would be back so soon, and I was telling Gray—"

Bearman ignored the man, but he knew Oliver was deeply affected by the fact that he just stood there. Bearman did not feel sorry for him. A man should do his job. When Bearman was satisfied, he took the currycomb back into the stable and replaced it on the shelf. He came out again to find Oliver still standing there with Dollar-Five, either looking at him or watching him, which, with Dollar-Five, was two different things. He gathered the mare's reins and pulled the bridle and headstall off the mare's head. "Come on, Dollar-Five, let's load up." To Oliver, he said, "If I owe you anything, bill me."

As he passed the anvil, Gray Dyer started to say something, but Bearman said, "No."

In the wagonyard, Bearman placed the bridle close up to the seat. He filled his cask with water, hammered down the lid with the heel of his hand, and tied it in the wagon. He checked the harness of the mules and walked around the wagon, checking the wheels, while Dollar-Five waited. Satisfied, he climbed onto the seat, gave the lines a shake, and guided the placid mules out the rear of the wagonyard and around into the street. He had to wait for two automobiles to pass, and he thought about having an automobile for distance and a horse for rough work. Then he thought about the time he had seen Annie Tinsley pass by an open door without looking at him. It must be mental, he concluded, *Surely that can be fixed.*

Everything on his list was already stacked by the side door of the general store, so he was quickly loaded and started southwest into a sun too hot for April. Despite his anxiety about Annie Tinsley, he let the mules walk most of the way down into the broad valley of the Rio Grande, and he let them rest after steep grades. He did not make Garrison's ranch by dark, nor did he attempt to reach it at all that night but bypassed it in the dark. Dollar-Five, aware of how close they were to a friendly place, trotted up to the wagon seat next to Bearman and whinnied.

"Not this time," he told her, and she snorted and ran ahead. He was afraid of bad news and the effect it would have on him in front of other people.

About eight miles above Stillwell's store, he found a level place near a dry wash, with good forage for the animals. Dollar-Five had preceded Bearman and the mules and was already in the wash. Bearman watered the mules and led them down into the wash, where he hobbled them, just in case, and the mare followed Bearman back to the wagon for a drink.

The animals taken care of, he made a meal out of the chunk of homemade bread from the restaurant. Then he pulled his bedroll from behind the wagon seat where he also carried his rifle when he traveled. He made his bed near enough to the rear wagon wheel that he could rest his back against the outer side of the hub, and for a while, he sat there smoking his pipe and thinking. Then he made a pillow of his coat and lay on his back to watch the stars, as if they could tell him something.

Such was his mood when the moon rose that he began to remember every callous thing he had ever said in his life. Whether retort or extended callousness disguised as exclamation or condemnation, each instance ran through his mind with a burning like that of a new hemp rope through an ungloved hand and made a blister not temporal in healing, but everlastingly fresh made and raw. Prone to self-examination and feelings of guilt and remorse, he did not wonder why he should remember these instances now.

He knew he had been rude to the blacksmith before learning the man's boy was sick with a fever, and when Gray Dyer had curtly offered the excuse, Bearman had been rude to him as well. The blacksmith had done a shameful job in letting the saddle and blanket fall from the sawhorse and lie in the dirt. To Bearman, at that time, it was a negligence that could not be excused, even by preoccupation with the illness of a child.

But now, as he shifted away from a fist-sized rock in his back, his rudeness burned in his consciousness. Considering what lay ahead of him, what had perhaps already happened in his absence from the Flats, he knew he had made a bad start.

"Well, Lord," he said aloud. "Forgive me my rudeness. I hope you see fit to heal the boy, and . . ." He paused, and his jawline hardened. So personal were the words, he dared not speak; he could not bring himself to burden God orally with his selfish desire. He turned his eyes away from the moon and drew no comfort from the skirt of smoky light with which she draped the mountains to the south.

Later, Dollar-Five came up out of the wash and stood near him while he slept, and coyotes continued an unresolved argument, miles away in the dark, unpeopled desert.

XII

Near Maravillas Canyon, April 1945

4/20/1945 No other way. Took her.

J Bearman

It was past the middle of the afternoon that day when Bearman rode into the yard of the Tinsley place, glad to see Tinsley's Dodge parked in the shade of a cottonwood. He wrapped the lines around the brake and jumped down from the high seat. He remembered thinking Yoakum dismounted with a bounce, but Bearman was too stiff to try it. He did not unhitch the mules, but led them to the concrete water trough that extended both into the corral and out of it again. Dollar-Five had already taken advantage of it and was now interested in the three horses in the corral. Bearman imagined the mare asking for news.

Although he seemed intent only on his animals, his eyes had swept the front of the house, counted the chickens in the yard, listened to the intermittent squeak of the windmill fan, and noted the otherwise silent aspect of the house. He was also aware of the exact moment Morton Tinsley appeared in the doorway in the deep shadow of the porch.

"Hello, Morton," he said, stepping into the shade.

Tinsley nodded and looked at Bearman's animals. "Mr. Bearman," he said, "it's a sorry state of affairs you find me in this day."

Bearman also nodded, his throat tight, feeling the older man's apparent agony above his own.

"Been to town. Heard about it."

"Getting supplies?"

"Yes, sir."

Bearman followed Tinsley to the wagon where the older man looked at Bearman's purchases as if he were thinking of buying something. "Yep. Beans are cheaper in the sack than in the can."

"I heard Mrs. Tinsley was in a bad way," Bearman prompted, now irritated by the man's distraction.

"I've never seen the like of it before," Tinsley said, returning to the porch. "Just quit. Won't do nothin'. Won't even look at the baby. Just slippin' away."

Bearman swallowed. "Hard thing."

"It is that. Doctor Burke said there was nothing wrong with her he could fix. He said her heart's gone out of her, the result of 'great distress and hopeless fear.' That's what he said. I don't understand it."

"What does she say?"

Tinsley shook his head. "Don't say nothin'. Don't talk. Won't look at you. Hasn't touched a bite for four days. By God, lately won't even get up to tend to her business. Bed is all fouled. Esperanza won't touch it. Mrs. Tinsley just lies there, not sleepin' and not awake."

At the thought of the vital woman he knew so broken, Bearman felt his own agony rise above that of the other man. It was clear Tinsley did not know what he had. For a moment, he focused on listening to the wind under the eaves of the porch. He stood so that he faced the rocky escarpments of the *Sierritas de Guadalupe* across the river in Mexico.

"Can't make her?" he asked shortly, with a different voice.

"I don't know how to make her. I don't know anything about birthing and womenfolks and what they go through. I tell you, I'm stretched to the limit out here."

"Doctor said you didn't see any use in taking her to the hospital."

"What for? What for?" he repeated. "I've got arrangements to make and people to contact. I've got a ranch to take care of. I can't be running back and forth between here and Alpine, if she's just goin' to die anyway. That costs money."

It was then Bearman understood that Morton Tinsley had given his wife no support during the delivery. Tinsley had been concerned about himself when she needed him so badly at one of those times when a woman was most painfully vulnerable.

"And the Mexican woman?"

"She won't touch her. Crosses herself, shakes her head, and tends to the baby. '*Es muerto, pobrecita*,' she says. I let her take the baby across the river with her when she went home over in La Linda. It's better off there than here until this mess is settled."

Bearman's muscles tensed at hearing Annie Tinsley's child referred to as *it* and her decline toward death as *a mess*. Nevertheless, he remembered his regret at his behavior the night before, and he held his temper.

"Doctor give you any advice?"

Tinsley did not answer, then he shook his head and managed, "Come inside."

Bearman hesitated. "I just stopped by to pay my respects."

"Well, come inside and look at what you're paying for."

Morton Tinsley's face was set and hard when he faced the house, his eyes too wide, with a glare of desperation or madness in them. Bearman took off his hat and followed him into the house. The front room was the largest and the coolest. Bearman remembered seeing Annie Tinsley walk across this room. Tinsley continued down a short hall to a closed door. He looked at Bearman, then opened it, and they went inside.

Bearman was instantly aware of the smell and the buzz of flies. Although the room was only slightly cool, the figure on the bed was covered to her hair with a soiled sheet, and a cotton blanket with an Indian pattern was twisted down to her hip as if she had cast it off. Both were soiled and stained with urine and feces. As if drawn against his will, breathing through his mouth, Bearman stepped around the bed. Flies touched his face and landed on his shirtsleeves. At the head of the bed, he stopped and looked down at the tangled clumps of brown hair above the sheet. His eyes moved down to her shoulders, watching for the movement of breathing and afraid he would see none.

"Go ahead. Pull that sheet back," Tinsley said from the doorway where he remained.

Bearman looked at him, his face pale, then reached two fingers down and drew the sheet away from Annie Tinsley's face. He started visibly. The haggard profile, turned into the yellowed folds of the pillow beneath her head, bore no resemblance to any woman he had ever met. Her mouth was open, her lips strangely slack, as if she were in deep thought or chronic pain. Her eyes were closed, but Bearman had the impression, unconfirmed by anything tangible, that she was neither asleep nor fully conscious.

A minute passed, second by second, then another, and Bearman raised the sheet higher, saw her shoulder, saw it move, saw something else, then drew the sheet down again as it had been. The skin of his face felt taut, and he knew he could neither breathe nor speak until he was again outside.

On the porch, Bearman said, "So, what are you going to do?"

"You saw her; what do you think I'm going to do?"

"Something."

"Something? Like what?"

> "*There's lots of things a man could do to save his true love and get them out of the danged mess they was in. Goshdarnit, don't you think so, Mr. Bearman?*"

"Anything is better than nothing. Get her help. Clean her up and get her out of that closed room. She's not dead yet."

Tinsley turned his back on Bearman. "I told you she won't let me. She fights me when I try to help her. Barely drinks a cup of water a day. The one time I tried to get her out of that bed, she screamed until she passed out. I thought she was dead then. I don't know—she's a real disappointment to me as a wife and mother, unfeeling as that sounds."

Dollar-Five turned suddenly from the corral and watched Bearman. She whinnied but stayed where she was.

"Let me take her downriver," Bearman said, surprising them both, his voice low, strange.

"What the hell, Bearman? Have you lost your mind, too?"

"Listen, Morton. What if she's not too far gone to save? You know Wally Yoakum?"

Tinsley nodded. "Supposedly a range detective and veterinarian, not that I ever heard he did any detecting—or doctoring."

"He lives back where the canyons run together, a long way from anywhere, but he knows a *curandera* the Mexicans call *la Mujer del Rio*."

"I've heard those stories. Mexicans think she's a witch."

"Let me take her to this woman."

"There's no roads back there for my car. I don't know how long I can be away, the baby and all."

"I'll take her. The *Mujer* knows I'm a friend of Mr. Yoakum. If you were there, we would never find her."

"Folks will think it ain't right, you taking her."

Bearman took a few quick steps off the porch like he was going somewhere, trying hard to be calm, then turned on his heel and came back.

"Morton," he said, "I know you for a peaceable man, but I promise you this: if you don't get straight in your mind right now the most needful thing, I'm going to knock you down and pick you up again until you figure it out."

"Hold on, Bearman," Tinsley said, backing away. "What's your interest, anyway?'

"I'm trying to help a neighbor whose life is in danger. That's all."

Of course, it was deeper than that. He had seen something besides her slow respiration when he pulled the sheet back from her shoulder. In her right hand, tucked under her chin, she was holding a small, black volcanic rock shaped like a valentine heart. He was not sure what it stood for in her mind, just that it was important to her, a kind of lifeline, but also a connection between them.

Faced with a confrontation, Tinsley quickly backed down. "Do what you want," he sighed. "I have to meet Esperanza at the river crossing upstream. She needs money to care for the baby. I'll probably spend the night in Alpine."

"If anyone asks a question, just say I took her. That ought to make you feel better. But don't you change your mind and come gunning for me."

"I got to go. If she's dead when I get back, so be it." Tinsley turned back into the house to get his hat and duffel, in a hurry now that he had an excuse to get away.

As Bearman crossed the yard, he was ready, at that moment, to follow any other plan than the one he had come up with. It was foolish, premature, and open to the worst kind of tragedy if Annie Tinsley were to die while in his care. But who else was there to make the continuing effort to rouse her from the dark place into which she had fallen? Tinsley had plainly given up on her and removed himself as the rightful caretaker. The doctor had used her case as a means of sympathetic gossip in a crowded public place. Bearman even doubted his own ability to help her, having failed to recognize the woman he knew.

Morton Tinsley left the house with a canvas duffel and climbed into his Dodge without looking at or speaking to Bearman. He started the Dodge and almost backed into the chicken coop. He corrected and drove away, scattering chickens as he went. Bearman watched him from Dollar-Five's shoulder.

"Didn't even offer his car to drive her over to our little rock house," he said to the horse. "I heard one time that a dinosaur's brain was so small, the creature barely even knew it was alive. You reckon that's Tinsley's problem?"

Dollar-Five bumped Bearman with her shoulder, and Bearman said, "All right."

Bearman untied his canteen from the wagon and tied it in the water trough to cool its contents. Drinking hot water was like taking medicine without the benefit of any relief. He considered his load stacked forward and thought about how to arrange it to accommodate the woman. Beside supplements for the mules and the mare, he had a fifty-pound sack of dried beans, a sack of flour, two pounds of cornmeal, a twenty-five-pound burlap sack of potatoes and various canned goods, including tomatoes, peaches, condensed milk, and yellow hominy, and a sack of purple onions. He had a carton of bullets for his .45 and a seven-ounce can of Sir Walter Raleigh pipe tobacco. He laid out the sacks along the sideboards and shifted his saddle to the right corner of the wagon bed, away from the water cask, to allow more room in the middle. His pistol and gun belt were in his saddlebag, out of reach, and he left them there. He was too preoccupied to realize his mistake.

That done, he went back into the house, leaving Dollar-Five to haze the chickens.

It was a different house without the presence of Tinsley's helpless anger and resentment, which had been big enough, it seemed to Bearman, to take the air out of the rooms. He stopped before going down the hallway to the closed door and took in the arrangement and decor. It was a house with rooms and windows, dominated by a woman with taste, and he saw by the fireplace a small framed print by James McNeill Whistler of Maud Franklin. The sight of it and the memory of his comparing her to a figure painted by Whistler strengthened his resolve. She was Annie Tinsley, after all. He took a smile of determination with him through the closed door.

She lay as before, barely breathing.

Bearman dropped some clothing out of a chair and sat down close to the bed. His initial shock and revulsion were gone. He almost never let other people's concept of what was right and proper influence him, whether he agreed with it or not. A sickroom was just a sickroom. Things were what they were. So this time, the room and the smell and the flies did not distract him from his study.

He sat for a long time looking at her, seeing again with both memory and vision the woman she was. He did not want to stay in that house, in that room, longer than necessary, but he figured he would have to go very slow with her. At the same time, he gradually became convinced that she knew he was there and who he was. A connection had been opened, as on a telephone line. There was something, whereas before, there was nothing. Watching her, he saw her seem to come back from the dead with a slight, impatient movement, almost a twitch of her head on the soiled pillow, not caused by a fly, and the slight opening of one eye. The hand holding the rock surreptitiously slipped down to her waist an inch at a time, as if she were deliberately hiding it. He was encouraged. He knew that it was not a time for sympathy, no matter how earnest or sincere, neither did he intend to show her the depth of his concern.

"Hello, ma'am," he said in a soft voice.

The eye closed. The flies buzzed. Bearman crossed his legs and fanned away flies while he critically considered the room in its present disarray. He began to sing in a low voice, as he often did when on the trail.

Did you ever hear tell of Sweet Betsy from Pike,
Who crossed the wide mountains with her lover Ike,
Two yoke of cattle, a large yellow dog,
A tall Shanghai rooster, and one spotted hog.

His voice and the lyrics had no effect. He started another verse:

They soon reached the desert, where Betsy gave out,
And down on the sand she lay rolling about.
Ike in great wonder looked on in surprise,
Saying, "Betsy get up, you'll get sand in your eyes."

She groaned. From the dark place that made her temples seem to swell with pain, Annie Tinsley was aware with mortification that Bearman was in the room and was once again causing her do that which she could neither explain nor justify. It was easy to fight her husband because he gave up so quickly. The doctor, like the one who had attended to her mother in San Antonio, had his standard impersonal protocol, which did not allow for personal examinations into the mind and emotions. But somehow, this man had a power over her she could not resist. For a moment, she was so far out of her despair that she was embarrassed by her condition before him. John Bearman was a man who did not quit.

"Excuse me, Sweet Betsy?"

No, she thought. *I won't. I don't want to. It's too late.*

The wagon broke down with a terrible crash
And out on the prairie rolled all sorts of trash.

"Please shut up," she mumbled against her will.

"Did you say something, Sweet Betsy?"

"Shut up. Shut up. Shut up."

"Sweet Betsy."

"Shut up!" she screamed, and Dollar-Five appeared outside the window, looking for Bearman.

Bearman uncrossed his legs and leaned forward. Screaming was good. Screaming was passion. He remembered from his two previous meetings with her that Annie Tinsley reacted to frustration with anger. She was a fighter, not this sunken, limp form of a woman, so hurt she had quit on everything, even on life itself.

"Sweet Betsy."

The sheet flew back. "That's not my name!" Her eyes, reddened and swollen, burned into his.

Bearman straightened in the chair and placed his broad hands on his knees. "I know it isn't your name, ma'am, but you sure answered to it. I wasn't being mean for the sake of it. I needed to know something, and now I do."

She did not ask him what it was.

"Listen, like it or not, you're going home with me to my 'little rock house,' as you called it. You're going to stay a while, so you need to get up now and get cleaned up and dressed and pick out what you want to take. I've got my wagon, so there is plenty of room for anything shy of furniture. Except maybe this chair. We'll need another chair at my place. All right? I'll be out front."

He stood up. Annie Tinsley pulled the sheet up to her nose with a snap, and it was Bearman who was suddenly embarrassed to be looking at her while she lay in bed.

"No," she said. "Not going."

"You surely are."

"Are you kidnapping me? Did you kill Morton?"

"No and no."

"Who are you?"

"I'll be out front," he said again and walked out of the room, leaving the door open.

Dollar-Five met him by the wagon. She snuffled him, and he stroked her jaw. Satisfied, she returned to the shade of the cottonwood and watched the chickens. Annie Tinsley's horse, Tyler, stood by the corral fence, his head over the rail, watching every movement in the yard. Bearman thought it would be a good idea to take the horse.

Dollar-Five already knew him, and being a gelding, he did not impress her.

Bearman went to the barn and came back with a saddle, blanket, and bridle. Rather than put the tack in the wagon, he bridled and saddled the horse. Dollar-Five appeared at his shoulder and pretended to nip at him or get between him and Tyler. "There are worse things," Bearman said, pushing the mare away with his elbow. Dollar-Five shook her mane and did the "haughty walk" back into the shade. Bearman tied Tyler to a corral rail and untied his canteen from the water trough. He placed it in the sun for evaporation to further cool the contents.

Bearman went back to the barn and took armloads of hay to the wagon for bedding. He did not expect her to ride beside him.

After twenty minutes, he went back in the house and looked in at the door. Annie Tinsley was still in bed. For a few beats, he stood with his hands on his hips, looking down at her with a frown, then he turned to the wardrobe and opened it to see what she had. He was completely unprepared for the effect that seeing her clothes had on him. He just looked, and then he fingered the sleeve of the white blouse she had been wearing the day he met her two years ago. Unable to make up his mind what to take, he pulled all the clothes off the rod and carried them out to the wagon. *I ought to Sweet Betsy her again*, he thought as he threw the pile in along the right sideboards.

It was worse with her gown and robe and underthings, things he was never meant to see, except, perhaps, for her .38 and gun belt, which he included in the pile. He ignored the temptation to stare and did what he needed to do. In a chest under the window, he found extra bedding, and he took that to spread on the hay and his bunk. He did not want her soiling his bed. *Would she do that?* he wondered. He found her boots and some slippers and put them in. Piled in the bed of the wagon, it seemed to him like a lot of clothes, but women needed clothes. He thought that was enough, but he supposed he could always come back for something if she needed it. The fact was, however, he did not want to face Morton Tinsley again, ever. The man's ineptitude disgusted Bearman.

All the time Bearman carried clothes and bedding outside, Annie Tinsley had lain with her eyes closed, not moving or caring what Bearman did, if she was even aware that he was still there. But after the loading, Bearman came in with his canteen, determined to get some water in her. He approached the bed slowly, anxious that she would slip so deeply within herself in such a short time.

"Sweet Betsy? Time to get up."

She seemed to press her head further against the pillow.

"Sweet Betsy. Sweet Betsy. Sweet Betsy."

She began to sob, and Bearman had mixed thoughts about that. Reaction had to be better than no action, at least to a certain extent.

"I've brought you some cool water," he said.

She shook her head back and forth across the pillowcase before she said, "No."

"Ma'am, you need this. You can't think straight if you've been without water for a time."

Annie Tinsley could feel him doing it again, stealing into her will and bending it. For a minute or two, she fought it off. Finally, she took a long breath of surrender, but then he poured water on her face. Later, Bearman thought, *spring loaded, spring released* as Annie Tinsley shot up from the waist, coughing and spitting. She turned on Bearman and tried to hit him, but he dodged away. Then she was crying and slapping the bed in something very close to a rage. Bearman stepped away from the bed and watched as she collapsed on the pillow, exhausted. Dust motes swam in the air.

He decided it was time to be nice. "Ma'am," he said, "I'm sorry for that trick, but you need to drink." He also thought she needed to get cleaned up and eat something. He wanted her to make him feel better about what he was doing.

She was crying softly. Bearman eased himself down on the side of the bed. Her face and hair were wet with tears and river water from the canteen. Bearman rested the canteen in the chair next to the bed and pulled loose the knot in the bandana around his neck. He used it to dry her eyes and cheeks and brushed back the matted hair at her temples, marveling at the unexpected contact.

"One time when I was a youngster, I got lost in the woods back home," he began. "It was East Texas and sandy. Pine trees grew so close together that every part of the woods looked like every other part of the woods. My father sold Watkins products, and sometimes, I would ride with him. I had no notion of where the road led in those days, but I knew one of the stops was at the house of a girl my age who loved toys and whistles. She had a jack-in-the-box we used to try to outguess."

Softly and slowly, like putting a child to sleep, he told her the story about a willful ten-year-old boy who thought he could cut through the woods to his friend's house instead of waiting for his father at one of his father's longer stops. The little girl knew he was coming that day because he had told her so. He had a plastic whistle he got in a box of Cracker Jacks, and he planned to surprise her with it. He had scorned the road and taken off on a deer tail that led farther into the woods and toward high ground, which meant less and less chance of water. With nothing but trees for bearings, he had been lost for two and a half days and was dizzy from lack of water before he was found.

"The next day, my father told me my little friend had also gone into the woods and gotten lost, looking for me. It was three more days before they found her."

Annie Tinsley lay perfectly still while he talked, but when he fell silent, she opened her eyes and abruptly grabbed the wrist of the hand that held the bandana. She stared at him, lucid and furious. Her grip was surprisingly strong, as if she wanted to tear his hand from his arm.

"Quit touching me," she said in a fierce voice.

"Ma'am, I'll be honest with you: you need a little touching."

"How dare you?"

"Up to this point, it was pretty easy."

She let go of his wrist and closed her eyes. "That's my scarf," she said.

"No, ma'am," he said. "It's my bandana. I found it where you left it." Then, after a pause, "Be best if you didn't cry anymore."

"I left it for you," she sobbed, though she had not wanted to tell him that. "What happened to the little friend?"

"She died. Will you take some water now?"

"No."

XIII

Outlaw Flats, April 1945

```
4/20/1945 Ambushed by Ornelos, MP,
one other.
Near Taylor farm. Shots fired. Ornelos
hit. AT spared by miracle.
```

J Bearman

Nevertheless, Bearman did manage to force Annie Tinsley to drink. She did not want to give in and accept the water, but this man of all men seemed to hypnotize her or bewitch her—she did not know what, could not think about it clearly except to feel so horrible that she could only wish the ground would open up and take her away. She fell back again on the dirty pillow after he released her head, and Bearman thought her color appeared to change, to darken into a flush, more like that of a living person than that of a china doll. He, however, was pale and shaking when he capped his canteen and stood away from the bed.

John, old boy, he began to admonish himself for what he was doing, but then he looked at the woman in the bed, her face calm in a kind of sleep, and he said aloud, "We need to get this little girl out of the woods, and if I'm the one who's going to do it, I might as well get it done."

He looked around the room to see if there was anything else he should take. The top of her dresser was cleaned off. Two pairs of shoes were surely enough. Then he thought of soap and such-like and found the bathroom. He liked being in that private room least of all, but he put such items as he thought were hers in a cloth bag. That was enough. He took the sack and his canteen to the wagon and stowed them away.

Dollar-Five started forward, but Bearman said, "Not yet," and she went back to the shade. She still seemed to resent the fact that Tyler was saddled instead of her. Bearman squinted at the sun to see how much time he had left before dark, and with that thought, he knew he was wasting it. For the work he had to do, he put on his gloves.

Back in her room, in that awful surrender of decency, Bearman tried to rouse Annie Tinsley. Nothing he said seemed to have any effect on her. She was not asleep—he was sure she was not asleep, but she was not in the waking world, either. He brushed back her hair. He grasped her shoulder and shook her gently, said her name. There was no response. Except for her slow breathing, there was no indication she was even alive.

Sho now, he thought.

The sheet lay at her chin, so jostling her, he pulled the cotton blanket up to that level. Where the sheet and blanket had become twisted, he pulled them straight, walking around the bed to do so. Satisfied, he caught the bottom sheet on the left and threw it and the covers back over Annie Tinsley. He did the same thing on the other side, effectively wrapping her with the bedclothes.

With one knee on the bed, he slipped his arms under her and lifted her off the bed. He regained the floor with both feet and shook her gently against his chest to better hold her. He carried her out of the house, kicking the door shut behind him. At the wagon, he had some trouble. He had left the tailgate down, but the best he could do with the woman was lay her sideways at the end of the wagon and climb over her to put her in the bed he had made for her from his purchases and her own bedding. Dollar-Five was very interested in what he was doing and twice bit the end of the cover as if to pull it off the figure wrapped in it or to pull the whole bundle off the wagon. Bearman rebuked her, but she did not go back to the shade. She knew it was time to go.

Satisfied, Bearman jumped down and closed the tailgate. He untied Tyler and tied the horse behind the wagon to a ring on the tailgate made for that purpose. As was his habit, Bearman used a knot that would give from a hard jerk. Too many things could happen on a desert road to effectively trap an animal with a hard knot. Dollar-Five began to half-circle around the gelding, as if to show her superiority, the same way she did in Marathon around tethered horses.

Bearman woke up the mules with encouraging nonsense, then climbed up on the high seat and started them homeward. Bearman liked the way the mules knew the road and never paused unless reined. He glanced over his shoulder at the sleeping woman to see that she was riding all right and the sun was not in her face.

Going along the rough road, past the site of Taylor's farm, Bearman felt his anxiety lessen. His mind had been full of dread since he first heard the pronouncement that she was dying. Now, the spirit of the future seemed to be smiling on him—or at least not scowling. He sang parts of the old Civil War song, "Lorena," and enjoyed the cool end-of-the-day feel of the air. He noted the sun had passed behind a mountain to the west that, in outline, looked like a fortress.

Then three men rode up from the river, their horses wet to the belly.

They stopped in the road ahead of him, and Bearman pulled up as well. He recognized two of the men. One was Marcos Pulaski. The other was Emilio Ornelos. All three were armed.

Marcos Pulaski and the third man moved outward off the road and separated while Ornelos sat his horse in the middle of the road. Up close, Ornelos was a handsome man, not quite a dude, but it was clear that he fancied himself a bit. When he took off his hat, his black hair was curly and trimmed. His eyes were wide apart and arrogant. His mouth was a line that, even in repose, suggested a sneer. He appeared to be more Castilian than Indian in coloration.

His clothes were new and clean, and neither he nor the other two were wearing chaps. This meeting was not about cattle. It was about Bearman.

Bearman did not say anything nor show any surprise. He should have been glad Pulaski was there, but he knew the man could do nothing to help him short of revealing his purpose or murder.

Bearman decided to let the other man speak first.

"Greetings, Señor government man. We meet in the sun this time."

Bearman knew Ornelos was sure of having the upper hand. He would convince him otherwise if he could. At the same time, he had Annie Tinsley to consider. "Not *el sol*, but *la sombra*, which scavengers and men like you prefer."

While Ornelos took the insult with his sneer of contempt, Bearman shifted the lines to his right hand and glanced over his shoulder at the woman. She had settled some in the wagon bed with the jostling, but otherwise had not moved. He wrapped the lines around the brake handle and was keenly, tragically aware that his rifle was under his feet and his pistol too far away in his saddlebag.

"You're on the wrong side of the river, *amigo*," he said.

"What river? The river flows; is it the same water? Yesterday's river is no more. Which river am I on the wrong side of?"

Bearman looked at Pulaski, then turned back to Ornelos, shaking his head. "That same old clever Latin trick again," he said. "Pretending ignorance while reciting a philosophy written on the wind with the dust of ages. You're a hundred years behind the time, my friend."

"You are not gracious," Ornelos said, straightening in the saddle at the new insult.

"What do you want?"

"So, we will not get to know each other."

"There will be no *mordida*, if that's what you mean."

"No. I can see that. You and I have—"

"Cut it," Bearman said. He wondered briefly where Dollar-Five was. "What do you want?"

"What do you have?" Ornelos sneered and gestured at the other two men to find the answer to his question.

They rode forward, Pulaski to the head of the wagon, the other man to the rear where Annie Tinsley's horse was tied. Bearman looked Pulaski in the eye, but Pulaski knew his role, and his face showed nothing. He saw that Bearman was not wearing his pistol, and he saw the buttstock of his rifle in the saddle scabbard on the floorboard under his seat. Pulaski knew that Ornelos saw it as well. He pulled it from under the seat and pretended to look at it.

Ornelos rode closer. "I will see his rifle," he said eagerly.

Pulaski said, "It is a *pinche* rifle for little girl bullets."

"Nevertheless, it is a Winchester. I will take it." Almost all Winchesters had been confiscated after the revolution and locked away in federal warehouses. The quickness of the lever action was prized over the bolt action.

"No," Bearman said.

"And who will stop me?"

"The same people who stopped your shipment of infected cattle."

"And who is that, you?"

"The United States government."

"And where is that?"

"You're looking at him. Say what you want. It's late, and I'm in a hurry."

"To go to your ugly *casita*? I wonder if it will be there."

The natural urge to protect his home surged through Bearman, but there was no outward sign of his anger.

"You have cost me many monies and a good man," Ornelos said. "I return the favor."

"You waited long enough."

The man at the back of the wagon realized the bundle of soiled bedclothes he was prodding amid the sundries hid the body of woman. "*¡Aiy*! *¡Madre a Dios*! *Es una mujer muerto, y tan cochina.*"

Pulaski reined his horse toward the other man, and Ornelos spurred forward. The clustered movement so close to Tyler made the skittish horse rear against the slip knot Bearman had tied in the reins, and the horse broke away.

"Do you plan all your disasters ahead of time?"

"*¡Consigue el caballo*!" Ornelos shouted. "Get the horse!" He wrestled his own disturbed horse against the high side of the wagon, observing the woman and the care in which she had been wrapped. He knew from the local gossip that this was the Tinsley woman who was dying after the birth of her child, just like a *gringa*. He could not guess in those hurried seconds why she was in the wagon of this man, but he knew she was important to him.

"This for my loss!" he shouted again. The words and the tone penetrated Annie Tinsley's awareness. She opened her eyes just as Ornelos put the barrel of Bearman's rifle over the sideboard in her face and tipped back the hammer from the safety position.

In those few seconds of desperate helplessness, Annie Tinsley knew how much she wanted to live. She began to strain against the constriction of the bedclothes that so completely bound her, but she was too weak to be effective.

A leer of triumph altering his features, Ornelos pulled the trigger.

There was a hollow snap when the hammer hit the firing pin, but no explosion. In that short space of time, Bearman threw himself over the brake onto the ground and reached over the sideboard to snatch up his Colt's and the gun belt in which it rested.

Ornelos, familiar with the Springfield bolt action popular in the revolution, had no way of knowing that Bearman never carried a live round under the hammer, that the rifle must be levered first. He was confused long enough to see Bearman pull his .45 free of the leather and to hear him cry out in a rough, loud voice, "*Sho now*!"

A red demon burst through the brush from the river and knocked the third man out of his saddle before twisting and rearing toward Pulaski, who jerked his horse into that of Ornelos to keep him from shooting either animal or person.

Without a clear target and in an effort to further confuse the situation, Bearman fired a round into the air. The mules squatted on their tails at the sound and jumped forward a pace. Annie Tinsley, hearing the gun so close by, began to scream in a hoarse voice. The sound of it was like a voice heard from the back of a cave, and it cut Bearman to a higher level of pity and anger.

Dollar-Five was not through. She turned at the tailgate and raced past Bearman to the mules, which she bit at and encouraged to jump forward again, thus upsetting all the players in their deadly game. By this time, the third man was on his feet and running toward the other two, his horse speeding away down the near slope toward the river from which the trio had come.

Bearman fired into the air again and called Dollar-Five back to his side. Even in the fury of her rage at being threatened, the mare instantly wheeled and came back. Ornelos, encumbered with a rifle he thought did not work, was trying to turn his mount toward the river.

Pulaski said, "*Volver al río, jefe*. Go to the river. I will take care of this *cabrón*." He pulled his automatic and fired three quick *crack-crack-cracks* in Bearman's direction, careful not to hit him. Annie Tinsley abruptly stopped screaming. Bearman thought he heard her sob and was strangely relieved. He did not think she had been hit.

"*Vete*," Pulaski said to Ornelos, deliberately jerking his reins back and forth to keep up the appearance of a struggle.

Ornelos had his horse under control and spurred down the road. Holding Bearman's rifle in his left hand, he shouted, "I leave you with your dead, *cabrón*."

Bearman answered with two quick, aimed shots, overcoming his natural disinclination to kill a man not immediately threatening him. He was mad enough to swing his pistol at Pulaski but lowered the barrel when he saw the surprise on the man's face.

Ornelos lurched in his saddle as if pushed, recovered, and spurred his horse away on the road about fifty yards before he cut down toward the water. The horseless rider was there and threw up his arms calling for help, but Ornelos, holding his right arm against his side and fumbling Bearman's rifle in the same hand as the reins, brushed past him and was gone.

Meanwhile, Bearman, now disregarding Pulaski, had circled the wagon and used the spokes of the near wheel to climb over the sideboard and check on Annie Tinsley. Dollar-Five followed him to the wagon and shook her mane at Pulaski's horse.

"How is she, *amigo*? Dead?" Pulaski asked in a low voice, holding close to the wagon bed.

Bearman could not answer. He knelt over the woman and put his hand on her face. Flushed from the sun, her face felt hot, but Annie Tinsley unconsciously turned her wet cheek toward him at his touch, and Bearman shook his head at Pulaski. *Just too tired to fight*, Bearman thought.

Pulaski said, "Do you want me to get your other horse, *amigo*?"

"No. I'll catch him with Dollar-Five or let him go back home. Go down the road a way and shoot at something that makes a noise when hit. I'll answer your shots one for one until I'm empty. Thank you, Marcos."

"I had no part in the destruction of your house. Know that. *Adiós*."

"What?"

Bearman called Dollar-Five and jumped on her back to be away from the wagon and the mules when he began to shoot the heavy .45. Pulaski turned in the saddle before going down to the river and firing his automatic. Bearman answered him shot for shot until Pulaski ran out. The man shouted deprecations and threats to Bearman and then was gone. Bearman heard Pulaski's horse hit the water and slog across, and that was it.

"Good old girl," Bearman said, patting the mare's neck. "You had fun back there, didn't you?"

They went slowly back the way they had come, the mare prancing for about ten feet. Bearman would have missed Tinsley's horse, but Dollar-Five followed its scent and turned down toward the river, where they found the gelding nuzzling the surface of the water. It was still skittish, but the mare crowded it until Bearman could get the reins. He jumped across into the saddle, and they went back to the wagon, with Dollar-Five running ahead.

After he had retied the horse to the ring in the tailgate, he climbed into the wagon and awkwardly knelt beside the woman, trying to stay off her clothes. He smoothed her hair and told her what had happened and that he would make sure it did not happen again. "I will fight for you," he said, and perhaps she heard him, but perhaps not. She made no move nor uttered a word. He felt a renewed sense of dread and again had serious doubts as to what he was doing. He climbed out of the wagon and up again onto the seat to drive his mules home.

"*Your little rock house.*"

XIV

Near Big Canyon, April 1945

4/20/1945-4/21/1945 Back at camp, riders sent to burn hut. Yoakum stopped raid. Kept their horses. AT in bad shape.

J Bearman

From a narrowing distance, Bearman's hut looked intact. The roof was still on it. The ramada still leaned. The spindly bars of the corral were in place, but there were now three horses in it, two of which were wearing Mexican stock saddles. The third belonged to Wally Yoakum. Bearman smelled smoke. The mules smelled the end of a journey and stepped lively over the last rise, and Bearman turned them onto the level in front of his hut.

Sitting there in the cooling air of the twilight near the firepit was Wally Yoakum. He spit and said, "Well, he arrives. I've been moping here singing 'Where Is My Wandering Boy Tonight?' for the last hour and wondering if I would ever see your painful face again."

Bearman jumped down from the wagon, and Yoakum noticed he was wearing his pistol and that there were empty loops in his gun belt. Bearman turned to the wagon bed and looked into it steadily, as if counting something. He left the wagon and let his gaze comb the corral and yard, the ramada, the hut, and Yoakum sitting in the lone chair Bearman brought with him when he first came to the river. The only things clearly out of place were a cloth sack of canned goods, four empty bean cans on the ground by the corner of the ramada, and two strange horses in the corral.

Dollar-Five considered the strange horses for a minute, but when they approached the rails to scent her, she turned away in disgust, standing by the wagon instead.

Bearman walked over to Yoakum and shook his hand. "Everything all right?" he asked, although he could see for himself that it wasn't. He was reluctant to hear Yoakum's answer. He was afraid it involved a killing.

"Relative," Yoakum said. "It's all relative. Just like at Christmas."

"I'm tired, Wally."

"I can see that, John. Ignore me if I'm inappropriate. I've always believed the best way to fight weariness is to laugh."

"Take another card."

Bearman moved to the doorway and could see through the increasing gloom of the interior that the hut had been ransacked. He stepped over the threshold beside Yoakum and looked around. His food cans and sacks had been dumped on the rock floor along with his clothes and equipment. A section of stovepipe had been knocked away from his wood heater and soot added its darkness to the gloom in that corner. The only irreplaceable possession in the hut was his Victrola, which he kept on the floor in the west corner under a wooden box, and it had not been touched. His bunk had been turned over and half of his bedroll hung off the edge of the deal table where it had been thrown. One of his kerosene lamps was on the table, absent its chimney, either broken or removed in preparation for lighting the lamp and starting a fire. Some of Bearman's firewood had been piled among the wreckage for that purpose. Next to the table, his two-burner kerosene stove was intact, for which he was grateful.

He did not look closer.

"I've been waiting on the cleaning lady to get started, but she never showed," Yoakum said, standing up beside Bearman. In a more serious voice, he said, "I wanted you to see what they done, if you ever came back."

"Who is 'they'?"

"Follow me. I'll show you."

Yoakum led Bearman away from the hut, and Bearman protested, "My mules."

"I see you got an extra horse."

"Him, too."

Yoakum kept walking. "Sometimes poor, dumb animals just have to wait."

"Where are we going?"

"Are you with me or not?"

Bearman did not answer. It was clear they were going straight to the outhouse. Yoakum yanked open the plank door, and Bearman found himself looking at two very uncomfortable vaqueros from across the river. Their hands and feet were tied, and they were placed so that their faces were against the raised seat.

"They done that themselves." Yoakum explained that he had been passing by when he noticed two strange horses tied to the corral and, coming around the hut, had found two Mexicans sitting in the shade eating beans.

"I came down on them like thunder and shot the can right out of the hand of one them. *¡Manos arribas!*" he shouted suddenly. "Let's show the boss here which one of you coyotes got his hand scratched."

"No *puede*, Señor," one said in an apologetic voice. "You know me, Señor," he said to Bearman. "I am Umberto Diaz. Anglos call me Berto."

"I got another name for you," Yoakum said. Then, "I tied them tight. It's the other one, with bean juice on his face and shirt."

Without saying anything, Bearman stooped and pulled their boots off one by one. He removed the spurs from one pair of boots. He tossed them behind him in the sand. The other pair of boots were well worn but had no spurs. He dropped the boots down the hole amid cries of protest and dismay. Bearman ignored the men and pulled his knife to cut the pigging strings that bound them. Yoakum drew his Colt's to keep watch in that crowded place.

When he had them on their feet—one of them wore no socks—Bearman told them they could either dig for their boots or walk barefoot back to whoever sent them. He would keep the horses. It was their decision. "*Puedes cavar por tus botas o caminar de regreso a donde sea que vengas. Me quedaré con tus caballos por un tiempo. ¿Cuál es?*"

The two men grumbled but said no audible word. It was clear either choice was no choice. They ended up walking away across the sand. The one wearing socks bent to get his spurs, but Bearman drew his pistol and fired a round that made the man hop away. Yoakum fired a round into the air for his two cents' worth. Dollar-Five snorted and huffed at the two men as they passed her, which further hurried their steps.

Bearman gathered the spurs and said, "Thanks for being here, Wally."

Yoakum spit. "I tend to take my fun where I can find it."

As they walked back up the hill in the now dark, they heard a cry for help from the river. "¡*Ayudate*! ¡*Ayudate*!"

Yoakum said, "It gets swift down there as the river goes into the canyon. Easy to get swept off your feet."

Bearman didn't respond, and Yoakum knew his friend was troubled by something beyond the attack on his hut. He saw Bearman shake his head two different times before they got to the wagon. As they passed the hut, Bearman tossed the spurs over against the wall by the bean cans.

Yoakum said, "I'll get the mules, John, and help you clean up the mess they made. Then we'll unload the wagon."

Bearman nodded. "There's something I want to show you first."

They went past the mules, their boots crunching the gravel, and stopped at the tailgate. Bearman slipped the knot on the lines of the Tinsley horse and led it over to the corral, where he tied it to a rail.

Yoakum stayed close to Bearman, watchful in his own way. They returned to the wagon, and Bearman said, "Wait here."

He walked over to the hut and went inside, sliding his feet on the flagstone floor lest he do more damage by treading on something unseen. He lit the kerosene lamp and held it up to find the chimney, which was intact but had rolled to the edge of the table that abutted the wall. He placed the chimney on the lantern, noticing even more destruction with the light, then went back to the wagon.

Yoakum had let down the tailgate and was standing away from it. When Bearman joined him, Yoakum said, "There's a live person in there."

"I know, Wally. It's Mrs. Tinsley. She quit after the baby was born. Her heart went out of her. The doctor said there was nothing he could do for her. Tinsley was willing to just let her die."

"The baby all right?"

"Said so. A girl."

"What did they name her?"

"Wally?"

"Sorry. Did you shoot Tinsley?"

"No. I convinced him she could be saved if I took her to *la Mujer del Rio*."

Yoakum was startled. "But John . . ."

"I know, but he doesn't. He was half out of his mind, anyway. He may regret this business later, but for now, I've got her away from that filth she was in."

Yoakum was silent, the mules patient. "How is she?"

Bearman knew he was asking for a diagnosis. "The past week, she's eaten nothing, lost weight. Takes a sip or two of water when forced. Didn't bother to get out of bed to do her business. Fades in and out, somewhere between knowing and not knowing. But she's a fighter, Wally, once she's stirred up. She's just quit, that's all. I couldn't stand to think of her going like that."

"Bleeding?"

"I don't know."

"Fever?"

"I don't think so."

Yoakum was silent, and Bearman lowered the lantern. He avoided looking in the wagon.

"That's her scarf you're wearing, isn't it?"

"Yes. It was hers."

"She's the one?"

"The best."

"Well, I think you done right. Win or lose, you had to try. 'For of all sad words of tongue or pen, the saddest are these: "It might have been!"'" Yoakum quoted. "We've got a job of work ahead of us."

"You'll help me?"

"I reckon. What's first?"

"All of it. We need to take care of the animals. We need to get Mrs. Tinsley cleaned up. We need to straighten the—" Bearman almost said *little rock house* "—hut so she'll have a place to sleep. We need to figure out what to do with all her stuff I brought."

"That her chair?"

"It was by her bed."

"Get another?"

"No."

"Dadgum." Yoakum spit. "The box again. All right, we can't do everything first, but we can get this poor lady out of your wagon and cleaned up."

"I don't have anything big enough to heat water in, and besides . . ."

"John, you're going backwards in years. Pretty soon, you'll be a baby. You've got the whole Rio Grande to bathe her in."

"But—"

"John, let me help you. Give me the lamp."

Yoakum took the lamp and began to rummage through the pile of Annie Tinsley's clothes. Bearman turned away for a minute to get his breath. At first, all he saw was darkness, but then the stars were bright above him in a clear sky, and the three-quarter moon, rising over Mexico, threw a brightening shadow away from him across the rocky ground.

There were things to do.

He turned back to Yoakum, who said, "I see you brought some bedclothes and at least one gown. That's good. A towel?"

Bearman shrugged. "Maybe."

"Well, get up in the wagon and let's untangle her from this mess. Smells worse than I did a year ago crawling through that brush and cow flop to get away from them smugglers. We had us a time that night and nothin' since. I wonder what that snake has been up to? It's been so quiet across the river that you know he's up to something. It takes cash money to run a ranch, even in Mexico where it's catch-as-catch-can every day. I'll bet two dollars Confederate money that—"

"Wally."

"What?"

"I'm all right. You don't have to talk so much."

"I like hearing myself talk, and you aren't the only one with a load of worry in your war bag. This is a nice lady, and she's in trouble."

Annie Tinsley had slipped and settled during the rough ride so that Bearman was forced to lift her from the shoulders and hold her there while he pulled at the tangle of dirty sheets and blanket. Yoakum did the same with her ankles and legs. Some hay dribbled down from the tailgate and sparked a memory in Bearman that faded before he knew what it was.

"I wonder if this is what that Carter fellow did when he found old King Tut."

"Wally."

"I know. It ain't the same."

The covers were tossed aside, and there she was, in the moonlight, apparently asleep, on her back with her arms by her sides and the gown she was wearing when she had given birth pushed up around her knees, her face pale and unlined, smooth as alabaster. Bearman looked for and found the small black rock Annie Tinsley had been holding. He slipped it into his pocket.

Yoakum said quietly, "This ugly country hasn't ever seen anything like this young lady, except maybe once before."

Bearman jumped down and unlaced and removed his boots, leaving them on the wagon. He did the same with his pistol, gun belt, and shirt.

"Wouldn't be any use taking the pistol." He shrugged.

Yoakum said, "Just holler. I'll hear you."

"All right."

Together, they maneuvered her into Bearman's arms.

"She feels light," he said, concerned.

"You would too if you ain't had nothin' to eat for a week." Yoakum paused. "Oh lordy, you're not going to feed her beans, are you?"

"It's protein," Bearman said. "And she's getting heavier."

"Well, don't just stand there. Take her down to the river and get her cleaned up."

Yoakum followed them as far as the hut.

"It'll be cold," Bearman said.

"Not if you stay close just downriver from the hot spring. In the meantime, I'll try to sequester your animals and make some sense of your housekeeping."

Bearman started away, then stopped. "And get a good fire going for when we get back."

"Already thought of it. I'll start with your bunk. Speaking of which, here, take the soap. Go."

XV

Near Big Canyon, April 1945

```
4/20/1945-4/21/1945 AT safe. Not happy.
```

J. Bearman

As he walked down to the river, Bearman did not look at Annie Tinsley but at where he was going. He did not revel in the fact that he held this woman above all women in his arms. Nor did he think to himself that of all the geography in the whole wide world, she was nowhere but in his arms. He only felt the living presence of her and the mysterious strength her contact gave him.

There was a patch of gravel, then sand, and, at the river's edge, a strip of limestone rocks and rubble whose edges had been worn by thousands of years of rolling in floodwaters. Beyond that lay the slab he and the brothers had always used for drying their clothes. He dropped the bar of soap there and stepped into the water.

Dollar-Five ambled out of the willow thicket from which she had watched the Mexican flail his way through a short length of rapids and followed Bearman into the water. The mare stopped when Bearman went deeper and watched him, flicking her ears for sound and occasionally looking across the river.

The stones demanded careful stepping, and Bearman moved cautiously with his burden deeper into the river, then upstream to the left, closer to where the hot spring pulsed from a broken stratum there in the limestone ledge. The flow of the spring at the present low level of the river created its own current, sweeping the bottom of the river free of pebbles and mud. The water brought relief to Bearman's tired, strained muscles, which he had pushed to the limit in the last two days.

When her feet and ankles slipped into the yet-cool water, Annie Tinsley reacted instinctively and began to kick and moan, as if to save herself in the midst of a nightmare. She struggled against Bearman's grip and rocked her head back and forth violently in a gesture of absolute negative.

"Fight it, ma'am," he told her.

Bearman held her firmly but gently, as if to reassure her that no harm was meant and she was in no danger. He spoke to her in soft tones, telling her where she was and what he was doing, but her continued lack of engagement or thoughtful response worried him. He slipped into the dark water that was over his beltline, still moving closer to the spring, and he lowered Annie Tinsley completely under water. She sputtered and fought upward and gasped. He almost lost his grip on her, but then she turned her face against his chest and raised her arms about his shoulders. The odor of her surrender in that hot, foul bedroom was slowly taken away by the current.

The moonlight was just touching the river's edge at that point, dappling the shoreline with silver ripples. The desert night was not quiet, but the sounds of animal or bird or wind in the brush were elusive, heard more in memory than in real time, overcome by the soft swish and gurgle of the current. Where the water drained from Annie Tinsley's hair, droplets caught the moonlight, and her face was like a cameo rising from black velvet sprinkled with glitter. Looking down at her upturned face, he was suddenly and fully conscious that he was indeed holding this woman in his arms in the river, in the moonlight, and that she was clinging to him to save her from the deep place she was in.

He laughed.

She was so light in his arms with the river sharing in the uplifting of her weight. Bearman began to turn in the water as if dancing, bending his knees and rising again to further sluice away the filth of her sickbed. At one point, her lips parted into what seemed a smile. Her head was thrown back, and Bearman longed to see the moonlight in her eyes. Then, surprisingly, she put her cheek again onto his chest and said, "No."

What that meant, other than a response to his thought, he could not guess.

He, who so seldom laughed, laughed again and spun with her in the current. It seemed to him that he could not perceive her with his eyes alone. He saw her there in the water, in her white nightgown in the moonlight, with his hearing, and the sound of her was the sound of his own heart driving the blood through his veins. He had no idea that he could breathe so deeply, that blood could surge so powerfully, that sight and hearing could turn one into the other, that taste and touch and fragrance could solidify into a quivering, breathing person.

He gradually let his arm slide out from under her legs, and as her feet dropped, she clung to him tighter, her body pressed against his. Bearman really seemed to be dancing with her now in the chest-deep water. He was relieved and glad that she was responding to the moment with conscious intention. He thought that perhaps she had given up in the first place because she had no reason not to. There was the baby, of course, but to her, the baby had been a source of sickness and weakness and pain, not to mention the extreme moral responsibility of bringing a helpless human being into a remote house on the bank of the Rio Grande. She had been made to suffer it practically and emotionally all alone. Later, the little girl would become a person, an image of the brightness of her mother. Annie Tinsley would have to see that.

She dropped her left arm from his shoulder, and looking down at her as she slumped against him in sheer exhaustion, he realized how little modesty the wet white nightgown allowed her. The bar of soap was still on the rock, but he knew he could not bathe her. He pulled her along with him into shallower water.

"Wally!"

Yoakum and Dollar-Five both met him at the river's edge.

"What happened?" Yoakum wanted to know.

"I can't bathe her," Bearman said, embarrassed.

"Why not? Lose the soap?"

"Look at her." Bearman lifted her out of the water.

"Oh."

"I'm the wrong person to carry for the rest of my life the memory of what that would be like."

"What about me?"

"You're the doctor, that's *what* about you, and you were married a long time. You're old and have less time ahead to remember. That's what *else*."

Bearman felt Annie Tinsley shiver, or seem to. The water was mildly warm, but the wet gown and skin out of the water were immediately chilled. Beyond her physical discomfort was a great reluctance to let a man bathe her in the dark nighttime waters of the Rio Grande, but she was simply too tired to protest, and she slumped in Bearman's arms.

"Let me get my boots off."

After he had stripped down to his pants, Yoakum took the woman from Bearman's arms and waded upstream. Bearman watched Yoakum carry the unconscious woman to the spring, then he and Dollar-Five walked up the hill to the hut. The temperature had dropped into the fifties.

Yoakum had a moderate fire burning outside the hut and a lamp lit on the table inside. Bearman stood in the doorway and saw the miracle Yoakum had achieved in such a short time. He focused on his bunk and saw that Yoakum had stripped the mattress and remade the bed with some of Annie Tinsley's clean bedding. He was touched that now a pink long-sleeved nightgown lay folded on the bed. The only thing that remained untouched by Yoakum's industry was the stovepipe on the wood heater. A dent in one section would have to be looked at.

Yoakum called from the river.

"John, bring me that clean nightgown and a towel."

Bearman snatched up the nightgown but could not find a towel. "What did you do with the towel?"

"I don't remember. Hurry up. She's cold."

Another fruitless search, then Bearman snatched the wool blanket from the bunk and hurried down to the river where he found Yoakum holding the pale form of the woman in the dark water to keep the chill breeze off of her. Annie Tinsley's wet, stained nightgown was on the bank.

Yoakum said, "Good. You brought a blanket. This poor woman is going to shake herself into pieces if we don't get her dry and some dry clothes on her. Spread that blanket on the ledge and get out of here if you don't want to be blinded by a vision from heaven. Go. And build up a good fire."

Bearman hurried back to the hut. He threw the wood that Yoakum had cleaned out of the hut onto the fire and went past it to the wagon, where he retrieved his shirt and boots. Dressed again, he climbed into the wagon and pulled out Annie Tinsley's chair. He placed it upwind from the fire, but close, and Yoakum met him there. Together, they placed her in the chair and wrapped the blanket around her, all but her feet and hair.

"God Almighty," Yoakum said, almost stepping into the fire. "I'm about to freeze to death."

Bearman, in much better shape than the other two, having only wet pants, volunteered to get Yoakum's clothes, but Yoakum shook his head, and after another couple of minutes by the fire, started off in the moonlight to get his stuff.

"Take that dirty bedding with you. I don't want her to have to see it again until it's clean."

"I'm already clean," Yoakum grumbled, but he took the bundle with him and left it with the soiled gown.

Bearman went to the wagon again to look for some socks. He remembered putting some in but could not find them. He went hurriedly to the hut and from his own duffel withdrew a pair of wool socks in fair shape, only the heels a little threadbare.

Annie Tinsley was slumped in the chair, which, thankfully, had arms, or she would have tumbled to the ground. Bearman knelt in front of her and put the socks on her feet after warming them. He could feel her shivering. He put his hand on the heavy wetness of her hair and was angry at himself for not finding a towel. In the end, he put one of his khaki shirts over her head after warming it by the fire. Then he knelt in front her again and rubbed her shoulders and arms, careful all the while not to block the heat from the fire.

Yoakum came back up from the river. He stopped by the fire and stared at the huddled form across the flames. "She looks like the headless horseman."

Bearman, ever watchful as he worked to stop the shivering, saw Annie Tinsley shake her head and felt her shrug her arms away from his hands.

"Ma'am," he said, "can you hear me?"

"I still have ears, don't I—What is this thing on my head?"

"It's my shirt, ma'am."

"I feel like it's suffocating me." She shook her head back and forth and tried to draw her arms out of the folds of the blanket.

"Your hair is wet. Best leave the shirt a while longer. A chill out here could lead to pneumonia."

"Then why did you try to drown me in the river? Get it off."

Annie Tinsley got one arm loose from the blanket and jerked the shirt off her head. She moved to throw it in the fire, but Bearman stopped her. He took the shirt away from her and handed it off to Yoakum, who put it on his own head and said, "I call that macaroni."

Bearman swallowed audibly.

Annie Tinsley stared at Yoakum, then at Bearman, then asked Yoakum, "Who are you?"

"My name is Yoakum, Mrs. Tinsley. You know me. I've been by your house many a time, helping your husband count cattle and check brands up near Bourland Canyon." He pushed the shirt back on his shoulders so that she could see his face.

She squinted at him without responding and bent her eyes on Bearman, who said, "Please don't ask me who I am."

"Why should I?"

"Because you admittedly have a habit of wanting to quirt something or somebody when you get mad."

She stared at him. "I said that once upon a time, didn't I?"

"You said it, did it, and admitted it. By the way, welcome to the little rock house," he added, hoping to win a smile.

No smile came.

She pulled the blanket back up on her shoulder where it had slipped and stared at the fire. After several minutes, she turned again to Bearman, who remained close, and said, "I also remember. . . I also remember asking you to excuse my behavior at the station in Marathon."

"You did, and I did."

Her lips trembled, and now the firelight, rather than enhancing her beauty, seemed to exaggerate every wrinkle around her eyes and mouth and above her brows, as if in an instant she had aged forty years. Her eyes swam with unshed tears. "What about now?" she asked him in a voice laden with exhaustion.

"Now more than ever."

"I'm a horrible person," she sobbed.

"Stop that. You are worn out, hungry, and been through all kinds of hell. No, listen. You want to go back to a place of misery, thinking you deserve it and why not anyway? I'm not you, but I've been where you are now. I wanted to quit, lay it down, and who cared anyhow? It was a long steep climb out of that place, but I did it, and you're going to do it, or by God, I'll know the reason why not."

"I second that motion from personal experience," Yoakum said.

Annie Tinsley shook her head, as if negating their words, and sobbed into the blanket, hiding her face. Bearman, helplessly angry, looked at Yoakum, who stepped closer, his trousers steaming from the fire. "Release valve," he suggested, nodding.

Dollar-Five, lingering in the shadows by the corral, moved up slowly behind Annie Tinsley's chair. The mare put her head over the woman's shoulder and huffed softly in her face. Annie Tinsley was startled, as well she might have been, and cried out. Yoakum turned his attention to Bearman for his reaction, but Bearman just stood there watching.

"What is your horse doing?" Annie Tinsley asked almost fearfully after Dollar-Five had huffed in her face again.

Bearman said, "She's giving you her breath, her spirit. You give yours back by blowing on her. She senses your need of strength."

"Dadgum," Yoakum muttered.

Annie Tinsley, half suspecting Bearman was making fun of her, blew in Dollar-Five's muzzle. Dollar-Five raised her head with a loud whinny and stomped her right hoof.

"Now shout *Sho now* as loud as you can."

"Why?"

"Just do it."

"What does it mean?"

"*Sure enough* made short. Scream it."

"I don't want to."

Bearman lowered his chin and stared at her.

"No."

Bearman waited. Yoakum watched.

"Sho now!" Annie Tinsley suddenly screamed into the night. "Sho now!" she screamed again. Dollar-Five reared up on her hind legs and came down with a scattering of gravel. She did her haughty walk with mincing steps over to the corral and back to Annie Tinsley, who was both astonished and amused. From there, she bolted for the river, and they heard her hooves in the rocks when she turned at the river's edge and charged back up the hill straight to Bearman, then back to Annie Tinsley.

"Like that," Bearman said.

Dollar-Five lingered in that watchful, protective way she had. Annie Tinsley wiped her face on the blanket and said after a time, "I'm thirsty," in a little girl voice, as if surprised and ashamed by the need.

Bearman brought her a cup of fresh water from the pump and told her it would be best just to sip it. She sipped about half the cup and held it in her lap. She shivered violently just once and then was perfectly still.

"Hungry?" Bearman asked.

Annie Tinsley stared at him without answering. "Did you . . . ?"

"Did I what, ma'am?"

She shifted inside the blanket and pulled the edge up to her chin. She stared at him timidly, and he said, "No."

She cut her eyes to Yoakum, who no longer had Bearman's shirt. Bearman hoped it wasn't in the fire or on the ground.

"I was the one bathed you, Mrs. Tinsley, but I had my eyes closed the whole time. You needed cleaning up, Mrs. Tinsley, and John here was too shy to do it. He's often too shy to bathe himself. One time—"

"Wally."

Bearman turned back to Annie Tinsley and said, "I couldn't leave you in that room, ma'am. It was no place for a woman who wants to do things."

Her eyes dimmed with tears again, but she said, half accusingly, half ironically, "You almost got me killed bringing me here."

"What's that?" Yoakum asked.

"Then you tried to drown me."

"By golly, tell the story or wash the dishes."

Bearman said, "Later. I want some coffee and something to eat."

"Not beans," Yoakum moaned. "Mrs. Tinsley, tell him you can't eat no beans."

Before Bearman left the fire to prepare a meal, he bent over Annie Tinsley. His nearness both calmed and disturbed her. Facing east, the light of the moon was in her eyes, and the flames from the fire made golden flickers across her smooth cheeks. The shadowed wrinkles were gone.

Bearman said very quietly, "Yes?"

She knew he was asking her more than what kind of food he should prepare. He was asking her if she was sound physically. He was asking her if he had done the right thing in bringing her to his hut. He was asking her if she was glad to be there. He was asking her if she felt alive again. He might not have known all the things his question inspired in her, but Annie Tinsley did.

"Yes," she said, just as quietly, and hid her face in the blanket until she felt the blush fade.

Bearman made coffee, and the three of them, now sitting close together, shared the cup, the men protesting when she did not sip her portion. They threatened to toss her in the river again or to pelt her with rocks if she didn't. As if she weren't sitting beside them, they started a ridiculous argument about what kind of rock would be best—limestone or flint—and who should throw the first one. Once, they made her laugh.

Bearman started with two cubes of chicken bouillon. He dissolved the cubes in a pot of water, and while it heated, he opened a can of Boston baked beans into a smaller pan. After it was emptied and rinsed, he and Yoakum made a coffee cup out of the empty can, which they shared. He made small balls of dough at the table while Yoakum talked too much across the fire from Annie Tinsley. He had caught up the box, his usual seat, and rocked back and forth on it. Bearman was sure that at any moment the thin slats would give way and catapult Yoakum into the fire.

Taking the Dutch oven out to the diminished fire, he thought, *Two days of travel and fear and battle come down to this: a peaceful night with good people, a bright moon, warm fire, chicken soup without the chicken, dumplings, and beans.*

Annie Tinsley, for her part, stared at the fire and tried to comprehend how six miles of separation could make such a difference in a life and in a world.

"*Yes.*"

XVI

Near Big Canyon, April 1945

4/20/1945-4/21/1945 Enemies across the river. Marcos P exposed. In danger.

J Bearman

Annie Tinsley sipped some of the chicken broth in her cup and ate the dumplings that landed in it from Bearman's ladle, but she was falling asleep in her chair as she did it. She seemed to like the salty taste of the broth, but after so many days of nothing, her stomach could not hold much. Bearman, watching her, rescued the cup as it slipped from her fingers. Her chin dropped, and Bearman believed she was now in the true sleep she needed.

"Wally," he called softly.

Yoakum tilted his can and set it down empty by the box as Bearman unfolded the blanket around Annie Tinsley and picked her up in his arms. She felt warm but not feverish against his chest. After the dark weave of the wool blanket, her pale pink nightgown seemed to glow in the moonlight; like the soiled gown, this one was made of cotton and reached to her ankles.

Turning from the chair, he waited while Yoakum gathered up the blanket, shook it out, and went ahead of him into the hut. Yoakum threw back the covers on Bearman's bunk and stepped aside. Bearman laid her on the bed and felt her feet and hair.

"Dry," he whispered.

"Breathin' easy too," Yoakum whispered back and turned to leave the hut. "You want I should bring in the Dutch and the coffee pot?"

Bearman moved away from the bunk. "It's best," he said.

Yoakum had already pulled the Dutch from the coals. He handed it off to Bearman, who put it on the wood heater in the corner. The coffee pot went on the kerosene stove.

"Wait."

Yoakum turned and leaned toward him. "What?"

"Should I leave the lamp for her?"

"Moon's pretty bright."

"In case she wakes up and doesn't know where she is."

"Women always know where they are and will tell you so."

"Wally."

"Yeah, leave it, poor thing."

"*Es muerto, pobrecita.*"

Bearman placed the lamp on the deal table against the wall, the wick turned low, but not enough to smoke. He started to follow Yoakum out the door when he remembered her unusual rock. He stood by the bed and pulled the valentine-shaped rock from his pocket and placed it gently in her right hand, which, as before, was tucked under her chin. In her sleep, she closed her fingers around it.

Bearman pulled the cover up over her shoulder. "Goodnight, ma'am," he said softly and went out. Before he closed the door, Yoakum handed him a pitcher of water to put inside.

"Women," he said.

For a while, the two men sat talking quietly by the fire, but as the coals softened and whitened, there were longer periods of silence. Neither man could refrain from keeping an eye on the door of the hut where Dollar-Five stood as if waiting for it to be opened. The moon got smaller and brighter as it rose higher. They took turns yawning until finally Bearman stood up, feeling the chill of the night.

"Are your britches dry yet?" he asked Yoakum.

"Pretty much."

"You have bedding?"

"Rosie's carryin' it behind the saddle."

"You ever think about taking the saddle off of her when you're through for the day?"

"She likes it."

They did not unsaddle the Mexican horses, but Rosie and Tyler were relieved of that weight and turned into the corral. Bearman had long ago built pegs in a corner of the western wall under the ramada to hang saddles on. A rail accommodated the blankets, but the bridles he hung from the ramada were on loops of baling wire to make it harder for mice to gnaw on the lines. Bearman thought about the woman sleeping in his bunk. He wondered what she would think of his little rock house once she had time to study it. He owned so little.

Since Bearman's army surplus cots were in the hut and they did not want to disturb Annie Tinsley, they decided to sleep in the wagon bed rather than on the rocks. The high sides of the wagon would block the chilly wind, such as it was, and the hay would be a bit more comfortable. They moved the supplies and Annie Tinsley's clothes to clear a space for their bedding. Spurts of smoke from the fire wavered in the moonlight like lost spirits.

Lying on their backs with the moon in their faces, Bearman told of his meeting with Ornelos and what had happened.

"If he hadn't taken my rifle, I'd have had him. I could reach it, but my pistol was behind me. My father gave me that rifle with his blessing. I want it back."

Yoakum was outraged. "John. Honestly? You thought you could go anywhere out here without wearing your pistol? I keep tryin' not to be ashamed of you, but it's uphill work."

"I had other things on my mind."

"Like bringin' Mrs. Tinsley here?"

"That was part of it. I was afraid she was going to die on the way."

"Bringin' her here was pretty crazy, John."

"You think so?"

"Don't get me to thinkin'. But I guess if I *was* to think about it, I'd say it was crazy, but the right thing to do."

"I hope so."

"Don't you know, I wish Marisa was here." Yoakum sniffed once.

"Having another woman here would make a difference. She's kind of at our mercy."

"Notice how touchy she was about who bathed her?"

"Any grown woman would be."

"I wouldn't, if I was dirty as she was."

"I said *grown woman*. What's your point?"

"It made a difference, that's all."

"She doesn't like me?"

"The opposite, I'd say."

"I don't want to think about it."

"Probably best."

As they talked softly, each one used "getting comfortable" as an excuse to lift his head up above the sideboard and check on the hut. The window was on the other side of the hut, but they could make out a little seam of light around the door. They used its persistence as a measure of Annie Tinsley's sleep. Inevitably, they raised up at the same time.

Lying back down, Yoakum said, "I believe your mare is really a dog, standin' guard like that by the door."

"I believe your mare is really a nag."

"She's not."

"Neither is Dollar-Five a dog."

They fell asleep before the argument was settled and were awakened at first light by someone shouting "¡*Hola*!" from down by the river.

Dollar-Five put her head over the side of the wagon and snorted.

Yoakum snorted in answer without opening his eyes. "More trouble."

"I'll take care of it."

Bearman sat up and pulled on his boots. He scooted to the tailgate and dropped down.

"Take your Colt's this time."

"Yes, Mother."

Bearman walked softly past the door of the hut, resisting the impulse to open it and check on Annie Tinsley. At the river's edge, he met two men and a misshapen little boy. The men were wet above their beltline and the little boy was completely wet. The men were the same ones he had sent barefooted across the river the night before. He was faintly relieved that the man caught in the rapids had survived. They were still barefooted. Bearman could see no weapons.

"*¿Que quiere?*" he asked.

The two men snatched off their hats and bowed slightly. As the boy was hatless, he just looked at Bearman.

"Señor, we have come to apologize for what we did yesterday. The *jefe* said to destroy the house of the *gringo* who cost him much monies. We do as we are told until the wild man come shooting his pistol and yelling at us. We are sorry for eating your beans and disturbing your *casita*."

"Well?"

"Señor, we did not know *la Mujer del Rio* is here. We ask her forgiveness and light many candles for her mercy."

"*La Mujer del Rio*?"

"*Sí*. She help many peoples along the river. My little girl she save from the cough."

"She is not here."

"Señor, forgive us, but we watch from across the river in the moonlight as *la Mujer* get her strength in the river as she always does when she help the sick."

"That was not her."

"Señor, forgive me again, but we see her. *La Mujer* make a light from herself."

"All right. I forgive you, but stay on your side of the river."

"Is only time we cross."

Bearman started to turn away, his mind a blur of thoughts, some comic, some tragic. The dirty bedclothes and nightgown from the night before still lay piled by the river, and now this.

The spokesman called him back. "But señor, *por favor*. We cannot work without our boots and our horses."

"Figure it out."

The two men grimaced, but the boy just stood there. Bearman wondered why they had brought him.

"*Sí*, but we have come to get the boots, *con su permiso*."

Bearman looked at the three and raised his eyebrows. "You want to get your boots? How are you going to do that?"

The two men looked at the boy. "Alphonso will get them for us. *Con su permiso*," the spokesman added.

"The boy?"

"Señor, Alphonso is not a boy, but a man, un *enano*, a midget. He will go down after the boots. We must have them—the rocks, the thorns." He shrugged.

"What does Alphonso get out of it?"

"There is more in the *retrete*?"

"I mean, why does he do it?"

Another shrug. "Is a favor. He is small; we are too big."

Yoakum walked up behind Bearman, and the men shifted warily.

"What is this?" he asked. Then, recognizing the two men, "Come to get more beans?"

"*Botas*," the spokesman said. "*Caballos*," the other said.

Bearman asked, "How is Alphonso going to get the boots?"

"He will go down the hole."

"Down the hole?"

"Remind me never to go to Mexico again," Yoakum said.

"*Sí, otra vez, con su permiso.*"

"If this ain't no trick, I've got to see it."

Bearman led the way to the outhouse, the barefooted men walking gingerly across the gravel and rocks. Yoakum followed them, noting the way the little man swiveled as he walked in a child's boots. He could not help but believe that it was a trick of some sort. He turned often and searched the river and the brush on the other side for danger.

Bearman threw open the door and stepped back. Alphonso went in and looked down the hole. "*No hay problema,*" he said in a voice that sounded like he was speaking from the bottom of his throat. He sat down and began to undress.

Bearman and Yoakum exchanged a glance and took another step back so that they were behind the Mexicans.

When Alphonso was completely undressed, the two men crowded in the outhouse on either side of the hole. They lifted the midget above the hole, one by each arm, and lowered him down into the muck. His wrists were the only part of him visible when the two men dropped him. Bearman heard the *squelch* from where he was standing.

"By God," Yoakum said.

"*Oye,*" Bearman called. "Do not dirty the *retrete.*"

A boot was handed up. "*Es de mio,*" the spokesman said. He stepped outside and laid the soiled boot down behind the outhouse.

So it was with the other boots, some worse than others.

"Now what?" Yoakum said. "Are they just going to leave that little jasper down there?"

A few sheets of a catalog were handed up. The spokesman shrugged. "Alphonso like the pictures."

"They're stained."

"He no care." The man leaned over the hole and shouted, "*¿Cómo esta?*"

"*Bien,*" came the strange, muffled voice.

Both men leaned over the hole, and when two wrists appeared, they each grabbed one and lifted the midget straight up and out of the hole without his body touching the sides. They backed out and carried him that way, dripping, down to the river and threw him in.

Yoakum started laughing. When Bearman looked at him, Yoakum choked and said, "I can't help it. I grew up with brothers. It looked like that muck had just given birth."

"That's enough of that," Bearman said.

The men came back, gathered up the boots, and took them down to the river to wash. Alphonso was sort of swimming, sometimes staying underwater for what seemed to Bearman a long time, otherwise apparently happy. When the men were satisfied with their boots, they put them on, came back up and gathered the midget's clothes, and took them back to the river so he could dress. They had to repeatedly call him out of the water.

"You going to give them back their horses?"

Bearman nodded. "I don't want to have to feed them."

Yoakum shook his head. "Too bad those infant sons of Erin weren't here to see this. Wouldn't it have given them somethin' to talk about?"

Bearman said, nodding at the group by the river, "They said they came this morning to apologize."

"They came for their boots and horses."

"They said they didn't know *la Mujer del Rio* was here."

"What?"

"That's right. They wanted her to forgive them. One of them said *la Mujer* had healed his little girl."

Yoakum shook his head and took off his hat, then shook his head again and put his hat back on. "She's still doing it, bless her lovely heart."

"She will be, Wally, as long as this river flows into the canyon country. Your Marisa is a legend now."

"She seemed mighty close last night. Mrs. Tinsley in that white nightgown, stains and all."

"They saw her."

"Those people are still leaving all sorts of doodads down yonder where Big Canyon starts."

"Are they?"

"Trinkets and little bells and scorpions made out of twisted wire, fossils, arrowheads. I can hear the halt and lame callin' out to her in the evenings. I take them back there and pretend I am helping *la Mujer*. Most of the time, it's just cuts, poor diet, or bites. Wouldn't do no good to tell them she's passed on, and it gives me a chance to ask them about their livestock."

"I just wanted you to know."

The midget pulled on his child's boots, and the three Mexicans came back up from the river to Bearman and Yoakum. More confident now, they left their hats on when they asked permission to get their horses. Their boots squeaked when they walked.

When Bearman let down the bars of the corral, Dollar-Five was there to see that only the strange horses were let out. The Mexicans got their horses, and with furtive looks at the closed door of Bearman's hut as they went by, they crossed themselves. Yoakum stayed behind to build a new fire. Bearman collected the spurs and followed behind.

At the river, he held out the spurs. He indicated the filed points of the rowels. "You use these on your horses?" he asked.

The spokesman nodded and said, "*Sí*. The cattle are fast sometimes. It is necessary."

Bearman did not respond. The second man took the spurs with thanks. He pulled the midget up onto his saddle, and Bearman and the spokesman watched as the two regained the other side.

"Señor," he said. "Thank you very much for to give us back our boots and horses, and most of all, the spurs, which you could have kept. It is strange to be here where you live and play the *musica*. Many times, we see you ride your tall mare along the river. We know you are *muy caballero*."

It was growing lighter now. Bearman was thinking of Annie Tinsley. He wanted to be there when she woke up. He could hear Yoakum breaking sticks. Across the river, the others had disappeared in the brush.

"*De nada*," Bearman said. He started to turn away, but the other man stopped him.

"*Oye*," he said. "You must hear this. There is another matter. I have heard around the fire at night when the riders smoke and drink a little, that the *jefe* try to kill the gringo on the road yesterday. The *jefe* had two hombres with him—Augustin and Marcos. Something go wrong. Augustin is knock off his horse by your mare. He run from there to catch his horse, but his horse, she is gone across the river. The *jefe* follow and leave Marcos to kill you. But you shoot Señor Ornelos. His arm no good now. Augustin say Marcos no kill you, but *habla* instead. He see you make a plan and you and Marcos shoot at nothing—bang bang bang. Augustin angry to be left to walk home. Last night, he say he tell the *jefe*, say Marcos work for the *federales* to kill the sick cows."

"Last night?"

"*Sí*. Augustin know we are angry at the *gringo*, pardon me, for having to walk *tambien*, so he talk the mouth. But, Señor, the *jefe* no at the *rancho*. He go to Zacatecas to bring some cows."

"Did Marcos go with him?"

"*Sí*. This is before we find out *la Mujer del Rio* is with you. Then we know not to make war on you, but Augustin, he don't believe in *la Mujer*. He is *muy malo* with the *muchachas tambien*."

"When will Ornelos be back?"

The Mexican considered. "Without the trouble, two, three days."

"You speak the truth?"

"Señor, *sí*, a thousand times. I would never lie in the presence of *la Mujer del Rio*."

"What is your name?"

"Umberto. *Gringos* call me Berto. My father and uncles make the wax. We have the talk on the road to sell my wax."

"*Bueno, gracias. Adiós.*"

Umberto nodded, mounted his horse, and rode slowly across the river, letting the horse find its footing where it would.

"What was all that palaver about?" Yoakum asked when Bearman joined him at the modest fire. The sun was fully on the ridge. It would be hot later. Bearman glanced at the door of the hut.

"Marcos Pulaski might be in danger." He told Yoakum what the Mexican had said.

"What are we going to do about it?"

"Go to Mexico."

"We got no authority in Mexico."

"I want my rifle back. That's my authority. Besides, you're a veterinarian. You can go where you want."

"It's just a rifle, John. Shoots pistol ammunition. Forget it and get you a .30-30."

"My father placed that rifle in my hands the day before he and my mother were murdered by the man my father hired to help bring in hay. The man was a marijuana addict. He didn't get far. When Father gave me the rifle, he said, 'Always use it for right.' I'm going to get it back," Bearman said and walked over to the closed door of his hut.

XVII

Near Big Canyon, April 1945

4/21/1945 Bringing AT out of "the room."

J Bearman

[notepaper]
He irritates me because he refuses to feel sorry for me. He is not afraid of my temper, but seems to encourage it. This morning, I exchanged what Mr. Bearman calls "quirts" with Mr. Yoakum. They simply cannot be serious. I want them to wallow with me, but they keep raising me up.

Bearman knocked softly on the door, waited, and knocked again a bit harder. Whether he showed it or not, he couldn't help but fear the worst where Annie Tinsley was concerned. He was tempted to go around and check on her through the window.

Her voice came clearly and firmly through the door: "Who is it?"

It was such a ridiculous question that he felt more relieved than alarmed. He decided to be ridiculous, too.

He said, "Wells Fargo, ma'am. I have a letter for you."

"What does it say?"

"It says, Dear Sleepy Head—"

"Go away."

Bearman waited, then knocked again.

There was no response from the hut. Bearman continued knocking.

"Who is it?"

"Me."

"What do you want?"

"The sun, the moon, and the stars."

"If I give them to you, will you go away?"

"You may have already done so."

Behind him, Yoakum sat on the box, poking at the fire, and laughed. "Children, playing games," he said to himself. "Scared to death to say what they really want to say."

A number of minutes in silence went by.

"Then why are you . . . why are you still here?"

"I live here occasionally, and it's time for breakfast."

"Is that other man still here?"

"What other man?"

"I don't remember his name."

Bearman turned to Yoakum with a grin. "You've been quirted," he said.

From inside the hut, Annie Tinsley called, "Are you making fun of me?"

"No, ma'am. A quirt is a serious thing. If I used one on Dollar-Five, she'd toss me into a cactus and run off and join the Mexicans. I wouldn't blame her."

The door swung outward, and Annie Tinsley stood there like the hut was her own. She had wrapped the blanket around her for a robe. On her feet, Bearman's socks had slipped down so that the toes looked like the points of deflated elf shoes. Her rich brown hair was tangled at the ends and matted on the top, the effects of P&G soap and hard water. The tones of her face were slack and drawn, the effects of dehydration and starvation following the birth of her daughter.

She waited for him to ask how she was and how she had slept, but he only stood there looking at her, answering his unasked questions.

"I need my clothes," Annie Tinsley said.

"Yes, ma'am. You want me to bring them to you, or do you want to go over there and pick them out?"

She studied his face for a moment. "You said the same thing about my horse that day."

"One of us might be forming a new habit," Bearman replied, glad she had remembered a time special to him.

"Or both."

"Or not."

He studied her face for a full minute.

"Don't stare at me."

"Your things are in the wagon," he said unnecessarily.

She shook her head. "I never want to see the bed of that wagon again in this lifetime. Or any other. I am sore from head to toe and was almost murdered in it."

"And your hair is a fright."

"Oh!" She backed away, pulling the door shut.

"Pick another card," Yoakum said.

Bearman liked the fight he was seeing.

"Ma'am," he said through the door, "our coffee and breakfast are in there with you. If you will let me, I can get them and put them on the fire. I'm kind of used to breakfast in the morning, even if it is leftovers."

"'Cept for beans," Yoakum put in.

Nothing.

"And I can bring your clothes from the wagon to save you a lifetime of worrying about being hauled again."

Nothing. Then, "Hauled?"

"There was a load in that wagon."

"I was part of a load?" Her voice was sharp.

"Yes, ma'am. The best part. And I still believe you'll never need a mirror to mess with the glory God gave you."

The door opened, and Annie Tinsley stood there as before. Dollar-Five had appeared from the river and wanted to be petted. Annie Tinsley obliged for a while, then gently let Dollar-Five know the mare had gotten all the petting she was going to get just then. Dollar-Five snorted at Bearman and went off again toward the river.

Bearman saw that his disparaged shirt had been pegged over the window for modesty, and he smiled at her. Annie Tinsley was charmed by Bearman's smile in spite of herself, although she tried not to show it. *Why couldn't this man just play the part she had chosen for him?*

"Well," she said, staring at Bearman, "am I terrifying you?"

"Scaring my own hungry self half to death," Yoakum said in mock fear.

"I was not speaking to you, Mr. Yoakum."

At hearing her say his name, he asked, "Now that we're friends again, can I sit in your chair?"

"No."

Bearman grinned and stepped up to Annie Tinsley as if he were going to butt into her, and she stiffened. Instead, he pushed past her for the coffee pot and the big Dutch.

"I thought you were going to get me my things from your horrible wagon," she said petulantly, wrapping the blanket more tightly around herself, although she need not have bothered. Bearman hardly glanced at her now.

"Where did you learn to talk like that?"

For a moment, she did not know what to say. She remembered once saying, "*I'm not like this*," but what if she were?

"Mind if I make coffee first?" Bearman asked in her silence, pushing past her again on his way outside.

"Are you seeking my permission?"

He stopped. "Used to giving it?"

"What does that mean?"

"It means being considerate does not indicate servility."

"Are you trying to make me angry?"

"Not really."

"What are you like when you really try?"

"Ma'am?"

"What?"

"Let me get your things, and by then, the coffee will be ready and the dumplings hot. How does that sound?"

"Like the backdoor slamming," she said, referring to the time she had accused him of being indirect.

"Well," Bearman said, "I think being angry at me is better than being angry at yourself. I'd about jump for joy if you took a swing at me. I can take the beating, but you've had about all you can take of beating up yourself."

Annie Tinsley's lips parted in confused wonder. *He knew.*

Bearman passed off the big Dutch and the coffee pot to Yoakum and went to the wagon. It was a mess of supplies and bedrolls. By the time he had decided to start by pulling out the bedrolls, Yoakum showed up at his side.

"Don't throw my bedroll on the ground," he said.

"Your bedroll is always on the ground. Last night was a holiday for it."

They pulled the bedrolls out and dropped them on the ground. Next came the sacks and supplies. When the way was clear, Bearman laid hold of a tangle of blouses and skirts, but Yoakum touched his arm.

"Hunh-uh," he said. "She'll be wanting her underthings first, as well as her toiletries if you brought any, which I hope you did. Her legs are near chapped raw. She'll want some shoes. These rocks and gravel are hard on tender feet."

"I rustled all I could find," Bearman said, moving toward the front of the wagon where his saddle was.

He gathered up the drawstrings of the bag holding bottles and combs and brushes, various strange ointments, and two bottles of pills with Annie Tinsley's name on them. He also found her slippers.

Before Bearman turned from the wagon, Yoakum stopped him. He had seen Mrs. Tinsley coming up the hill from the outhouse, followed by Dollar-Five. The woman went into the hut and closed the door. He wanted to save her any embarrassment.

To Bearman, he said, "I was watching you play Mrs. Tinsley like a violin this morning and last night too. How come you know so much about how to handle a woman in a bad temper?"

"Whose crazy idea was it to throw rocks at her if she hesitated to drink her share of the coffee last night?"

"Well . . ."

"Although, I will admit it did make her laugh."

"But I was married a long time. Marisa taught me not to pay attention to temper. Who taught you?"

Bearman nodded toward the hut where Dollar-Five had again taken up a vigil.

"Oh. Hold on. The mare or Mrs. Tinsley?"

"One time in particular, I remember my mother being very angry with my father. We endured a day of her silence before my father brought her a flower growing out of a dried cow patty. It was such a completely wrong thing to do that my mother started to laugh. Then we all three were laughing. Mother kept the flower and told Father the patty was his supper. That made an impression, but there are times when you just know things," Bearman concluded.

"And times when you don't," Yoakum said, shaking his head.

Bearman moved Dollar-Five away from the door and kicked it with his boot, his hands being full. Annie Tinsley opened it immediately. She stood to the side in her long light pink nightgown. She had folded the blanket and put it on the bunk.

Bearman was surprised to see she had abandoned the blanket, but only said, "This is the first load. Holler when you're ready for the rest."

He started to go back out, but she stopped him with a hand on his arm. Her face had made that change again to an expression and complexion that were serious without being sad or angry. She had been meditating on certain things.

"Ma'am?" Bearman waited.

"You are the only one who is not afraid of my—" She groped for the word. "—*breakdown.*"

He looked at her, knowing she was understanding something important about her situation.

"Maybe I just don't show it."

"What's the difference?" she asked with the ghost of a smile.

"A thing is either a thing or it's not."

"If I want a fire to go out, I don't put any more wood on it."

"Have I been doing that?"

"Somebody has."

She smiled again, and Bearman took the smile with a lighter heart. "Holler," he said as he went out and closed the door.

Annie Tinsley took her time getting ready to face the men again. She was both hungry and thirsty, but she also was just vain enough to want to show Bearman and Yoakum her best side. She furiously brushed her hair, feeling again Bearman washing her face with her own red scarf. She smiled and then grimaced to remember how angry it made her that he should be the one to minister to her. "*You need a little touching*," he had said, and she knew she had been waiting for one who would do it—anyone. No. *Someone.*

She studied herself in the hand mirror he had included among the toiletries. Would she ever stop being surprised at his thoughtfulness? She looked like she had been sick: pale and drawn, yet to reclaim her figure, dark circles under her eyes.

She hollered his name.

"Just a minute."

Bearman kicked at the door and stepped back. Annie Tinsley opened it to see him half hidden behind an armful of hopelessly wrinkled skirts and blouses. On top and trailing the lines along beside him was Dollar-Five's bridle. Her expression changed.

"It was Wally's idea."

"Who is that?"

"You've been quirted again," Bearman said over his shoulder.

"Dadgum, and we were getting along so nicely. Mrs. Tinsley, your chair is just sittin' here empty."

"Keep it that way," she said without looking at him. She was looking at Bearman, waiting to hear him say something about her hair. "Well?"

"That's a deep subject," Bearman answered.

She stepped to one side, frowning, and snatched the bridle as Bearman passed. Bearman dropped her clothes on the bunk, spreading his arms so that the bundle fell flat. When he turned, she was holding the bridle and flipping the lines as if she was in the process of coiling them, and they had snagged on the stone doorway.

"Ma'am," he said and stopped, staring at her as if seeing her for the first time, or perhaps seeing her as she was when they first met.

To cover her blush, she said, "What's left?"

She had to say it twice.

"Your boots and pistol."

"You'd better leave those for a while, don't you think?" she said and threw the bridle out the door.

"I try not to think. Wally tried to think once upon a time, and look where he is right now."

"Who?" she asked.

From outside, they heard, "Dadgum."

"Breakfast is ready when you are." Bearman walked out, closing the door behind him. He picked up the abused bridle and tossed it to Yoakum with a grin. He turned and knocked again.

"What."

He opened the door a crack and said, "You didn't need a mirror for that work of art."

Bearman and Yoakum had moved under the ramada for shade from the rising heat of the morning sun. When Annie Tinsley finally opened the door to the hut and appeared at the corner of the ramada, still in the morning sunlight, both men lowered their coffee cans and stared. To cover her blush of satisfaction, she hurried over to her chair, where Bearman had placed his one enamelware cup on the seat. She was wearing a dark green riding skirt and a brown blouse with a blue scarf tied around her throat. On her feet, she wore her sensible walking shoes. Her hair was fixed and her face washed. To the men, she did not look like an invalid.

Yoakum said, "The sun done come up twice today."

"Thank you, Mr. Yoakum."

"Call me Wally."

"Thank you, Wally. And you may call me Annie. I do not feel very much like 'Mrs. Tinsley' right now."

"Well, Annie, that's settled. What about John over there?"

Annie Tinsley glanced at him, sitting there smoking his pipe, one leg crossed over the other knee, his face both placid and touched with amusement. He was waiting for her answer.

She said, "*Mr. Bearman* is just fine for him as he persists in calling me *ma'am*, as if I were a fifty-year-old serving woman in a boarding house."

"Ho!"

"Don't say it, Wally. We'll tally the scars when it's all over."

"Was that a quirt?" Annie Tinsley asked innocently.

Although the dumplings were soggy and dissolving in the broth, Annie ate well, claiming the saltiness tasted good to her. The men were glad to hear it. Bearman knew the saltiness would cause her to drink more water, which she needed.

They had been sitting there the better part of an hour when Yoakum stood, stretched, and shook himself in a way that made Bearman smile. "I think I've got some washing to do before it gets much hotter," he said.

"You mean you're not going to claim man's privilege and wait for the woman to do the washing?" Annie Tinsley asked.

"Annie," Yoakum said, "it's true women was given the vote twenty-five years ago, and that that enfranchisement has since been often misused, but this is the Rio Grande country. The only dividing line in duties is wellness and skill. The story is that your husband spent a week trying to loosen a reverse screw nut when, had you been consulted, the problem would have been obvious to you at a glance. Therefore, you should be in charge of nuts and bolts, not the man. Gender has nothing to do with it. The desert knocks on the door of everyone who dares live here—man, woman, or child."

"I was not being a cat, Wally. Can I still call you *Wally*?"

"Till the ends of the earth."

"You mean *end* of the earth," Bearman said.

"That too," Yoakum put in.

"Thank you, Wally," she replied, "but you've done enough washing."

Annie Tinsley tried not to carry her thought past the bedding, but she included her bath in the "washing." She blushed, and the men looked out of the shade at the slope in the bright sunlight. A minute went by in silence, then she said, "But you and Mr. Bearman can decide who will do the dishes."

At that, she got up, went inside the hut for her hat, and came back out. Without saying anything, she went to the wagon and retrieved her gun belt and pistol and put it around her waist. She searched the wagon bed for any more of her belongings, but all she saw were the remains of Bearman's supplies that had yet to be unloaded and her boots.

She rejoined the men. "Where are the things that need washing?"

"I left them down at the river, Annie."

She blushed again and was grateful her hat threw a shadow across her face. *When would she just accept the last night's necessity and quit being so embarrassed?*

"Soap?"

"Yep," Yoakum said. "Are you sure you're up to it?"

The truth was she felt a little wobbly but was also determined to rise to the men's expectation of her.

Bearman, watching her, said, "Holler if you need something."

"With Dollar-Five down there?" she said over her shoulder. She decided as she went that she would ask Bearman what he meant by *holler*.

Dollar-Five, having heard her name, joined Annie Tinsley past the stand of river cane and flood debris, where she stopped in confusion. There on the rocks by the river were her bedding and nightgown. They were spread with small rocks on the corners and were now dry. They had been scrubbed clean, and the sunlight had returned to them the rich cotton smell of items dried by that purifying light. She thought Yoakum must have been teasing her.

She went down to the river's edge, and as she stood there, she saw that there were some trinkets placed around the edges of her nightgown. There were three religious medallions; others were beads and colorful duck feathers. There were insects made of twisted copper wire and doll-like figures made of cane stalks and cloth. In a strange way, they frightened her.

Suddenly, from across the river came the sound of children singing. She saw them emerge from the brush and stop at the river's edge. She did not know the song they sang, but the sound of their immature voices reminded her with the force of grief that she had an infant daughter she had abandoned. She choked on a sob and ran back up the hill to the hut, crying and trying to catch her breath. She stumbled across the threshold and flung herself face down on the bunk.

"What in the world?" Bearman asked.

The men hurried to the door of the hut, but Annie Tinsley did not seem to hear their questions or acknowledge their presence.

"She's back in her room again," Bearman said. "Something at the river."

XVIII

Near Big Canyon, April 1945

4/21/1945 *La Mujer del Rio* returns. A relapse.

J Bearman

[notepaper]

I broke again.

They left her and went down the hill. They saw the bedding washed and dried, and, going closer, the trinkets and the children moving back into the shade of the mesquite and catclaw, but not leaving. A rider appeared, his horse wet to the belly. It was Umberto. He took off his sombrero, waved, and rode into the brush, joining the children in that shade.

Bearman returned the salute and said to Yoakum, "You know the meaning of this better than I do. I'll gather up this stuff. You go see if you can explain this to her."

"Her name is Annie."

"Not to me. Go. We can't let her slip again."

"All right, John."

The memories of his Marisa freshly played in his mind as he went up the hill to the hut. Yoakum stopped in the doorway, his throat tight. Annie Tinsley was quiet now, sniffing back the congestion in her head from crying.

“Annie, it’s me, Wally. I want to tell you something, and I want you to listen. Can you do that?”

She turned her head toward him. “Oh, Wally,” she said, her voice broken. “The children were singing.”

“Were they?”

“I feel like such a terrible person. It hurts so much. Oh, why did Mr. Bearman bring me here?”

She sobbed and seemed about to start crying again.

“Don’t,” Yoakum said. “Now isn’t the time for tears.”

“What can he think of me?”

“I’ll tell you that in a minute, but first I want to tell you something else. Will you listen?”

“Yes.”

“Wipe your face.”

Yoakum went out and got his peaches box, then came back and set it close to the bunk, the peaches girl uppermost. He sat down and cleared his throat.

“When the stock market broke in ’29, it seemed my wife Marisa and I had next to nothing and no prospects. Sure, we had a small ranch and my brand-new veterinarian’s license, but cattle weren’t worth anything; no one could afford a veterinarian, so we packed up our necessaries, including all kinds of medicine I had on hand. We sold our little place in the hill country at a loss and came to the river, which we hoped would provide us food and a place to shelter. Nobody cared much who squatted out here in those days as long as they left other people’s stuff alone. We got by with deer meat and fish, and there was a man named Taylor who used to grow vegetables and suchlike we could barter for.

“But a hideout is not the only reason we came. My Marisa suffered from rheumatoid arthritis, the kind that cripples a person with knots of bone and swelling. It affects a person’s innards, too. There is no cure for it, but we heard that the hot springs along the Rio Grande can ease the pain and stiffness. We found one back where Big Canyon meets the river. We built a little grass and cane hut there—nothing too permanent because we both knew she didn't have much time.

"She loved that spring, Annie. I'd love to show it to you. She would lie in it for hours, sometimes nap in it. When she could no longer walk, I'd carry her down to the spring in her white nightgown. The spring was only partially shaded, and she burned easily. Pretty soon, some Mexicans discovered us, sometimes visiting us when the river was low. They brought the children to see *la Mujer*, as they called her.

"Then one day, she noticed a little boy about ten with boils on his legs and back. She took that boy into the spring, and after he had had a good soak, she lanced those boils and had me put salve on them. At the time, we had more medicines than food. A week later, or thereabouts, the Mexican women began to bring their sick and ailing children for *la Mujer del Rio* to cure. They also began to bring us foodstuffs and leave little trinkets and weavings around the pool. All the children wanted to kiss her. That last year I could hardly stand it, watching her give hope to others while she had none for herself.

"Somebody saw you in the river in your white nightgown last night, and they thought *la Mujer* had come back. Tell you the truth, holding you in the river while I bathed you brought her back to me. Don't be shy about it. You needed it, and I thank you for the chance to sort of be with her again.

"Anyway, I guess while we were eating, they came across the river to honor you, even sing for you, just like they did for Marisa. For a while, it used to tear the heart out of me to hear it, but now I just smile to know Marisa was that loved."

"Oh, Wally, I am so sorry for you."

Yoakum nodded acceptance of her sympathy. She was thinking of someone besides herself. "John brought you over here to help you get strong again. He helped me, and he's got a dozen stories from his own life like mine and yours. We need to honor that effort and compassion. Look how far you've come since this time yesterday."

Annie Tinsley was quiet for a minute, sniffing a little, her hand unconsciously stroking her belly. It was true that something, some way of being had changed her. She was staring out the open door but seeing only memory.

Then she said, "How does Mr. Bearman make such a difference? I do and say things around him that I never thought I would do or say to a man I hardly know. Is it some kind of hypnosis? One time I saw a hypnotist in San Antonio make a society woman snort like a hog every time she heard the word *hello*."

Yoakum chuckled. He knew what it was, but he said, "John makes you want to do things just by being John. I've thought about it a little bit, because I enjoy comin' over here. He works on you just by being who he is. Everything seems quicker and deeper when he's around."

"Wally," she said again suddenly, touching the sleeve of his shirt. "What must he think of me?"

The doorway darkened, and Bearman stood there. He was holding the folded bedding with her nightgown and the trinkets and crafts left on the river bank on top of the clean sheets. Yoakum cleared his throat, stood up, and moved out of the way, taking the box with him.

Bearman said, "I'll tell you what I think. I think you need to give me some room on the bunk for this stuff so I don't have to walk around carrying it or drop it in the dirt."

She turned her face away from him, ashamed of herself. She swung her feet off the bunk and moved to the foot of it. Bearman placed his load on the bunk and said, "Ma'am, I want you to come down to the river with me."

"I can't," she said, feeling the pull of his personality. "Please leave me alone."

"You may not want to, but you can and you will, if I have to carry you. It'll be either in my arms or over my shoulder."

She shook her head, her face turned away. Yoakum, emotional after the telling of his story, left the doorway. Bearman took a step closer to her, their knees almost touching, she sitting, he standing.

"Ma'am," he said softly, "these people along the river don't have much. They live in huts of sticks and grass with dirt floors. They sleep on the ground and lack furniture of any but the rudest kind, handmade from whatever is available. They don't have minds and hearts cluttered with temporal fantasies from the outside world. They cook and eat on fires without Dutch ovens or ladles or plates. They toast their tortillas on flat pieces of scrap metal. Their religion is mostly superstition, but they hold to it. Simple things they weave or have been given are treasures to them, more meaningful than money. Wally's wife Marisa was both vision and miracle to them. I asked Wally to tell you about her because I wanted you to know what this means." He nodded at the bedding and nightgown and offerings from the people across the river. "Her presence out here made them feel cared for and protected."

Annie Tinsley shook her head again, still refusing to look at him.

"I'm not worthy of that," she said, her voice raspy and broken. "I'm a woman who has deserted her child. It is better that they know now they were mistaken. Wally's Marisa or *la Mujer* or whoever has not come to live here on the hill above the river. I cannot face them, knowing the truth of what I am."

"The only person you've deserted is yourself. Come."

"No."

With a sudden movement, Bearman bent and turned her toward him by her shoulders. He had a glimpse of her startled face—eyes wide and lips parted—but he paid no heed to her apprehension. Maintaining the direction of that initial pull, he lifted her up from the bunk until he could catch her legs, his left arm around her waist, then straightened with Annie Tinsley in his arms. Her perfect hair feathered his cheek, and once again, in spite of everything, she was overcome by his scent.

"You're going," he said.

She slapped him with her left hand, her face going from sadness to anger, and Bearman hefted her to a more comfortable weight against his chest.

"That's a girl," he laughed and carried her outside. "You are on your way."

Yoakum was standing nearby. When Annie Tinsley began to kick and twist against Bearman's grip, Yoakum said, "You'd better get her pistol, John."

"Put me down," she said, her voice now strident with fury.

"You've been reading too many romances," Bearman said. "It takes more than that to make the bad man put the woman down."

"You're hateful."

"Keep it up," he said, turning toward the river.

Dollar-Five came up from the river at the sound of raised voices. Annie Tinsley, seeing the mare, shouted, "*Sho now*!"

Dollar-Five neighed loudly and stomped her right hoof. She ran at Yoakum and made a circle around him, then ran to Bearman but stopped beside him and put her forehead against his shoulder. She nudged him, then turned her eyes. She huffed in Annie Tinsley's face and held there until the woman choked on a smothered laugh—the sound of surrender and broken anger. She returned the huff, and Dollar-Five was satisfied.

So was Bearman.

"Would you put me down, please," Annie Tinsley said. Her voice was weaker now. She was not strong enough to suffer repeated extremes of emotion.

"Can I carry you past the cane? Dollar-Five wants to go with us."

"Yes," she said. She put her head against his chest. The images conjured by Yoakum's story revolved in her mind.

At the river's edge, he put her down gently and steadied her until she was firmly on her feet. He stepped away.

She wouldn't look at the river or across it but stood in the bright sunlight, hatless and humble, until the children started to sing again, their childish voices tracking across the river like the ripples of sunlight in the shallows of the flowing water. Dollar-Five neighed loudly at the sound and shook her mane.

Then Annie Tinsley looked and waved. There was an instant reaction across the river. The children began to dip and weave their bodies in circles as they sang, under the direction of an older girl. The rider again took off his sombrero and waved it. He shouted something friendly, but the words were lost to her in the voices of the children.

She turned to Bearman and stepped close to him. "Will you take me back now, Mr. Bearman?" she said, her voice subdued.

"Wave one more time."

She lifted her hand to those across the river and said, "I really think I am about to faint."

She did. Bearman caught her up in his arms again and carried her back to his little rock house, where she slept most of the rest of the day.

XIX

Near Big Canyon, April 1945

```
4/22/1945 To the top of what she
calls a mesa. AT stronger.
```

J Bearman

[notepaper]
We went up on the mesa today. I could not help but feel at home there.
Mr. Bearman has a way of changing my mind.
He is so . . .

The weather was mild, with high clouds and a wavering east wind on the second day after Bearman brought Annie Tinsley to his little rock house. It was nearing the end of the random April cold spells, and soon the winds of May would lift sand across the Texas basin that would dust and grit everything not sheltered or covered, including food being cooked and open liquids not being drunk. May would also begin the season of rising temperatures during the day and cool breezes in the night.

On this day, Bearman alternated restlessly between the ramada where Annie Tinsley sat and the river's edge, hoping to see Umberto again with news of Pulaski and Ornelos. He and Yoakum unloaded his wagon and pulled it by hand alongside the corral near where the ridge sloped away toward the river.

Bearman said, "If we're two mules, you're the off mule."

"And if I was drivin' this wagon, I'd sure put some attention on the right-hand mule that keeps driftin' me toward the edge of the slope."

After that, there seemed nothing special that needed doing, so they sat under the ramada and told stories—Yoakum mostly—and smoked, hoping by their presence to keep Annie Tinsley focused on the immediate moment.

They found her to be muted but attentive. Sometimes she put in a short anecdote from her childhood or an observation, but in moments of silence, she simply studied her surroundings as if trying to memorize the layout of the camp Bearman had established. In a rough but thoughtful way, he had created the perfect habitat for living in the desert along the Rio Grande. Yet, although she scanned and rescanned the hut and corral and the wagon, she was most often drawn to the ridge above where she sat. From its unknown height, her eyes would drop to Bearman when he returned from the river and sat to smoke his pipe and (she knew) observe and measure her well-being.

It seemed to Bearman that Annie Tinsley had come to terms with the misplaced homage of the Mexicans and their gifts. It was difficult for her, but she had twice returned to the river's edge to wash the big Dutch and had gathered the curious objects she found there. Touched but no longer self-condemning, she displayed them on Bearman's table. Whenever he went inside, he looked over the growing assortment, thinking to see her heart-shaped rock among the tokens, but it was not there.

Yoakum offered the opinion that she could open a gewgaw shop in Marathon and sell her collection to tourists.

"For shame, Wally. They're gifts. A person doesn't sell gifts."

"I wasn't being crass. I was thinking you could leave the people money by the river."

“What use would they have for money out here?” Bearman asked. “Money is for the rancho over the mountain and the long road to Zacatecas.”

“And what reason would I have for coming all the way out here to leave a few dollars?”

Yoakum could think of one reason, but he kept it to himself. Instead, he turned and looked over his shoulder to where his horse was idly staring at the inactive mules. “Come around, Rosie,” he called. “We done wore out our welcome. Folks gangin’ up on me, and me havin’ to desecrate the peaches girl by sitting on her box. I’ve got splinters all over my—”

“Poor Wally,” Annie Tinsley interrupted.

Bearman laughed. “He’s about as poor as I am rich.”

“Are you rich, Mr. Bearman?”

He looked steadily at her and smoked for a minute, then said, “Sometimes, ma’am.”

She blushed and pretended to fan a persistent fly away from her face. She thought how much easier it would be for her if she did not understand him so well, but she knew the understanding worked both ways. It was what charmed her most about John Bearman. She was not used to it.

“By the way,” she said, having again studied the height of the ridge, “would you take me up on that mesa sometime?” The upward trail was plain to see from where she sat, and she wondered where it led.

Bearman leaned forward to better see out from under the overhang of the ramada. “It’s not really a mesa,” he said.

“Nevertheless.”

“You feel like it?”

“Yes.”

“We’ll go after lunch, if you feel like it.”

The morning passed, and by noon, the breeze had cooled and shifted to the north. They sat against the west wall to eat their lunch, their plates in their laps. Annie Tinsley was again aware the men were covertly watching her. She was happy to please them by cleaning her plate.

"Beans," Yoakum said in disgust.

"Eat and be glad," Bearman told him.

"But to serve beans to a lady?"

"She's not a lady," Bearman said. Annie Tinsley gasped, and her fork slid off the edge of her plate. "She is a certified honorary River Rider, and it is her duty and privilege to subsist off the same fare as her fellow men in service. Isn't that right, ma'am?"

Later, when Bearman was putting the saddle on Dollar-Five, getting ready to take Annie Tinsley up on the mesa-that-was-not-a-mesa, Yoakum asked him, "Did you see her face when you said she was not a lady? I thought there was going to be a killin' for sure, and the worst part is I wasn't sure which side I was going to be on."

"She needs shocks like that, Wally. Little ones to rearrange her thinking. The only person who can keep her out of that terrible room is herself."

"You mean Annie."

"You know who I mean. She's Morton Tinsley's wife," he said, although he didn't like to think or speak it. "You keep on about that and it's beans for supper."

A movement at the door of the hut drew their attention. Annie Tinsley stepped out into the sunlight like an idealized vision of Western womanhood. She was wearing brown boots stitched with a paisley design, her brown riding skirt with a narrow belt, and her gun belt and pistol that Bearman insisted she wear as a condition to going, although he did not say why. Her blouse was khaki and topped by a blue bandana scarf. She carried her hat in her hand. The sunlight was in her perfect hair.

They stared at her as she crossed the gravel, dropping her hat on her head at a rakish angle.

"Just shoot me," Yoakum said. "I believe in ghosts."

"How about I shoot you on general principles?" Bearman replied, then said softly as Annie Tinsley drew near, "Keep your eye on things. Fire a round if there's any news from across the river."

"Will do."

"I am ready, Mr. Bearman," Annie Tinsley said, stopping before them, her hands on her hips.

Bearman thought her room of misery was getting smaller and smaller, fading. He was increasingly proud of her and affected by her.

"Are we taking Dollar-Five?"

The mare knickered.

"It's a bit of a climb. Dollar-Five can carry you if you get tired."

"You can't carry me?" she teased.

"No, ma'am."

"Uh-oh," Yoakum said and turned away to spit, lest they read his face.

Bearman's blunt reply made her feel awkward. "If it's too much trouble—"

"Let's go," he said, and shouldering his canteen, he started around the corral to the trail that wound up the slope toward the top, Dollar-Five beside him.

Annie Tinsley looked at Yoakum, but his face was now blank. He nodded at the trail and started back to the ramada and his choice of chairs. She drew a deep breath and hurried to catch Bearman, determined not to need Dollar-Five's saddle if it took her all day to reach the top.

The narrow trail they followed was made by wildlife and Reagan brothers cattle drifting down to the river after a day of foraging the hills. The higher they went, the more the trail became low shelves of limestone, and the view was increasingly panoramic and beautiful. She stopped where the trail began to wind around the mesa-that-was-not-a-mesa and rested, enjoying the view.

Below them, the Flats opened up in thick, green growth along the floodplain of the Rio Grande and to undulating hillocks away from the river where creosote created the deception of fruitful green across the tan of the desert. Rising to a level of the distant walls of Big Canyon, Annie Tinsley could see the humped formations of the mountain split in Texas and Mexico by the river. The wall of the *Sierritas* in Mexico as they rose up made her think of a gigantic wave about to crest. What she had seen from a hazy proximity became sharp and breathtaking in height and distance. Across the river from Bearman's camp, in the brush, she caught glimpses of Mexicans going about their business. The smoke of fires in two wax camps rose lazily and dispersed quickly. Deeper in, she could see the white rooftops of several buildings. She was surprised when she noticed three buzzards floating on the air currents at a height lower than where she stood.

She heard Dollar-Five come up behind her with Bearman.

"Tired?"

She had decided not to speak to Bearman until they reached the top, but once again, his influence broke through her resistance.

"No, just a little sore. Can I have a drink?"

Bearman stepped down beside her, unslung the canteen, and gave it to her. While she drank, he noticed her face was tinged with the healthy color of exertion, and her posture was erect and balanced on the uneven rocks of the trail. She was quickly becoming again the woman he knew.

She stoppered the canteen and gave it back to him. "I've never before been this high out here." She lifted the tail of her scarf to dry her lips. "It is amazing how close those mountains look when I know they are miles and miles away."

Bearman had his own awareness of "miles and miles" away, but he didn't say anything.

She shielded her eyes with her hand and said, "I don't see Wally."

"Want to make another bet?"

She smiled. "Will you cheat?"

"Nope. Scout's honor."

"What then?"

"I bet you a dollar, five that Wally is under the ramada trying out our chairs."

Sensing contention, the mare put her long face between them and snorted. Bearman said something to her, and she took a step back.

"A dollar, five again?"

"I'm a cautious gambler. I stick to a winner."

Annie Tinsley thought about it. "No deal on the bet. Modify it and let's bet on whose chair he decides to sit in."

"I bet it will be mine."

"That was fast. Why not mine? It's padded."

"Can't tell you until it's over."

"I bet mine."

"Shake."

Once again, her gloved hand slipped into his, and the contact was much different than even the times that he had carried her—but equally affecting.

True to her resolve, she declined to ride Dollar-Five to the top. Once she got there, it was a mild disappointment. The top of the mesa-that-was-not-a-mesa was like all the rest of the desert: gravel and sand and creosote bushes that waved their branches in the breeze. They were seldom harvested anymore for medicinal purposes and contributed to the lowering of the water table, but accomplished little else. The farther spread of the ridge revealed it was not freestanding like the giant mesa downriver from the mouth of Maravillas Canyon. Annie Tinsley had felt an urge to walk high ledges.

The view, however, did not disappoint.

"How far do you think we can see from here?" Annie Tinsley asked, seating her hat more firmly against the increasing breeze.

"Looking upriver, we can see the outline of the mountain cut by Maravillas Creek. See the hump that rises in the middle? That's at least thirty miles. Half a day's travel by automobile; all day by mules, especially by mules that walk in their sleep."

She looked and then lowered her gaze, and Bearman realized she was looking for a place to sit. He led her over to a ledge on the lip of a shallow arroyo, and they sat while Dollar-Five explored the familiar landscape.

After a few minutes of silence, Bearman asked, "All right?"

She looked at him, their shoulders touching, for the smoothest edge was narrow where they sat. "Yes," she said, dropping her eyes. "I was a little winded by the climb. I'm afraid my poor body . . . has a ways to go."

"Did you overdo it?"

"Maybe a little."

She began to play with the end of her scarf, which had lifted against her cheek in the breeze. Bearman sensed the reason she wanted to climb the mesa-that-was-not-a-mesa had little to do with the landscape. The white track of a road below them was the same one that led past her house.

"I like your place," she said, after a pause. "Your little rock house."

"It's a good place."

"It's a good place to be."

"Ma'am?"

She dropped her hands to her lap and looked without seeing into the far distance. Bearman had the impression she was shrinking beside him—not away, but down.

"I have to go back. You know that, don't you?"

"I'm glad you realize that," Bearman said without emotion.

She stared out at the vast landscape before them and spoke as if to it rather than Bearman.

"I met Morton eight years ago in San Antonio. He ran an insurance agency that my father had a policy with. After my father died, there was an irregularity that had to be worked out. Mother and I visited with Morton at the office, and he asked permission to visit us at home. I hadn't met many men once I finished school. Men found it obvious that I was uncomfortable in social situations. Morton's attentions were pleasant to me. We became engaged.

"After two years, Morton decided he did not want to live in the city anymore. He and the rest of the country wanted to go into the *glorious West*. Although neither of us had ever been farther west than Kerrville, I felt the same way. When he saw a listing for the Reynolds' place, he investigated and bought it cheap. He really had no idea how to run a ranch or live far removed from tradesmen. Most of the things he tried to do were costly failures.

"One time a rattlesnake got in the house, and I had to kill it. He was afraid to try, went from room to room looking for a solution until I finally killed it with my pistol. Then, I had to carry it out and throw it over the fence. It was a horrible time for me, not just the killing and handling, but because I had to do it at all. And I had no idea how the bullet would ricochet off the cement floor into the wall. He complained about that. Actually, there were two bullet holes."

"She is a great disappointment to me as a wife and a mother."

"When my time had come, I was so afraid something would go wrong with the baby. It hurt so much, and Morton was so useless. I was terrified, but he wouldn't stay with me. I felt absolutely alone in that way that is not just *by yourself*. After I knew the baby was all right, I . . . guess I just quit. I could not get away from a sense of loneliness or uselessness. The fear would not go away, but only got stronger because I knew the neglect was never going to change."

"Do you feel that way now?" Bearman asked quietly in a voice of concern that touched her deeply.

"No. When that man put the rifle barrel against my head, I knew how much I wanted to live."

Bearman drew a breath and looked out across the miles. "That was my fault."

"I don't accept that," Annie Tinsley said.

They were silent for a while. On top of the ridge the breeze was stronger, the mountains to the west more lonely. Cloud shadows ran across the river and up over the ridges as if they had to be somewhere. The stark beauties of the mountains, the river, and the desert revealed themselves in the movable light. Annie Tinsley felt she had never seen this landscape before. From somewhere below them, she heard the whistle of a bird.

"What kind of bird is that?" she asked. When Bearman admitted he could not identify a single bird out of so many along the river, she was slightly peeved. It reminded her of Morton Tinsley's habit of negating anything that drew her attention.

"Listen," she said.

It came again and clearly sounded out the words *Bob White*. There were quail sifting through the draw below them. "Bobwhite quail," Bearman told her.

"It's beautiful," Annie Tinsley said.

Bearman shifted uneasily. Her appeal had never been so hard for him to resist as it was then.

Annie Tinsley returned her gaze to the horizon. "Can I tell you something?"

"Go ahead."

"I made a mistake, Mr. Bearman. How bad a mistake, I didn't realize until we moved out here. There has been a cold emptiness inside of me. I never should have married Morton."

"Ma'am."

"I'm little more than furniture to him; some days, he doesn't say ten words to me. He's never once asked what I was thinking or how I was feeling. He would think I was crazy if I told him I wanted to come up here to this beautiful place. Can you understand the kind of loneliness that being ignored can create?"

Bearman nodded but did not speak.

"He didn't treat me any differently than usual during the pregnancy, but I suppose I still hoped, deep down, that when I really needed someone, he would be there. For me, and for the child. And when he wasn't . . ."

She lifted the tails of her bandana and touched at her eyes. Bearman knew she had more to say, and he waited for her to go on.

"We lived out here for four and a half years before my mother got sick, and I had to return to San Antonio to care for her. She would not consider coming out here, even though the doctor recommended the drier climate.

She never gave a convincing reason not to come. After I got back, I wondered if she wanted to stay in the city to avoid seeing me with Morton, if maybe she could sense how unhappy, how . . . stifled I felt with him. I've been feeling my loneliness more, these last few years . . . and then the baby . . . Many times, last week—Has it only been a week? —I wished I could have died with her."

"I hate to hear that."

Each sentence Annie Tinsley spoke had an odd effect on Bearman; a kind of weight seemed to be increasing on his shoulders.

They were quiet, breathing, sharing the effect of loss, remembering. For Annie Tinsley, it was a sweet quietness, and she felt somehow appreciated. It had always been a rare thing in her life.

"You were coming home that day we met at the train station?" Bearman asked quietly.

"Yes."

"I apologize for my behavior."

"Should I apologize for mine?"

"There was nothing wrong with your behavior."

"If there were, I want to blame it on you. I had no idea I could behave that way to a stranger." Annie Tinsley's voice changed when she began to remember.

"We kind of wrote our own script, but I don't think we were acting. Do you remember how many other people were on the platform while we were—whatever it was we were doing?"

"Daring each other," Annie Tinsley said. "I think there were three or four others there."

"There were at least two dozen. As I told you then, it was part of my job to know who got off the train."

"Oh," she said. "That makes it worse."

Bearman laughed shortly. "By whose standards?"

"You're right," she said, thinking about it, then added, "But that was how I was raised, don't you see? I was a city girl, trained in decorum to be proper at all times, even at home."

"You told me that when you came out here, you were hoping you could do things, like having an adventure. Well? You're in one now."

"Are you suggesting I am having an adventure by suffering a breakdown, deserting my newborn daughter, and being kidnapped from my own bed?"

She got to her feet in dismay, angrily dusting off the seat of her skirt. Bearman's comment struck her as criticism. It came too soon after the confidences.

"Sit down, ma'am."

"No. I don't want to. I'm not going to. I'm going back down now."

She stomped her foot, which made Dollar-Five look up from where she browsed and whinny. Annie Tinsley glanced at the horse, shook her head and sat down again.

"I wish you would quit doing that," she said with a sigh.

"Doing what?"

"Making me do things I don't want to do."

Bearman smiled. "I used to know a kid back home who was always afraid of getting in trouble if we swam in the creek. If the rest of us wanted to go skinny dipping, he would put his hands on his hips and tell us not to in a voice that sounded just like his mother when she scolded, which she did a lot. But he wanted to go swimming as bad as the rest of us. It was like he was two people, two very different people, neither one very happy. You've been like that, don't you think? I tell you to sit down when one of you gets angry and then you sit down because the other one of you, the stronger one, really wasn't insulted at all and wanted to sit down."

"I'm getting angry again."

"No, you aren't. In fact, I think you are well on your way to becoming the daring you, the strong you. It feels good, doesn't it?"

"Which one slapped you yesterday?" Annie Tinsley asked, trying to regain her balance. Bearman's insight caught her off guard.

"That slap was a little bit outrage and a little bit weary daring. I think your natures ganged up on me that time."

"Part of me is sorry for it."

"You don't need to be. That slap made me glad."

Annie Tinsley pushed up her hat and touched her temples like she was getting a headache, then she lowered her hands and looked at him, her face changed—serious, but not angry or sad.

She said, "Why did it matter to you? Why did you bring me to your little rock house?"

Bearman hesitated, unwilling to tell her the whole truth, because once the words were spoken, they could never be taken back. His mother had been an attractive woman, and he remembered the neighbor who tried to take advantage of her. The man's actions were in vain, but they angered and sickened Bearman. He resolved he would never be a man who stood between a husband and wife. *Irony often controls our lives*, he thought.

He said, "That day at the train station, I found out you had a fighting spirit. I was frankly delighted. I could have spent the whole day sparring with you. Once or twice, you acted like you were going to hit me, which I probably deserved. I admired you for it. I was in Marathon again on Thursday and overheard a doctor say you were dying."

"I didn't like the doctor."

"I can imagine why. I stopped by your place on Friday to pay my respects. I had no idea of bringing you here, but ma'am, you weren't fighting. Like you said, you had quit. It made me crazy to think it, so I convinced Morton to let me take you to *la Mujer del Rio*."

"So, in a sense, you were taking me to myself."

"That's one way to look at it."

"Did you know Wally was going to be at your place?"

"No, but I wasn't surprised. He wanders down from the Canyon pretty regularly now that he's alone."

"How hard was it to convince Morton?"

"One battle at a time. Let's save Morton for another time."

"Which means it wasn't hard. Then what?" Annie Tinsley asked, her voice low and hesitant as Bearman's had been. She was waiting to hear what she was afraid to hear.

"Then I bundled you up, almost got you killed—"

"What really happened?"

"Ornelos didn't know I never carry a round under the hammer. If there had been one, you would now be beyond all worries. I shudder to think."

She looked down and pressed the material of her skirt on her leg. Her hand moved back and forth as if she were drying her palm. Then she said, "And you brought me here."

"You needed to be in a place where you could heal and grow strong."

She said, in a voice as cool and soft as the breeze, "Why, oh why, did it take you so long?"

She rested her forehead against his shoulder in acknowledgement of her rescue, and she took in the strength of his scent. Bearman resisted the urge to embrace her, and she straightened slowly, neither ashamed nor sorry. She had gotten her answer and had given her reply.

At that moment, Bearman's eyes were drawn to movement on the road. Below them and out from the ridge by several miles was an automobile heading their way.

Bearman stood up and said, "We have to go."

He whistled for Dollar-Five.

XX

Near Big Canyon, April 1945

```
4/22/1945 Brothers return with news.
Tinsley brought sheriff with charge
of kidnapping. AT wonderful.
```

J Bearman

[notepaper]

I know I have to go back. I want to go back. Not today.

Dollar-Five came up and Bearman held her while Annie Tinsley mounted.

"Do I need to shorten the stirrups?" he asked. "Downhill looks pretty steep from the saddle."

Caught up in his sense of urgency, she shook her head.

"I'm going first. Stay behind me. Keep a tight seat where the trail is steep and Dollar-Five has to hop down the ledges. It'll feel like she's trying to buck."

"Who is it?" she had to ask. "Is it Morton?"

"Follow me."

Crossing the ridge to the trail, Bearman tried to see the automobile again, but even from this height, it was hidden by deep draws and creek beds. When he gained the trail, he moved faster than a walk but not quite a run. Because of the rocks in the trail, he was forced to keep his eye on the ground in front of him lest he turn his ankle on a loose chunk of limestone. In places he went downhill sideways, sliding in gravel. He heard Dollar-Five behind him and kept going.

When the corral came in sight, he could see Yoakum and two men standing under the ramada. The men looked familiar. One of them saw him and Annie Tinsley on Dollar-Five behind him. The man raised a shout. "Hello, Mr. Bearman. Tell Mr. Yoakum not to shoot us."

Relieved, Bearman passed the corral and said, "You can shoot them if you want to, Wally, or wait until after supper."

"Shoot us now," Brother said.

"No, stupid," Steve said. "We brought our own food."

"Oh yeah. Could we wait until after supper?"

"Maybe," Yoakum said.

Annie Tinsley, still on horseback, listened to the already familiar banter about Bearman's diet and thought, *Why don't all these men go away—except one?* She felt herself blush.

Bearman turned to her and, reading her expression, said, "Did you ever imagine you would be outcast on a lonely ridge along the Rio Grande with four men, and strangers at that?"

She shook her head and whispered, "Not since I was seventeen." When he was close, with his back to the others, she said, "But you mean seven men," with a bold smile.

"Seven?"

"One of the men is worth four ordinary men. That makes seven."

"I hope I'm the one to live up to that kind of arithmetic."

"You have so far."

"Let me introduce you."

They walked together to the ramada with Dollar-Five following. She stood outside the shade and watched the men. Yoakum and the brothers had eyes only for Annie Tinsley, a fact Bearman and she were aware of. Bearman shook hands with Steve and Brother. Annie Tinsley, now slightly embarrassed, stepped forward, and Bearman introduced her. Then he said, "Ma'am, these two young fellers helped me build my hut. This is Steve, and this is his brother, Brother."

She nodded and, in spite of herself, asked, "Brother? Don't you have a name as well as a relation?"

"His name is Phineas." Steve laughed.

"Aw, here we go again," Brother said. "Every time we meet somebody. Why'd you have to tell her that?"

"She asked," Yoakum said, having danced to that music before. But this time the raillery seemed forced.

"I think Phineas is a perfectly good name," Annie Tinsley said. "It has been around for thousands of years and exists in forms from Egyptian to Hebrew to Greek and Irish."

Brother smiled and said, "How about that?"

Bearman tipped his hat back and said, "Where did you two get this Ford?"

"We traded the truck for it, and some other things," Steve said.

"You came all the way out here on that road to show it off?" Bearman asked.

"No. We came to help you, Mr. Bearman. We been hearing some bad stuff about you in Marathon."

"Bad stuff?"

The shade under the ramada took on a tense heaviness, and the group shifted. Annie Tinsley, with a sudden sense of dread, felt her situation take on a tragic darkness that made her draw a pace away from Bearman. Yoakum stepped to the edge of the shade and spit. He remained there beside Dollar-Five. Brother moved behind Steve and stared at Annie Tinsley. Steve felt called to account, as if he had done or said something very wrong. Bearman felt the skin of his face tighten. It was as if a cold wind had touched each in turn, one by one.

"What kind of bad stuff?"

"They say you kidnapped Mrs. Tinsley after threatening her husband. That you had stopped by the house to visit but would not leave until Mr. Tinsley had to, to get his baby. When he came back to see how Mrs. Tinsley was doing, she and all her clothes were gone."

"And her horse," Brother said, then took a step back, ashamed.

Steve added, "The blacksmith and Preacher Dyer said you were acting crazy and threatening last week. They—I'm sorry, Mr. Bearman. They went to the sheriff, and they're headed this way to arrest you and rescue Mrs. Tinsley if she was still alive, which she almighty is."

Steve stopped and avoided looking at the woman.

Bearman turned to Annie Tinsley. Her face was pale, and her lips were trembling. There suddenly seemed to be miles and miles between them. Dollar-Five took a step forward, but Yoakum held her back.

"Steady," Bearman said in an aside, and a smile trembled on Annie Tinsley's lips.

"Part of me is ashamed and wants to cry," she admitted softly.

"I want you to fight," Bearman replied.

On hearing the whispered words, the brothers gave each other a look, Steve half-turning to see Brother. When he turned back around, he said, "Well, we come to help you, Mr. Bearman, but we won't do anything unless you tell us to. We brought our guns and plenty of food."

"And the sheriff and Tinsley are coming?"

"They was getting ready when we left town. Maybe Oliver and Preacher Dyer too. They was both pretty mad at you."

"What else?"

"You know what a gossip Sam Oliver is. He's been talking all kinds of bad, like that he once saw you flirting with Mrs. Tinsley at the train station a year or two ago."

"How is his boy?"

The brothers looked at each other. "We didn't hear nothing about his boy."

"Figures."

"Can I ask you something, Mr. Bearman, without having my eyes shot out by Mr. Yoakum?"

"Go ahead."

"I mean, I see Mrs. Tinsley here and all, but—excuse me, ma'am—are those things true they say?"

"Yes," Bearman answered.

"Mr. Bearman," Annie Tinsley said softly.

"You know they're true. You were there," he said to her. To the brothers, he added, "Remember that day I met you boys at the livery to haul all my stuff out here? You were nowhere in sight."

"We went over to the Gage for something to drink," Steve said.

Brother added, "We was thirsty, and we couldn't go in the store. The storekeeper won't let us go inside together anymore because one time me and Steve got in an argument and knocked over a keg of nails."

"It wasn't but about half full."

"It was more than half full. Nails went all the way to Ladies' Wear."

"How do you know what goes on in Ladies' Wear?"

"John?" Yoakum said.

"No," Bearman said. He went on. "All right, but you remember that day. That same day I met Mrs. Tinsley at the train station. She was coming home from San Antonio after caring for her sick mother."

"Did she get well?" Brother asked.

"She died," Annie Tinsley said.

"I'm sorry," the brothers said together. Steve added, "We lost our mother, too."

"She was awful sick."

"But she didn't get well, either."

"The doctor said her appendix burst."

Yoakum said, "John?" but Bearman ignored him.

"I knew that day in Marathon what a wonderful woman this is, to come and be a neighbor on the Rio Grande. When I heard she was dying,

I couldn't believe it. I went to Tinsley. He said . . . " Bearman stopped and looked at Annie Tinsley.

"It's all right," she said.

"He said there was nothing anybody could do for her, and he was late for an appointment. I'm sorry you have to hear that, ma'am. I asked him to let me bring her here, that *la Mujer del Rio* could heal her."

"We heard of her before," Steve said.

Yoakum said, "Humph," and Dollar-Five huffed in response.

"Mr. Tinsley said I could do what I wanted."

"What did you say, Mrs. Tinsley?" Steve asked in a friendly way, not judgmental, just curious.

Bearman answered for her. "She screamed at me and tried to hit me."

"That doesn't sound good," Steve said. "Are you all right, ma'am?"

"Please call me Annie or Mrs. Tinsley. Mr. Bearman is the only one who refers to me as *ma'am*. I'm all right. The day Mr. Bearman came to get me, I was out of my mind, and Mr. Bearman can be very persistent." Annie Tinsley smiled.

"He is about food," Brother said, and the tension broke at Bearman's expense.

Bearman glanced at Yoakum for some kind of help. He felt the explanations were too long and too personal. There would be time for that kind of talk soon, but not now. Yoakum nodded his understanding but did not say anything. He had already twice offered to shoot the talkative brothers.

"Mr. Bearman saved my life," Annie Tinsley said into the silence.

Steve nodded at her. "That's the kind of stuff he does all the time." To Bearman, he said, "Tell us how we can help."

Bearman knew the calming and distracting power of action. He said, "Steve, back your Ford around even with the outside edge of the ramada. Park it there and unload whatever you want to. If you can stay a few days, you are welcome. The ramada can be your camp. Ma'am, if it's all right with you, go inside and wait for me. We need to talk about what is going to happen. Wally, unsaddle Dollar-Five for me, will you?"

"If she'll let a commoner like me handle her."

"She will."

"John?" Yoakum said after the brothers went to their car. "Are you going to let her go back to a man who practically threw her away?"

Bearman shifted his hat. "It's up to her, Wally. She needs to be with her baby."

"*I will fight for you.*"

"I know it, dadgumit. Maybe you could kidnap the baby and bring the child over here."

"I just don't want anything to happen that causes her embarrassment or pain. If anything like that happens, I want it to happen to me. If I have to go to Alpine, so be it, but I will not have her criticized or shamed."

"I can obey orders only up to a point," Yoakum said.

"Thank you, Wally. I'll hunt coyotes with you any time."

"There's no shortage of them creatures, whether four-legged or two."

"Keep an eye on the brothers, too, will you? Don't let them get into trouble, and don't let them get behind you with loaded pistols. I've seen them shoot."

"How about I just shoot them now and be done."

Bearman ignored that and said, "By the way, which chair did you sit in while we were on top?"

"Yours, of course. Annie's chair is for Annie, not for the likes of me."

"Thanks."

Before he joined Annie Tinsley in the hut, he stepped away from it and studied the road. The landscape of flats and mountains so familiar to him had become the setting for a confrontation against which he had no defense. The white bones of the road were a harbinger of tragedy. In the distance, dust rose behind another traveler.

Bearman found Annie Tinsley looking out the window that faced upriver and the road. She heard his boots on the doorstep but did not turn.

"Ma'am?"

"I knew more this afternoon how much I would have to go back—and how much I would leave behind when I did—than I knew yesterday. Yesterday was like a dream of protection and peace. My life frightens me now, and I did so want never to feel that kind of bottomless fear again."

She turned and looked at him. Her eyes were dry.

"You are too brave to fall back into that now," he said.

"I'm not brave at all."

He took off his hat and held it in his hand at his side. "Every time I've been around you, I have seen your courage. That first night, as shivering and heartbroken as you were, you laughed at the antics of Wally and me. To laugh at that time was an act of sheer courage."

"Or forgetfulness."

Bearman smiled, and Annie Tinsley felt it as well as saw it. "Don't let that be a quirt."

"What?" she asked.

"Forgetfulness."

"There are things about these last three days I'll never forget."

"Nor I," Bearman said. He looked around the hut and considered how her possessions, so hastily gathered from her home, filled it in a way beyond just space. A confusion of softness lay here, a bit of color there, a subtle, more efficient way to use his table and boxes, a smooth fold where there would have been a wrinkle.

"Tell me what you want to do," he said, standing close in front of her.

"Don't ask me that. If I try to tell you, I think I will collapse again."

"Try anyway. I need to know."

"I want to see my little girl and hold her. I want to go home and clean up the wreck I left there. I want to come back in a week and show you the baby. I want to sit with you under the ramada and look up to the mesa-that-is-not-a-mesa and remember our talk there. I want you to ride home with me and say goodnight at my doorstep. I want to stay here always in another life and play games with Dollar-Five. I want to meet the children across the river and hear them sing again."

She clasped her fingers together as if they were cold and shook her head.

"I don't know the person I used to be. I want to dare, and I want my daughter to grow up daring. Do you understand?"

"I do, and I'm proud of you."

"Are you?"

"Yes, but tell me: when the others come, will you stay or go with them?"

Yoakum was at the door. "John," he said, "we got company."

"I'm coming." He put his hat on his head and started out the door, then stopped and took off his gun belt. "There's not going to be any shooting," he said. "I don't want anybody to get the idea there might be."

Bearman put the gun belt and holstered pistol in Annie Tinsley's hands. She held them to her breast. He smiled at her and said, "Go or stay?"

"One more night . . . maybe two?"

"Yes. Wait inside for a little while, then come out. You'll know when."

He left her at the doorstep, and Yoakum fell in beside him as they moved up the hill to where the road ended and the car stopped. Yoakum muttered something under his breath that Bearman didn't catch, and all four doors opened. The sheriff was driving, with Morton Tinsley sitting beside him. Sam Oliver and Preacher Gray Dyer were in the back.

Bearman heard steps slow down behind him and said, without turning his head, "Watch the brothers." When the four men got out of the sheriff's car, Bearman nodded at the sheriff and said, "Kind of a long way from town, aren't you, Henry?"

The sheriff moved around the hood of his car and stopped to lean against the fender in a nonaggressive way. He noted the layout of Bearman's camp and the other automobile without comment. He straightened his back and folded his arms across his chest. In silence, he studied Bearman without coming to any conclusion concerning the present situation, remembering the one he had derived the first time he met the River Rider: Bearman was a man among men, a loyal friend and a serious enemy.

The other three from town stood behind their open doors and searched the camp for a sign of Annie Tinsley. They were clearly nervous.

"What do you think, John?" the sheriff said. "Should I arrest the county commissioners for the crime of letting the road out here get in such terrible shape? Hello, Wally. I've seen those two young fellers around town. You boys being good?"

Neither one knew what to say, so they said nothing.

Bearman said, "The maintainer doesn't get used much, as dry as it's been." Ignoring Morton Tinsley, he said, "I can guess why you and Morton are here, but what are the other two here for? Pick them up on the way?"

"Wanted to come along to see if everything was all right."

"Uh-huh," Bearman said. With all the men watching for different reasons, he walked closer to the car, turning slowly on his way to show he carried no weapon. Yoakum nodded once, thought, *that guy,* and glanced at the brothers to make sure their pistols were in their pockets.

Bearman stopped on the nearer side of the sheriff's car facing Sam Oliver, the blacksmith. "Hello, Sam. How's your boy?"

Sam glanced at the sheriff, who stared impassively back at him, both curious and amused.

Sam said, "What boy?"

"I thought you had a sick boy. Thursday, he was too sick for you to take care of my stock, and now here you are a day's ride from town, and you ask me 'What boy?'"

Preacher Gray said, "The boy had a passing fever. Your actions and words were far from passing."

Bearman said, "Shut up, Preacher. Save it for your sermon, and do a better job next time. And look at yourself in the mirror. See if you can do anything about that log." He turned back to Sam Oliver and said, "This is a personal matter between me and Morton under the eyes of the law. It does not concern you in the least unless you choose to make it so, in which case I will oblige."

They all knew a threat from John Bearman was a gilt-edged promise. Sam Oliver swallowed visibly.

"Get back in the car," Bearman took a step closer to him.

"I come with the Sheriff," Morton said.

"Get back in the car."

"Sheriff?"

"Better do what he says, Sam. This is Mr. Bearman's property."

Sam Oliver looked at the men arrayed against him and climbed back into the car.

Bearman said, "Close the door and roll up the window."

"It's hot," Oliver protested.

"We did not come out here to be bullied," Preacher Dyer added.

Morton Tinsley interrupted, "Where is my wife? Is she alive or not?"

"That's what we come to find out," Sam said.

"Why bully the man for his compassion?" the preacher asked.

BANG! Yoakum fired his pistol into the air and said, "Sorry, sheriff. It won't happen again."

"Ai yi yi!" the brothers whooped.

The sheriff said, "Wally, you owe me for the one year of my life you just scared out of me."

Bearman welcomed the ensuing silence. Dollar-Five came up from the river where she had gone and stood outside the group, swishing her tail and watching Bearman. Gunfire meant trouble to her.

"Roll the window up," he said to Oliver. "You, too, Preacher. Get in the car and roll the windows up."

When both of the complaining observers were in the back seat, windows up, Bearman turned to Morton Tinsley and said, "Say what you've been planning to say all the way out here."

"You know damn well what I've got to say. You kidnapped my dying wife—"

"That's a lie. I stopped by your place because I heard she was in a desperate way, and your wife was lying in a bed of filth. I wouldn't treat a sick dog that way: filthy, dehydrated, starving."

"The doctor said there was nothing to be done."

"And you used that as an excuse to do nothing. I asked you to let me take her to *la Mujer del Rio*, and you said go ahead. You couldn't be bothered. You had other things to do. You said—remember what you said?—she was a great disappointment to you as a wife and a mother."

"I never said that."

"You're a double liar. I don't walk past liars. You lie to me again, I'll knock you down, Henry or no Henry."

"Mr. Bearman," the sheriff said. "So far I have no problem. Let's keep it that way."

Tinsley said, "I just want to know, is she alive? Where is she now?"

As if in answer, the standing men heard the voice of Mimi's aria from the third act of *La Bohème*, faint and scratchy, from inside the hut. Yoakum said later that he felt he heard Marisa's voice from the spring. The sheriff thought he heard an angel call his name. When Annie Tinsley stepped out of the hut, Brother said, "That's her. That's the woman in the song." Bearman looked down and shook his head, a smile on his face.

"Wait inside for a while. You'll know when to come out."

The aria continued to play as she came forward to where the men were grouped. She stopped in front of her husband, nothing showing in her expression, but Bearman detected a tremor of emotion in her otherwise still body. She was holding something in her right fist.

"Hello, Morton," she said.

He said, "My God, Annie, you look—"

"Like a *disappointment*? Hello, sheriff."

He nodded, staring. "Miz Tinsley."

She turned back to her husband. "How is the baby?"

"It's fine, doing well. I can't believe—"

"*She* is not an *it*. Why are you here, and why has the sheriff brought you?"

Tinsley hung his head. "People in town—"

"Tell the sheriff," she said. "He deserves an apology too." But before he started, Annie Tinsley herself addressed the sheriff. "Sheriff, did I hear Mr. Bearman call you Henry?"

She's letting me know she heard it all, Bearman thought.

"Yes, ma'am. My mother give me that name."

"Can I call you Henry?"

"Yes, ma'am. I'd be pleased."

"You're a politician, aren't you?"

"I'd be pleased anyway."

"You can call me Annie," she said and cut Bearman a look. "Go ahead, Morton," she said to her husband, who had been shifting from one foot to the other, impatient and bewildered by his wife's dialogue with the sheriff.

"People kept asking me how you were and did you die and why was I in town instead of at the ranch, so I told them Mr. Bearman had kidnapped you, and I didn't know where he had taken you. He said I could use that excuse. When Sam and Gray heard about it, they thought I ought to go to the sheriff. And here I am."

"Slow day, Henry?" Annie Tinsley asked with an arched brow.

"I was obligated to oblige."

"Where is the baby?" she snapped at Morton.

"Esperanza has it—*her*."

"When is the last time you saw her?"

"I don't know. Day before yesterday, I guess."

Annie Tinsley shook her head in frustration and disgust. She was close to tears, but she turned to the sheriff. "Henry, do I look like a woman in distress?"

Bearman caught Brother's attention and nodded for him to go take the needle off the record when it went silent.

Henry said, "Oh, no more than any woman nowadays, I guess."

"Is that a joke?" she asked.

"I ride with Wally now and then."

"Dadgum."

"Are you coming back?" Morton asked.

There was a heartbreaking pause before Annie Tinsley said, "Yes, but not today."

"Annie, you have no business staying here alone with these men. It isn't seemly."

Annie Tinsley held Bearman back with a lifted hand.

"Tell her, Henry," Morton said, sensing protection.

"You know what, Morton? I think this matter now stands outside the law. I was willing to acknowledge, based on what you and those two busybodies claimed, that there might have been wrongdoing. Something certainly unusual has taken place, but I see no evidence of a crime. In fact, based on how you described her condition, a miracle has happened. I know Mr. Bearman, and I've seen your wife. I'm going back to town."

Bearman said, "Thanks, Henry. I'd ask you to stay for supper, but I'm not wasting food on these other skunks."

"Even if it's just beans," Steve muttered with a smile.

"That's all right. Next time you're in Alpine, buy me lunch. Annie." He nodded, touching the brim of his hat.

Tinsley turned to Bearman. "I'm not leaving without my wife."

"Get in the car."

"Sheriff?" Morton appealed.

Bearman shouted "Sho now!" and Dollar-Five burst forward to his side, looking for the threat. The only standing stranger was Morton Tinsley, so she trotted up to him, flashed her teeth in a wicked whinny, and let her chest force the car door closed on him. Morton dropped in the seat and leaned away from the window.

Bearman moved up beside Dollar-Five and said to Morton, "And if you come back without being invited, I'll run you off with a lash."

"She's my wife."

Bearman said, "I make no claim on her other than sympathy for a person in dire need. She is free to go whenever she is ready."

Tinsley could not think of anything to say to that. He knew he had been bested. It was just one more point in his long list of self-inflicted failures. He gave his wife a tough-guy look that was wasted on her. She turned away from him. The sheriff, his door open, leaned back and told his passengers that he was going to hold his pistol in his lap and the first goose that squawked was going to get shot and left beside the road.

As the sheriff backed his car around, Annie Tinsley turned to Bearman and said, "I must sit down." She started to take a step and fell into his arms. She immediately recovered, as if she had only stumbled, and he walked her to her chair under the ramada.

Yoakum turned to Steve and said, "Bring me a cup from the pump." He was watching Annie Tinsley's face. When Steve brought him the cup, it was empty. Yoakum said through his teeth, "Put water in it for Mrs. Tinsley."

"Oh." Steve went back to the pump.

Bearman knelt in front of her chair as he had that first night. He held her empty hand without asking permission and asked her if she was all right. He told her she was magnificent. Yoakum handed her the cup of water, and the men made a circle of concern and admiration around her.

Yoakum said, "Annie, you'll do to ride the river with. I never saw anyone more controlled than you were in a trying situation like that. John, did you notice she was still wearing her pistol?"

"I guess I didn't. She never needed it, that's sure enough."

The brothers agreed noisily, quoting and misquoting what was said.

After she drank and dried her lips with the tails of her scarf, she gave the cup to Brother and said, "Wally?"

"Yes, Annie?"

"While Mr. Bearman and I were on the mesa, did you sit in my chair?"

"Not even for a second."

Bearman said, "Tell her why not."

Yoakum blushed. "I told John, 'Annie's chair was for Annie, not for the likes of me.'"

"Come here, Wally. Give me your hand."

"Which one?"

"Your right hand."

Yoakum put out his hand, and Annie Tinsley took it and kissed the back of it. "Thank you, Wally," she said. "Thank you all," she added. "You make me feel like someone special."

Wally took his hand back and turned away, sniffing. "Dadgum."

Brother said, "Even Mr. Bearman?"

She smiled at him. "I may have a few words for Mr. Bearman."

When the others had moved away, Bearman said, "Forget words. You owe me a dollar, five."

"You cheated me again. You knew what he would do."

"Sometimes I'm wrong about people. I had no idea you would do what you did. How do you feel, really?"

"I think I'm ready for what comes next."

"That's supper. They expect beans. Feel like helping me surprise them?"

"What do you have in mind?"

"I want you to find out what the brothers brought in case we want to add it to the menu."

She did, and they did. Supper was a success. Bearman had bought potatoes, and the brothers had a wheel of what they called "rat cheese." The brothers rolled the big Idaho potatoes in mud and placed them under the coals of the fire pit. Annie Tinsley made a kind of dipping sauce out of a can of cream of mushroom soup which, with the cheese, made a fine topping.

By the time they had finished eating, it was dark on the ridge, and the fire felt good. They talked about the day, replaying what was said in the confrontation with the men from Marathon. Steve and Yoakum gathered the dishes and carried them down to the river to rinse them out. Bearman smoked his pipe and watched the way the flickering firelight animated Annie Tinsley's face. Steve and Yoakum came back from the river. Steve took the dishes over to the pump, and Yoakum found his box.

Abruptly Brother said, "Mrs. Tinsley? Was that you singing on Mr. Bearman's record?"

She smiled across the fire. "No, Phineas. I have been curious about his Victrola since the first day I was here. When I found his records, I wanted to listen to Mimi's aria. Musette also sings a wonderful aria, but I didn't feel like a Musette. She had a way of putting herself forward. I wondered what kind of man would bring a Victrola and his record collection to a place like this."

Brother said, "Mr. Bearman is a mysterious man."

Bearman laughed and Yoakum said, "Gotcha."

"Mr. Bearman never would tell us what she was saying," Steve said, returning to the fire.

"She was saying goodbye and giving away her things," Annie Tinsley said.

"Where was she going?" Brother asked.

After a while, Annie replied softly, "She was dying."

Steve said, "Mr. Bearman told us it didn't matter what she was saying. I guess that's why. We got the idea, anyway."

Annie Tinsley looked at Bearman in the firelight, and he understood the recording was also played to tell him what she had decided.

"Another woman's voice."

"I knew I had heard it recently," Annie said. "The Mexican children were singing their own words to the up and down of Mimi's aria. They had apparently heard it before."

"Many times, Mrs. Tinsley. Many times." After several minutes, Brother asked, "How come you didn't feel like this Musette person?"

Bearman said, "Brother."

"Sorry, Mrs. Tinsley."

"You are forgiven, Phineas," she said and looked at Bearman. "I think I've done all I want to do today. If you men will excuse me, I will go to bed."

When she stood up, all the others did too, saying "goodnight" in a chorus. Bearman followed Annie Tinsley to the hut to retrieve his and Yoakum's cots. Yoakum remained by the fire, giving the two at the hut a moment alone. Bearman went back to the hut for bedding. Annie Tinsley was standing with her back to the door staring at some of the trinkets that had been left for her.

"Was it all a little bit too much?" Bearman asked.

She turned and looked at him. Her expression was serious but not angry or sad. After two or three minutes, she said, "No. It was a good day."

Bearman smiled. "Goodnight, ma'am," he said.

XXI

Unidentified Mexican Village, April 1945

4/23/1945-4/24/1945

[notepaper]

Mr. Bearman was taken by Ornelos riders. Mr. Yoakum plans to get him back with me as la Mujer del Rio, and with him and Steve and Phineas to what he calls "ride shotgun." I feel like an actress on a stage who doesn't know her lines.

On the morning of the fourth day in Bearman's camp, Annie Tinsley was slow to leave the bunk and get dressed. When she finally opened the door, she found that all the men were seated around the fire pit with plates on their laps and forks in their hands. They immediately got to their feet. For a moment, she felt shy to be the center of their attention. Then Yoakum took her by the arm and led her to her empty chair.

The brothers said good morning, and Bearman smiled at her.

"Goodness," she said. She may have blushed, but later she only remembered how validated she felt. She was unaccustomed to being treated like a person who mattered. The feeling lasted through the day.

"How do you feel?" Bearman asked her after they were all seated again.

"All right," she said, returning his smile. "A little tired."

"We'll take it easy today."

The day was warm but windy. The brothers patched a flat tire on their Ford and afterward went exploring farther from camp than they had been before. Bearman told them to bring back firewood. He and Yoakum took turns keeping an eye across the river, waiting to hear news from or about Pulaski. Annie Tinsley worked in the hut, cleaning and arranging. When the brothers came back, she asked them to take the stove pipe outside and try to straighten it where it had been dented by the two men sent to destroy "the little rock house." They did a fair job and felt that the two new dents were small and not very noticeable if the pipe were rotated so that the damage was in the back. She also got them to remove the mouse nest she found behind Bearman's trunk.

After a spare meal at noon, the brothers hit their cots for a nap, and Yoakum dragged his cot under the ramada and joined them.

Bearman and Annie Tinsley walked along the river looking at rocks where the river had left them exposed after floods. Dollar-Five wanted to sniff the rocks Bearman picked up, but after a while, she wandered back to her favorite place in the willows.

"Look," Annie Tinsley said. She pointed to three ducks drifting in the current approaching the bend in the river. They were brightly colored and paid no attention to the two people on the river bank.

"They will drift down until they reach the rapids," Bearman said. "Then they'll fly back upriver and do it again."

"What a lovely way to spend an afternoon. I could drift down here and then go back and do it all over again."

"Ma'am."

"I wish you had a boat," Annie Tinsley said, watching the ducks go by.

Bearman picked up a rock with lines on its surface. He held it a moment, turning it in his hands, then threw it in the river. He started to ask Annie Tinsley if she still had her heart-shaped rock but changed his mind.

When the sun went behind the chain of mountains that included the mesa-that-was-not-a-mesa, Steve and Yoakum built a fire from a stack of limbs the brothers had foraged that afternoon. Bearman started supper. It would be chicken and dumplings again without the chicken. Nothing was said about beans.

After they finished eating, they sat close to each other around the fire, pensive in the twilight, each with his or her own thoughts about the day and their part in it. Yoakum was happy simply to be in the company of people he held in such affection. The brothers were arguing over whether there was such a thing as "almost certain" and was it the same thing as "pretty sure." Yoakum said it was just a manner of speaking and they should talk about something else, so they began to argue the difference between dogs and cats as pets. Steve claimed dogs would fight for you, but cats would run away and hide. Brother defended cats as being useful by killing rats and snakes. Annie Tinsley was trying to reconcile her desire to be with her baby with her reluctance to return home. Bearman was cleaning the blade of his belt knife on the leather of his boot.

Annie Tinsley said, "Let me borrow your belt knife. I've a loose thread that's been bothering me all day. The walls of your little rock house have a way of snatching one's clothes when she walks by."

Just then, an "¡*Hola*!" came up from the river.

The men were startled, except for Bearman. He flipped his knife by the blade and caught it again by the hilt. "News. If you guys drink all the coffee before I get back, make some more for me. It might be a long night. Ma'am, I leave you in charge of these outlaws."

As if to emphasize her authority, he handed her his knife. He would soon regret it.

No one spoke around the fire after Bearman left. Yoakum was deep in memories. Steve was flicking small pieces of gravel at Brother's back while Brother was poking the fire with a mesquite branch. To Steve's delight, Brother thought the little taps were insects and shook his shoulders each time a fragment of rock touched his back. Annie Tinsley was wondering about her little girl.

"Wally?"

"Yes, ma'am? I mean yes, Annie?"

"Did you and Marisa have any children?"

Yoakum gave the brothers a warning look, then turned back to Annie Tinsley. "Just one, a girl. She would be about your age."

"Where is she now?"

"Before Marisa and I moved out here, she was living along the coast at Rockport."

"She ever visit you?"

"No. She didn't want any part of what she knew would happen."

"She doesn't know?"

"Nope, but after being around you, I'm starting to miss that little girl who used to ride my shoulders."

"I've heard children can make a homing connection with their parents."

"I reckon they do. Maybe I'll use that to try to find mine."

"Maybe you should."

"Maybe I will, Annie."

They were silent again. The brothers were hesitant to say anything. Yoakum was lost in new memories. About twenty minutes went by. Annie Tinsley was thinking about Bearman and realized she had been hearing Dollar-Five neigh for several minutes. She looked across the fire at Yoakum.

"Wally," she said, "Mr. Bearman wasn't wearing his gun."

"Dadgum that boy." Yoakum jumped up from his box. "Where is it?"

"Inside. I'll get it."

But Yoakum followed her to the door of the hut. He took the gun belt from her and said, "Put yours back on."

He went off into the darkness. He came back shortly with a restless, nervous Dollar-Five behind him.

"There's no sign of John anywhere," he said. He gave Annie Tinsley Bearman's gun belt and said, "Keep this handy. We may need it."

⬩◆⬩

Umberto was at the water's edge when Bearman got down to the river, but there were also two horses. Dollar-Five was standing back from them and occasionally snorting with disfavor. She knew they belonged on the other side of the river.

"*¿Que pasa*?" Bearman asked.

Umberto looked at him as if asking forgiveness, and another man stepped out of the shadow of the line of cane. He had a long-barreled pistol in his hand, probably a .45. Although his face was shadowed by his hat, Bearman recognized him even in the gloom as the third man when Ornelos attacked him and Annie Tinsley that day on the road. According to Umberto, the man's name was Augustin. He did not believe in *la Mujer del Rio* and was brutal to young girls. He had become one of Bearman's least favorite people in the Big Bend country.

"*¿Que quiere*? What do you want?" Bearman asked, turning his back on Umberto.

"The *jefe* wants to see you, so I come to get you."

"With a pistol pointed at me?"

Bearman took an unexpected step toward the man, who took one step back. Then Bearman knew something about him—Ornelos wanted him alive.

"We should go," Umberto urged.

"Why the rush?" Bearman said.

"The *jefe* waits."

Bearman knew that he could shout and three—maybe four—guns would come down the hill. But Augustin held his pistol with his finger on the trigger. How many of his friends would be shot after he was down? He could call Dollar-Five into action, but he couldn't stand the thought that the first bullet would be for her. To Augustin, she was not a spirit horse, just another being he had power over while he held the gun.

Augustin read his hesitation. He said, "You have no *pistola*. What can you do?"

"Give me yours, and I will show you."

"It would be sad if something happen to your horse or your friends. Maybe *la Mujer* will remain to take care of me someday, eh, *cabrón*?"

No thought other than to smash the man's mouth for his foul suggestion caused Bearman to crowd the man again. This time it was an unplanned response, and Augustin took another step backward. He raised his gun to Bearman's chest, and Bearman knew something else about the man. He was a coward. He was afraid of what would happen if he fired his pistol, but so was Bearman.

Bearman said, "A coward, afraid to face his enemy, hides behind what his enemy loves."

"*Cállate, cabrón.* We go across the river now. Tie his hands, Umberto. *Date prisa;* hurry up."

"You don't need to tie my hands," Bearman said.

Augustin spit. "Oh, *sí.*"

"What are you afraid of?"

Augustin growled at Umberto, and the reluctant partner held up a piece of rope. Not wanting his hands behind his back, Bearman put forth his wrists with closed fists. Umberto tied them in a skillful way that included a slack loop under the coils that would cause the wrappings to come apart if Bearman failed to clamp his fingers on it. Umberto stepped back with the loose end in his hand. Augustin told him to tie it to his, not Umberto's, saddle horn. When that was done, Augustin holstered his pistol and mounted his horse. Bearman was still unwilling to call out to Dollar-Five and his friends. He kept seeing Annie Tinsley's face.

When they went down into the river, Dollar-Five started to follow. Augustin drew his pistol again. He remembered what a force the mare could be. He said, "If your horse follows us across the river, I will kill it on the other side."

As the dark water closed around his thighs, Bearman turned and spoke to Dollar-Five. She shook her head and turned a circle, then seemed to nod—a gesture which in a horse is not a nod at all. She did not like to see Bearman go with the strangers, but she was nothing if not obedient. She remained behind, watching.

When Augustin jerked the rope to deliberately trip Bearman in the water, Dollar-Five put her front hooves in the river. In that moment, she was in more danger than Bearman, who was now being dragged in the river, his legs pushed by the current close to the high-stepping hooves of Umberto's horse. He struggled to keep his head above the water.

On the other side, he used the tension on the rope to pull himself up out of the mud. One last look behind him revealed Dollar-Five with all four legs in the river, neighing repeatedly for a call or an answer. Then Bearman was pulled into the brush, and they did not see each other anymore.

Back at Bearman's camp, Yoakum stopped by the fire and said, "That boy is less a prisoner than a man with a mission: he wants his blasted rifle back."

"And we want *him* back, goshdarnit," Steve said. "Come on, Brother, let's get our stuff."

The brothers went to their Ford to get their pistols, but Annie Tinsley was beside Yoakum, at his shoulder. "Tell me what you saw, Wally. Was Mr. Bearman hurt?"

"All I saw was two darker spots on the bank where two wet horses stood, then went back into the river."

"Maybe he went with them on his own, as you said, to get his rifle."

Yoakum turned and faced her. He put his hands on her shoulders and said, "Annie, I need you to think about what you are saying. I, also, want to imagine the happiest explanation, but it won't be the right one, and it muddies up our response. Do you know what I mean?"

"Yes, Wally but—"

"No. There aren't any *buts* that fit the facts. John has been taken across the river by riders in the employ of the man that put a rifle to your head and pulled the trigger, a man John is certain he wounded, and a man who probably has either killed or made a prisoner of a federal agent that John befriended. Now, go talk to Dollar-Five. That mare is as upset as a child, and I want to think about what we need to do."

"We need to go after him is what we need to do," Annie said fiercely.

Yoakum turned away from the light of the fire, feeling a knot of dread for his friend and the danger he and the rest would face in going after him. He wanted to go by himself, but he dared not suggest it. He knew he would have to tie up Annie Tinsley to keep her from going, and the brothers would not allow that to happen. *Annie herself would not allow it*, he thought with a smile. He tried to mentally estimate the number of people who lived in the two wax camps and the men who rode herd. He had no idea how many there were. He knew that some of them still believed in his Marisa—*la Mujer del Rio*.

They would need horses. He had three. The mules did not count. He turned back to the fire and caught Annie Tinsley's look from where she stood with her arm reaching up to Dollar-Five's mane. Three horses. *By God*, he thought. *Annie can do it.*

"I'm ready," Steve said, approaching the wavering light of the fire. He spun his pistol by the trigger guard, and it spiraled off his finger to clatter on the ground.

Yoakum shook his head and said, "God save us from idiots and Irishmen. They are the best poets in the world but have the practical knowledge of a duck."

Brother said, "You know, Mr. Yoakum, sometimes the things you say are not very nice."

Yoakum ignored him. "Listen up, children. I've got a plan. First of all, we've got three horses that need to be saddled."

"If you're thinking about leaving me behind, you can think again," Annie Tinsley said.

"I *was* thinking that, Annie, and I was going to say so, just to enjoy the fireworks, but John and I agreed we would stop thinking."

"Huh?" Brother said.

Yoakum ignored him again. To Annie Tinsley, he said, "You're going. On Dollar-Five. I need you to get John's gun belt and the nightgown you were wearing when John stole you from the bosom of your family. Tonight, you are going to be *la Mujer del Rio* to save John's life. Boys, do you have a flashlight in that Ford? Does it have batteries? Bring it. Let's saddle up."

When the trio left Yoakum by the fire to carry out his orders, Yoakum said quietly to himself, "Sho now, boy. *Sho now.*"

Bearman was more annoyed than anything else as he was pulled in wet clothes along a well-beaten trail through the brush behind Augustin's horse. His boots had water in them, which caused his feet to slide from heel to toe and back again. But the *jacales* they passed along the trail were interesting to him, having never crossed the river there, although he had seen similar dwellings in other places. Cooking fires were dying out, goats were penned, and he heard children's voices. The turquoise and rose glow of twilight had faded in the sky, and the brightest stars were dropping into place above him. Bearman was surprised at how dark it was on the flat in the brush compared to the light from the moon and stars reflected by the rocks on his ridge.

Such thoughts kept him from being overwhelmed by the tight spot in which he found himself. He knew he could cast off his bonds at will, but he hoped that meeting Ornelos might also help him locate his rifle. Besides the emotional connection to the gun, Bearman hated to lose things.

People seemed to be going in the direction Augustin was taking him, with a rider now and then moving them like cattle toward some specific point. Half a mile from the river, Umberto turned off, presumably to join or collect his own family. To Bearman, this meant that whatever Ornelos planned was to be public, both spectacle and warning.

"*Lo siento mucho*," Umberto said over his shoulder. "I am very sorry."

"*Miedica.*" Augustin shouted after him and laughed. "Coward!"

Bearman said, "You forget running away after you fell off your horse, calling '*¡Ayudate!*'"

Augustin prodded his mount and jerked Bearman off his feet. He rolled as he fell and landed on his right shoulder. He quickly rolled over onto his back, the easier to keep his face and chest out of the dirt of the well-traveled trail. After being pulled over two unseen rocks that hammered his lower back and hips with the force of a kick, he rolled over onto his stomach and immediately began to feel his belt buckle plowing the trail and filling his pants with dirt, which clotted from his wet clothes. Once or twice, that made a positive difference. He was now able to twist away from most of the occasional rocks that showed pale against the dust raised by Augustin's horse, but some he could not avoid. Loosened from the pulling and being wet, it was all he could do to keep the rope from slipping off his wrists into his hands. It wasn't time.

His eyes and mouth were choked with dust when Augustin pulled him toward an open area lit by a bonfire. Now he could dimly see men, women, and children gathered together. Some of the men were obviously drunk, others nearly so, and still others solemn and quiet. Before Augustin came to a stop, Alphonso the midget jumped awkwardly on Bearman's back and pretended to be riding a horse. There was loud laughter from the drunks, who were mostly riders loyal to Ornelos; head shaking from the nearly so, who were sometimes friends of the riders; and averted eyes from the rest, who were the families of the wax camps. Bearman coughed and sneezed and rolled the midget off his back. There was more noise, more almost noise, and more turning away.

Augustin unwrapped the rope from his saddle horn and gave his end a few stiff jerks. "Hey, *caballero*!" he mocked. "Time to get up."

Bearman shook his head to clear his senses and pulled himself to a bruised, tottering stand. Augustin immediately jerked the rope forward, pulling Bearman off his feet again. He did it twice more, but the joke had worn thin, as Bearman showed no emotion and made no sound other than involuntary grunts of impact.

Before anything else could be done to him, he looked with interest at where he was. He was standing to the left of a freshly lit bonfire and in front of a row of adobe and rock huts not unlike his own but with flat roofs. One of them was a chapel, another a store of some kind, and another a *taverna* with a Dutch door and a ramada attached. Three others were just simple adobes that may have been dwellings. A corral of horses seemed to be in the shadows beyond the last building, but there were four others tethered to the side of the bar and random animals scattered among the people. To the right of the fire was a single Mexican ash that, at almost forty feet in height, must have weathered many droughts. It shaded a primitive well. Descending from a mostly horizontal limb were two ropes, and two bare-backed horses were held close by.

Perhaps three dozen people were standing in front of the chapel's closed door; others were grouped randomly. The whole area was beaten dirt with no ground cover at all. Bearman realized he was in a village, and had it been elsewhere, the buildings would have formed a square. As it was, they were in a straight line of descending importance away from the chapel on either side.

He faced the dark outline of the mountains. He thought of Annie Tinsley and how she loved far vistas.

Bearman was aware that Augustin was speaking to him in that same mocking tone, but his attention now was on the Dutch door of the *taverna* and the man who came out of it. The man was wearing a sling made of a dark silk scarf on his right arm. On his left hand he wore a tight black glove. Bearman saw that Ornelos was not wearing a gun. In his arrogance, he surrounded himself with men who would do his shooting.

People fell silent at his appearance, then the volume began to rise again. This was Ornelos, a *jefe*, who ran the simple people of his ranch the same way he ran his cattle, sick or well, tended or killed. Behind him came two men supporting a third: Marcos Pulaski. Smoke from the bonfire blew across the men, but Bearman could tell Pulaski had been beaten. Bearman turned his gaze on Augustin with such intensity that it made the other man flinch.

Before Augustin could jerk the rope again, Bearman twisted and pulled hard enough to snatch the end out of Augustin's hand. He then rushed the man and bumped him with his right shoulder. Augustin fell in the dirt. If Bearman expected a commotion, he was disappointed. Silence fell on the crowd again. Augustin got his feet under him and ran doubled over to tackle Bearman, but Bearman dodged to the side, pushed down on the man's shoulders, and hit him in the face with his raised knee. Augustin fell again. Bearman started to bend for the knife in his boot, then remembered he had given it to Annie Tinsley.

By then, Ornelos was close enough behind Bearman to kick his legs out from under him. He fell on his back, and the combined injuries from being dragged and falling left him momentarily immobile. Augustin, on his feet now with a bloody nose, kicked Bearman repeatedly as he lay on the ground. This time there was a general shout of approval. Bearman curled up lest one or more ribs were cracked or broken.

"*Bueno*," Ornelos said. "*Bastante*, Augustin. Get the *cabrón* on his feet."

With one more kick, which Bearman fended on his hip, Augustin pulled Bearman to his feet. Bearman's chest cried out with the hollow pain typical of bruised ribs, and he struggled to get his breath. Although he faced Ornelos now, he ignored the man and his sneer of triumph. Closer to the fire, he saw Pulaski watching him. Pulaski's face revealed a complete surrender to the inevitable, or perhaps he was in a daze from the beating. He seemed to have given up all hope of rescue. Bearman hated to see a good man beaten down, just as he had hated to see Annie Tinsley giving up on life.

"¡*Oye, hermano*!" he called, his voice strained through lack of a deep breath. "Where there is life, there is hope, eh?"

For a few seconds, there was complete silence. Then Ornelos struck Bearman in the face again and again with his gloved palm until Bearman lost his ability to see and hear. He swayed on his feet. Because of the pain in his chest, his breathing was as diminished as if he were inhaling through a soda straw.

In Spanish, Ornelos said, "You see the ropes hanging down? Look at me. You see the ropes? There are two, eh? There are two. Whose ropes are they? Are they mine? Are they yours? You do not know? Does Marcos, that dog of dogs—that *traidor*—know? Did I bring you here to hang you?"

"I want my rifle back."

"Oh. What good will it do you? I use up the bullets. Where can I get more? Right now, I carry the rifle on my horse to remind me of my victory over the United States government."

"It shoots a .45 pistol round," Bearman lied.

"I did not know that. The bullets say 38-40 on the brass. *No le hace.* There are many things I do not know. I do not know who those ropes belong to. That is up to you."

Bearman began to lean forward at the waist. Ornelos jerked him back upright.

"You will not hang tonight, you and the *traidor*, but someone will. Look around you, choose someone to take your place. Who will it be? Augustin? No. It is clear you do not like him. No, he is loyal to me. So, who?"

"I will not choose," Bearman said.

"Not to choose is a choice. You leave it up to me?"

Ornelos called a name and gave instructions. Two of his riders pulled a young girl, about sixteen, from the crowd and dragged her to Ornelos. She wore a simple dress of blue gingham that hung down to her ankles. Her feet were bare. Her hair was loose and long.

"How about this *chica*? Should I choose her?"

Over by the fire, Pulaski cried out. Bearman looked closely at the girl's terrified face. She had Pulaski's eyes. It had not occurred to him that Pulaski's family might be in this dangerous place.

"Not this one," Bearman wheezed.

"Yes. I think this one. Such a shame, too, eh, Augustin?"

"Let me have her first," he leered.

"Take her to the horse," Ornelos commanded the two riders.

"Take me instead," Bearman offered.

Ornelos shook his head. "You see? That is not the choice. Oh, you will die, but later. My people must know the price of betraying me. It is high and hurts many people."

There was silence except for the wailing of the girl's family and the snapping of wood from the fire. Pulaski collapsed between the two men who held him. A rider came out of the darkness and lifted the girl by the back of her dress onto one of the waiting horses. She struggled, and the dress nearly split in half before she was placed on the horse. She was crying until another rider fixed a rope around her neck, then she fainted, and the man held her upright.

Ornelos called another name, and the two riders ducked into the silent crowd and pulled out a screaming woman, the wife of Umberto.

"You make war on women?" Bearman hissed, frustrated by his inability to interfere.

"It was not my choice, but yours and the *traidor's*."

Another rider brought more wood and put it on the fire to make the hangings more visible. Umberto's wife was still screaming. Umberto had to be held back. The woman was taken to the other horse and thrown onto its back. She, too, fainted when the rope was forced over her head. It was the moment when all hope was gone. Umberto was sobbing, unable to speak in the face of such horror. He broke loose from those who held him, and another rider clubbed him down with the butt of an old Springfield.

"Now we see—" Ornelos started to say, but he was interrupted by a sound, distant but growing stronger. It was the voice of a woman singing what sounded like Musette's aria. After several minutes, a figure on horseback dressed all in white appeared at the end of the row of adobes where the horses were corralled. In that darkened place, she seemed to glow in her white nightgown, an effect created by Steve walking beside Dollar-Five, but not close, holding his flashlight on Annie Tinsley. An errant breeze caught locks of her unpinned hair, lifted them from her shoulders, and twirled them around her pale face. Her voice and the melody she chose were haunted and sad as Musette proclaimed her hopeless love. The words seemed to tremble from her lips and mingle with the smoke of the fire to drift away into the night. They had a different but equally strong effect on Bearman.

The crowd was awed with superstitious fear. No one moved. No one spoke. Burning branches snapped in the fire as the heat drew moisture from them. The horse holding Pulaski's daughter was tossing its head.

Then the families from the wax camps near the river recognized *la Mujer* and were briefly lifted from the horror Ornelos had planned. With reverent hesitation, the children began to sing as Marcos had taught them. Amid their simple words were growing whispers that united the adults in the assembly: "*¡Es la Mujer del Rio*!" The figure in white advanced slowly toward the crowd. The magnificent mare she rode seemed to prance haughtily with short mincing steps. Even Ornelos was silent.

Now, Bearman thought, and he shucked the loosened coils of rope from his wrists. Augustin stood beside him, but he, too, was entranced by the vision, despite his avowed disbelief in the reclusive healing woman. His gun was at his side, held loosely. Bearman, with a quick follow-through, bent, grabbed the man's wrist, and twisted so that with a yelp, Augustin let go of the pistol and was flipped in the air, his boots striking Ornelos as he went down. He landed on his back and immediately started to get back up, hatless and angry. Bearman recovered the pistol, reversed it so that he held it by the long barrel and clubbed Augustin on the temple, hard. The man dropped and stayed down.

When Ornelos shook off the flailing boots of Augustin, he jumped away and faced Bearman for only an instant, his sneer exchanged for a look of confusion, anger, and fear. Then he turned and ran toward the *taverna* and his horse, as was the way of the coward he was. Bearman struggled after him, the pain in his chest stealing his breath. He was afraid to cough lest he spit blood.

A quick glance to the left, and he saw Annie Tinsley swinging down from the saddle while Dollar-Five was looking everywhere for him. Steve was beside her, obviously protecting her, but so far, no guns had been raised. To the right, past the glare of the fire, he saw the men holding Pulaski drop him in confusion at seeing the *jefe* running away with the *gringo* behind him. Beyond Pulaski, he saw Yoakum and

Brother advancing in the shadows. He also saw nooses being pulled from around the necks of the two women, semi-conscious now and sobbing.

Annie Tinsley saw the two women's peril at the same time she saw Bearman hurrying awkwardly after another man. Bearman was holding his left arm against his chest like a folded wing. Ignoring all else, she grabbed Dollar-Five's bridle and pulled the mare's face around until Dollar-Five saw Bearman, then Annie Tinsley screamed, "*Sho now*!" and again, "*Sho now*!"

Dollar-Five neighed and rose on her hind legs. She seemed to shake all over and turn into a wild beast of some deep canyon legend. The people hurrying toward the supernatural protection of *la Mujer del Rio* gave way before the mare as she bolted straight to Bearman.

At that moment, Yoakum and Brother stepped out of the shadows, and Yoakum began his litany of battle. "¡*Manos arribas*!" he shouted and fired his pistol in the air to show he meant business. His taunts and jeers and threats chased the echo of his gunfire. Brother showed he could follow orders and likewise let off two rounds in the air.

Across the village, Annie Tinsley and Steve also fired in the air. Ignoring the danger, Annie Tinsley led Steve into the crowd to help Bearman, who had stopped in pain and shortness of breath to look in despair at the two women. With relief, he saw that Umberto, Pulaski, and some of the others were frantically holding the frightened horses abandoned by the riders and trying to untie the ropes from the tree. Riders began to run from the midst of the people, offering no real resistance. Their threat was in their number and Ornelos's cruelty. Very few of them wore pistols, relying instead on the rifles they carried on their saddles. Bullies and flunkies, every one of them, they thought only of getting to their horses and going back over the mountain to the safety of the ranch headquarters from which they could regroup and come down on the village with greater cruelty.

There was so much confusion of movement it was hard to tell

the riders from the men of the wax camps other than by the presence of children who had stopped their singing to run with their parents. Yoakum realized this. He turned to Brother and said, "Son, we're in Mexico. Try not to kill anybody, but if some of these rascals try to kill you, shoot the hell out of them. Look out for anyone wearing chaps."

But they soon found themselves among non-fighting families hurrying away toward the river. Yoakum saw the men frantically untying two women and the ropes noosed around their neck and pulled Brother that way.

"*¿Que pasa*?" he shouted.

Pulaski held his daughter in his arms and said, "Señor Bearman needs your help."

"You look like you could have used some help yourself," Yoakum said.

"Were these women criminals?" Brother wondered out loud.

There were random, unaimed shots by the chapel. Yoakum nodded at Brother. "Come on. John needs some help."

"I will come quickly, *mas o menos*," Pulaski assured them painfully, and they sought the shadows again and moved toward the chapel.

As the riders with corralled horses tried to reach them, Steve pulled a resisting Annie Tinsley behind a safe corner of the nearest adobe and turned the riders back to run unhorsed through the brush. Annie Tinsley took advantage of gunplay between Steve and a single rider to duck away from the corner, still trying to reach Bearman. Her gun belt increased the power of her presence. No one challenged her except one little girl who ran to her and hugged her, asking her to save them. The simple act in the midst of such turmoil made her think of her daughter. She wanted to cry. The little girl pressed on her a bracelet woven from horse hair and rejoined her family. They went off into the dark.

When Dollar-Five reached Bearman, she reared and snorted and charged anyone who happened to come close, then she stood with her shoulder against his. Bearman looked for Annie Tinsley but could not see her. Nor could he see that his own gun belt was in the saddle bag beside him. The two women were off the gallows horses and into the arms of their families.

Umberto appeared beside him. "*Gracias,* Señor. How can I help? *Por favor*, pardon me."

"Your wife?"

"Safe, thanks to *la Mujer del Rio*."

Bearman heard the shooting near the chapel and recognized Yoakum's .45. The fighting was becoming sporadic, but Ornelos was once again getting away, lost in the shadows of the ramada.

Bearman turned to the mare and wheezed, "Dollar-Five, rope!" He pointed at the ramada. He had no idea if a rope was there, but he smiled grimly at the chaos Dollar-Five would create. Unlike her antics in front of the store in Marathon with the horses tethered there, she was now stirred to a fighting pitch. She plunged into the ramada, scattering the riders, who were trying to free their lines and mount the saddles of their salvation. They dodged into the shadow beyond the ramada, and Ornelos joined them there.

"Take this," Bearman told Umberto, holding out Augustin's pistol. "Protect your family."

"*Bueno*," Umberto said. "*Vaya con Dios*." He joined others from the wax camps who were making for their *jacales* along the river.

"Shoot the horse! Shoot the horse!" Bearman heard Ornelos shouting.

But none of the men did. Their rifles were on their wildly pitching horses. There were Texans in the camp who had guns in their hands. This spirit horse had no gun. Let it rear and neigh.

Dollar-Five seemed to remember that voice and hated it. She leapt toward Ornelos, who dodged around the bar and came out of the shadow of the adobe into the blaze of the bonfire in time to see Bearman follow the reins to the bridle of Ornelos's disturbed horse and jerk his beloved rifle from the scabbard on Ornelos's saddle. Dollar-Five came behind the man and butted him farther into the light. Somewhere, she had found a piece of rope.

Bearman dug through the grit in his pants pocket and pulled out a 38-40 cartridge, the one he always carried to replace the one left unloaded. Ornelos, distracted by Dollar-Five who was trying to bite him, did not see Bearman wipe the cartridge clean and slip it into the magazine. Bearman levered the round and left the hammer back.

"Dollar-Five," he called, and the horse came to his side, angry but obedient. Bearman fought for breath and said, "I don't walk past people who make war on children and women. And make money from sick cattle."

"What will you do?" Ornelos sneered, edging toward the Dutch door of the *taverna*.

Just then, he heard Annie Tinsley scream his name, and he saw Augustin dragging her in front of him from the shadows. His face was bloody, and his eyes caught the firelight like the eyes of a feral animal. His grin showed bloody teeth.

"You have no bullets," Ornelos said, keeping an eye on Dollar-Five.

"Hey, *caballero*. I am going to enjoy your woman," Augustin said.

"I will fight for you."

For a moment, Bearman was back in a barn in East Texas facing the man who murdered his parents, his rifle in his hand. Now, as then, without hesitation, he raised the rifle to his cheek and shot the man in the head.

"Enjoy hell," Bearman said.

The dead man pulled Annie Tinsley down with him, and she struggled away from him, blood on her shoulder and in her hair.

"So," Ornelos said, closer now to the Dutch door. "A surprise."

Bearman saw Pulaski, Yoakum, and Brother pass in front of the chapel. From the other end of the row of adobes, Steve stepped out of the shadows, holstered his pistol and helped Annie Tinsley to her feet.

Everyone else was gone. The fire was burning down, and smoke ran along the fronts of the adobes before it lifted away into the night sky.

"So, *traidor*, what will you do now? Arrest me? I am not afraid. I have many friends. What will you do?"

Pulaski, like Bearman, was having trouble standing erect. He said, "You did not give me a choice tonight."

"So?"

"I choose you," he said.

He put out his hand, and Yoakum passed him his Colt's.

"This is murder," Ornelos quavered, his arrogance dissolving.

"No. It is justice," Pulaski said, and, as Steve turned Annie Tinsley away, Pulaski shot Ornelos. The bullet was high and hit Ornelos in the shoulder, knocking him back against the wall. Pulaski shot him again, this time in the heart. The federal agent stood without moving for a minute, then seemed to awaken and handed Yoakum his gun back.

"There were two bullet holes in the wall."

And then there was a strange hush where before there had been noise and confusion. Annie Tinsley pulled away from Steve and went to Bearman. Her nightgown seemed to draw light from the fire. Later, whenever he thought about her, he would remember her as she stood in front of him at that moment: the white gown with the blood of a villain staining the shoulder, her hair in disarray, her eyes moist with concern, and an expression on her face of some kind of harsh victory and gentle gladness. His breath, already shallow, was completely taken by the vision she made.

After a moment of the strange silence and frozen movement, he smiled and said, "You were wonderful."

The men agreed to move away from that place to the chapel where they could sit and make an accounting. The responsibility for everything that had happened that night would fall on Pulaski's shoulders. Yoakum wanted to know what would happen next, particularly since it had all taken place in Mexico and they were foreigners. The brothers shook hands and started telling their own stories to each other.

Bearman and Annie Tinsley left them at the door and walked over to the heap of red coals and dancing yellow flames, all that was left of the bonfire. Dollar-Five followed behind. She seemed nervous and wary but patient. Aware by his posture that Bearman was having difficulty, Annie Tinsley offered to carry his rifle and took it from his hand.

"Now I know why you wanted your rifle so bad."

"You do?"

She nodded. "You wanted to save me. Again."

"It was you who did the saving. You're the reason we won this fight."

He stopped and held himself rigid. He wanted to shiver, but the heat felt good. Turning a little away, he spit into his palm and held it to the light. There was no blood.

"You are not all right, are you, Mr. Bearman?" she asked.

"I think I have some cracked ribs and enough bruises to make a baker's dozen. Other than that—" He tilted his head in lieu of a shrug.

"And you're filthy."

"Are you going to tell me to jump in the river?"

She blushed and put a hand on Dollar-Five. "She's waiting for you."

Bearman stepped up to the trembling mare, and she blew in his face. He returned the action. "Good girl," he said, and she nickered.

"I think I am standing with the two most amazing females in the whole Big Bend of Texas."

Annie Tinsley gave him the serious-but-not-sad look.

Then he asked abruptly, "What are you wearing under that nightgown?

"I beg your pardon." She grasped the rifle with both hands, a little of her old self remaining.

"Give me the rifle."

"Why?"

"*Ma'am.*"

She gave it to him. He said, "Are you still wearing your riding outfit from this afternoon?"

"Yes." Her voice was tentative.

"Then it's time to get rid of that gown. Take it off and throw it in the fire. It has served its purpose."

She smiled and unbuttoned the bodice. She started to pull the nightgown over her head, but it clung to her skirt and blouse. Bearman helped her as best he could with one arm, and, at the last pull, her hair lifted and spread and fell again. Bearman was not ready for the effect that had on him. Even Dollar-Five seemed surprised and curious.

Annie Tinsley balled up the material, avoiding the blood spray, and tossed the bundle onto the coals, where it smoked, caught with blue flames, then burst into bright orange fire.

"No more quitting," Bearman said. "You've had your trial by fire and proven yourself."

"Does that mean I've earned my official River Rider badge?"

She stepped up to him as if she would embrace him, but stopped. "Sometimes you can only make me *want* to do something without my actually doing it."

"You did that on your own, ma'am," he said and smiled. He took a halting step to Annie Tinsley and gave her a one-armed embrace. For a moment, he felt her hair against his cheek and the surrender of her shoulders.

Around them, men appeared from the brush, men from the wax camps who had come back to see what had happened. They did not disturb the couple by the fire. Seeing the bodies of Augustin and Ornelos by the wall of the *taverna* and then candlelight through the open door of the chapel, they went that way.

Bearman released Annie Tinsley with a groan and said, "I've dirtied your blouse."

"I have another." She smiled. "Shall we join Wally and the brothers?"

"Did y'all make more coffee before you crossed the river?"

"Yes."

"Then let's go home."

"To your little rock house?"

Bearman slid his rifle into his saddle scabbard with great satisfaction. He would look it over for damages in the light of the coming day. Annie Tinsley helped Bearman up into Dollar-Five's saddle. He left the stirrup empty for her, and she climbed up behind him, her hands on his hips. They rode slowly, following the way Bearman had been dragged, and as they neared the wax camps, men, women, and children came out of the brush and watched them go by. Some of the children began to sing.

Annie Tinsley dropped her forehead onto Bearman's shoulder. She did not stop crying softly until they had crossed the river.

XXII

Near Big Canyon, April 1945

4/24/1945

[notepaper]

Coming back from Mexico, Mr. Bearman confessed his feelings directly.

Out of the river, they came to a stop by the fire circle. Bearman was surprised to see the coals of the fire fanned red by the night breeze. It seemed to him that it had been many hours since he left it and had been taken. He thought there would have been only white ashes. The blackened coffee pot was there. Faint whiffs of steam rose from the spout and drifted with the wood smoke. Moonlight lay on the camp and deepened the shadows. Dollar-Five blew and waited.

Annie Tinsley said, "Can you get down?"

He felt her lean away from his back, the breeze cold in the space she left.

"Yes."

He did not move in the saddle. Half playfully, she asked, "When?"

He kicked his wet boot free of the stirrup. She found the stirrup and swung down. She stood beside the mare to help him if she could, but he just sat there, his face raised to the bulk of the mesa-that-was-not-a-mesa. Then he looked at her.

"All my life I have faced hardship and danger. The man tonight is not the first man I have ever killed. I'm not worried about that. I don't have feelings about that, except I had to stop him from hurting you. And then there was you, ma'am, you, singing 'Musette's Waltz,' riding into that danger. I've known want and loneliness, some moments of happiness, but I have never felt the way I do right now, coming into camp with you in the moonlight. A thousand, thousand lonely dreams could never equal this moment."

Her tears caught the light of the moon. "Oh, John," she said.

Hearing his given name in her husky whisper recalled him to his resolve. "No, ma'am," he said. "I'm sorry. Not John tonight."

Realizing how far she had strayed, she nevertheless remained by his side to help him down from the high back of Dollar-Five.

"When?" she asked again softly.

"You'll know when." He swung down from the saddle, leaning against the mare to catch his breath, which was still shallow.

"I will try to be good till then," she said, and they both smiled.

They stood looking at each other for a full minute, then Bearman changed the mood by saying, "As for me, it's coffee first, then a swim to get cleaned up."

"My hair needs a good washing," Annie Tinsley said. She had gotten past her shyness.

"Want to borrow my P&G?"

She shook her head. "The naphtha in your P&G dries out my skin, like bathing in kerosene. Fortunately, you brought some of my own soap."

"Foresight. I plan for my disasters ahead of time."

"I believe you do, Mr. Bearman. Shall I unsaddle Dollar-Five?"

"You can loosen the cinches. Steve or Brother can take care of the saddle when they get back."

"Then coffee and the river."

She kissed Dollar-Five, loosened the cinches, and went to Bearman's chair to get his enamelware cup and fill it. Bearman reproved himself for his emotional speech, but he was glad she took it in stride—part of the night's demand for courage.

When Yoakum and the brothers splashed across the river and rode into camp, they found Bearman and Annie Tinsley sitting side by side in their chairs close to the renewed fire. Annie Tinsley had her hair wrapped in a white towel and wore a loose-fitting blue dress. Bearman was wearing a clean shirt and pants; moccasins covered his feet. It was obvious they had both been in the river, but none of the men commented on it, although they exchanged raised eyebrows.

"Where have y'all been?" Bearman asked in a hoarse voice when they had assembled around the fire.

He had been cleaning the Winchester with an oil-stained rag but now propped the rifle against the arm of his chair and dropped the rag on the ground. His emotions, already at a high pitch of sensitivity, were further stirred by the fact that his friends had come through the confusion unharmed. He did not tell them that under his shirt Annie Tinsley had bound his chest with one of her long scarves and fastened it with a safety pin, giving him some welcome relief.

Yoakum said, "We met a man named Mezcal and were detained."

Brother giggled.

Bearman asked, "Bring him home with you?"

Yoakum went to his horse and came back with a bottle wrapped in woven reeds. He gave it to Bearman, who pulled the stopper and took a drink. He took two more swallows and put the bottle on the ground by his chair. He had needed it.

Yoakum found his peaches box and said, "Pulaski has a story that leaves us out. There is so much gratitude across the river right now that we could pretty much get away with anything."

Steve, who had been silent, looked across the fire and said, "Are you all right, Mrs. Tinsley?"

"Yes, Steve. Thank you for looking out for me. You did a good job."

Steve blushed and mumbled, "You're welcome."

Brother said, "Uh-oh," and burst out laughing.

"Shut up," Steve said.

When it looked like it was going to go further, Yoakum said, "You boys behave and go unsaddle the horses. Don't stand behind Rosie while you're doing it, or you'll find yourself in the river again."

"Is that true, Mr. Bearman?"

"It might be."

"Why do y'all ride mares?"

Yoakum said, "They're loyal and protective, and the trouble they stir up is never vindictive."

"How do you know that?"

"Go unsaddle the horses, but don't try to corral Mr. Bearman's pet. Then come back and drink some coffee."

Annie Tinsley laughed. She was surprised she could.

Steve led Rosie and Tyler to the ramada, while Brother took Dollar-Five. They stripped them of saddles and blankets. Brother removed Dollar-Five's bridle and turned her loose, but Steve waited until he had the other two in the corral before he took their lines.

One of the mules in the corral did a strange thing. When Steve was closing the gate, the mule walked up to him and looked at him, flicking its large, unlovely ears back and forth. Steve started to ask the mule what it wanted, but then remembered it was a mule.

"Love at first sight," Yoakum whispered to Bearman, nodding at Steve. "You ought to name those mules Steve and Phineas."

The three at the fire watched the brothers without further comment, drawn only to their movements. Finished with tending to the horses, the brothers soon joined the others around the fire. No one said anything as they sat, watching their lives in the firelight. Annie Tinsley dropped her eyes away from the fire now and again, seeing the memory of the bonfire in the village.

After an extended pause, Bearman said to Yoakum, "Pulaski all right?"

Yoakum nodded and spit. "About like you, I guess. He said the business in Zacatecas was shut down. He had *federales* comin' up behind him to shut down Ornelos. They should be here tomorrow or the next day. Hopefully, foot-and-mouth in this part of the Big Bend is going to considerably decline."

"I got a letter to that effect when I was in Marathon last Thursday. There's a feeling that River Riders along this stretch of the Rio Grande won't be necessary much longer, but the truth is that it will be epidemic until Mexico quits importing infected cattle. And then there's the decline in the bovine population. Overgrazing is making it impossible for a rancher to have more than a few cows. Herds along the border may be a thing of the past."

"Then what?" Annie Tinsley asked quietly.

"I don't know. I may have to get a dog and start raising goats. What do you know about goats, Wally?"

"Baa Baa."

"That's sheep."

"Same difference."

"Have some more coffee before I start quoting Brother."

"What did that child of Erin say?"

"He said a thing was either a thing or it wasn't."

"As profound as the depths."

"Drink some more coffee."

Steve went to the Ford and brought back a sleeve of saltine crackers that they passed around. It did not last long, so he went back to the Ford for another.

Yoakum asked, "Got some peanut butter?"

"No, sir."

"Dadgum."

When the wax papers came back to him, Steve threw the empty sleeves in the fire, and everyone watched them burn. The sudden intensity of light made each of them lose his or her train of thought.

They talked then about things they had heard and seen, about the War—

"Ever regret not joining up?" Yoakum asked.

"Sometimes."

—the national Depression that had put most people financially behind scratch, the decline in the local deer population, a dog that barked at lantern light—other things present and past, until the moon had reached its zenith and the fire was just a random puff of smoke now and then. The coffee was gone.

Bearman and Yoakum were silent for some minutes, then talked about how a man like Ornelos could achieve the kind of Nazi power he had over the valley. They came to no definite conclusion.

Annie Tinsley listened to the men talk, enjoying it, silent by choice except when invited in. After a while, she took the towel off her head and brushed her hair without shyness.

"Look at that," Yoakum said at one point, pretending to see something in the night sky behind her.

When the brothers went to the Ford to get their cots, Yoakum stood and stretched. "I'll get ours," he said as Annie Tinsley started to stand.

When Yoakum came out with the two army surplus canvas cots, she leaned toward Bearman and said, "Wouldn't you rather sleep in your bunk? It has a mattress, such as it is." She had winced at the sight of the bruises and abrasions when she wrapped his chest.

"No. I've got a quilt in my footlocker for padding and my bedroll. If you'll get those, Wally will set up the cots. Here. Stand my rifle inside the door."

Under the ramada, the brothers started arguing about which one would sleep parallel closest to the wall. Steve said it would be him because he was the oldest. Brother accused him of only wanting to be closer to Mrs. Tinsley. Steve told Brother to watch his mouth. Brother reminded Steve that he was the one who lost their flashlight.

Yoakum stopped stretching the cots and said, "You boys shut up that racket or you'll both sleep in the corral."

"Who's going to make us?" Steve asked, dropping his bedroll on the ground.

"Wally," Bearman said.

"All right," Yoakum said to Bearman, "but keep a close eye on Mr. Mezcal. It's drinking water to an Irishman and poison to those around him."

The brothers stared for a minute, then decided they could both bed down next to the hut if they turned their cots longways, perpendicular to the wall.

Bearman took another drink and got stiffly to his feet. He watched Annie Tinsley come out of the hut with his bedding and make his bed. Dollar-Five evidently approved, for she merely looked on from a discreet distance. Annie Tinsley stood beside the cot, waiting to help Bearman if he needed it. But since there was no way she could help him without touching a bruise or abrasion, she merely stood aside while he lowered himself onto the cot.

"Want me to help you with your shirt?"

"No thanks."

"Then I'll say goodnight."

Bearman eased himself down until he was flat on his back. Annie Tinsley helped him with the cover.

"I'm sorry," he mumbled.

She paused. "For what?"

"For not walking you to your door and saying goodnight."

"Maybe another time?" she said.

He did not reply and after a few minutes, seemed to be asleep.

Three pairs of eyes pretended they did not see Annie Tinsley lean over and kiss his forehead, but they were closed in sleep when she got up after the moon set and, wrapping herself in a blanket, left the hut. She told herself she only wanted to check on him, but in truth, she just wanted to be near him. She picked up her chair and moved it next to his cot. The noise of Yoakum's snoring covered the sound her slippers made on the gravel.

She sat wrapped in the blanket as she had the first night and studied Bearman's face by the light of the stars. As if roused by her nearness, his eyes opened. He was at first confused by her presence, as if he were again in that first night, then he remembered. She whispered, "How do you feel?"

"What time is it?"

Annie Tinsley shook her head. "I don't know. The moon has set."

"After four then. How do you feel?"

"I asked you first."

"Are you checking on me?"

"Turnabout. You checked on me that first night."

"I reckon you needed it, ma'am."

"Do you hurt much?"

Bearman lay without speaking for several minutes. "About what you would expect," he said finally. "Tired of lying on my back. You?"

She understood that his shoulders and hips were too sore to take his weight. "I'm fine," she said. "I couldn't sleep. You have at least two mice in your little rock house. Until now they haven't bothered me, but tonight they have been a bit too insistent."

Bearman closed his eyes. "Kangaroo rats."

She said, in a different voice, but still a whisper, "Have you ever been married, Mr. Bearman?"

"No, ma'am. Have you?"

"I'm serious."

"So am I."

She thought about it. *Was just living with a man being married? Or was he referring more specifically to the person she now considered herself to be? Had that person ever given herself to a man?*

"Ever come close?" she dodged.

"Let's talk about something else."

They fell into an easy silence. At last, Annie Tinsley said, "Am I to forget all you've done for me, all we have shared?"

"No. But, you see, ma'am, we didn't stop with the friendly part. We kept right on going, and now we can't go back to where we started: two strangers caught up in a moment."

"Is that what all of this has been?"

"No. There's more. You have a baby to raise."

"Ah."

"It is an amazing thing to think that now there are two of you."

"Do you mean that?"

They talked sporadically and then yielded to weariness. The first light of the coming dawn revealed Annie Tinsley asleep there in her chair by Bearman's cot. Dollar-Five was at the river keeping watch across the water. Yoakum and the brothers were still asleep. Down below the spring, a canyon wren was singing reveille. Bearman, as was his habit at daybreak, woke up, then turned carefully onto his side and stared at Annie Tinsley's perfect face.

XXIII

Near Big Canyon, April 1945

4/24/1945 Quiet. No action across the river.

J Bearman

[notepaper]
Has it really only been five days? The desert or the river or the mountains hurry up human activity by stripping it of nonessentials. The desert can kill a person in three days. Can it also restore a life in four? God, what he has done for me, and how much I love him.

On the day before Annie Tinsley was to leave, Bearman was not only the first person to wake up, but also the first person to get up. Besides being stiff, he felt much better physically than he had during the night. He kicked off the covers and swung his legs over the side of the cot, the wooden rail touching the bruises on his thighs. He took a deep breath and felt no worse than after a day digging postholes back home. "Thank God," he whispered and stood up.

The other men were still asleep. Mezcal had that effect. It would put a man to sleep and keep him there. Annie Tinsley was also still asleep. Bearman looked at her, wrapped in a wool blanket, slumped sideways, her lips parted, her hair tied in a gypsy knot, making her face look younger—the whole fragile, beautiful form of a tired, heart-sick woman turned warrior. He wondered briefly how many languages combined it would take to build a vocabulary that would capture the way she looked that morning of her last day, with the sun yet to top the peaks of the *Sierritas de Guadalupe* in Mexico and the flat where already smoke rose from cooking fires. He knew it would probably take a Shakespeare and a Cervantes, at least. As for painting, no Whistler could do it; maybe a Sargent could, or a Koerner; perhaps a camera, but he doubted it.

Bearman stooped, and with a stifled grunt, lifted her from the chair, carried her into the hut, and tucked her into his bunk. He smiled when she did not seem to awaken. How many times had he already carried her? Her lips curled in her sleep, as if even then she could read his mind. He went out and closed the door behind him.

He was breaking sticks for the fire when Yoakum rolled off his cot and stood up. He disappeared and came back, watching Bearman's posture and movements closely. Bearman's left eye was turning black.

"They give you a beating, didn't they?" Yoakum said. "I can tell by the way you move they hurt your chest."

"Kicked," Bearman said and added more sticks to the fire. "The earliest known act of a man without honor."

"Uh-huh. Let me see. Sit down a minute, John."

With a glance at the door of the hut, Bearman unbuttoned his shirt and took it off before he sat in his chair.

Yoakum noted the scarf, which had slipped somewhat overnight. "Making a collection of women's apparel?" he asked.

Bearman grimaced. Yoakum unclipped the safety pin and gave it to Bearman to hold. He felt Bearman's ribs, prodded and pushed a little and noted the duration of Bearman's discomfort by the timing of his tightened grips on the chair arm. They were brief.

"You took most of it on your arms, didn't you?"

Bearman nodded. His arms were black with bruises.

"Your ribs are all right. Two days from now, you'll hurt."

Two days from now, she'll be gone.

"Third day is always the worst for this kind of stuff," Yoakum concluded. "I'll wrap you again, and you can put your shirt back on."

The door of Bearman's little rock house opened, and Annie Tinsley stepped out into the morning. Bearman, with a newly awakened sense of her leaving, was glad to see she was wearing a blue dress rather than her riding outfit. Her leaving would be postponed by how long it would take her to change.

The men greeted her, to which she replied with a nod of her head. Her eyes were full of sleep. She looked around for the brothers and found them still in their bedrolls.

Bearman asked her how she felt, thinking of her night in the chair that was still placed beside his cot.

She looked at him but did not reply, which gave him a feeling of separation, as if she had already gone. She picked up her chair and brought it closer to the fire, for the sun was slow to reach Bearman's camp. She placed it across the fire from Bearman rather than beside him. She had yet to say anything but seemed to intentionally ignore Bearman and Yoakum, who exchanged glances.

"The ways of a woman . . ." Yoakum muttered for Bearman's ears only when the awkward silence went on.

"I heard that," Annie Tinsley said. "Who made you an expert on the ways of women? Go ahead, finish the sentence."

"Are beyond understanding," Bearman said.

She gave him a close look and said, "I guess you're the expert now, Mr. Bearman?"

"That's one," Yoakum said.

"Be careful you don't fall off that box," she said.

"That's two," Bearman said.

"Dadgum."

Annie Tinsley ignored them again and looked to where the brothers still slept. Turning back, she saw a millipede rippling along the stone bench. She watched it fixedly.

"I'll make the coffee," Bearman said. He was confused, as perhaps Annie Tinsley wanted him to be. He got up and walked past her without looking at her. She was staring at the millipede.

"Need some help?" Yoakum asked at his back, standing.

"Evidently."

Annie Tinsley continued staring at the millipede.

Inside the hut, Bearman could smell the faint scent of Annie Tinsley's shampoo. He wondered how long it would last once she was gone. Yoakum came in, looked over his shoulder, and said, "She's not happy this morning."

"Her holiday is almost over."

"Either that or she slept badly," Yoakum added.

Bearman took the percolator from the big enamelware coffee pot and handed the pot to Yoakum. "Fill it at the pump, will you?"

Yoakum took the pot and went to the pump. He took a long way around the fire circle, around the cots, halfway to the brothers' Ford, then to the pump, where he made as much noise as possible rinsing the pot and filling it. As he passed the ramada on his way back, he hawked as loud as he could and spit. Both of the brothers bolted upright and looked around to see where the trouble was. He started singing the first verse of "When Irish Eyes Are Smiling" and went on to the door of the hut.

Bearman was standing just inside, watching the still figure in her chair by the fire.

He made biscuits and put them in the big Dutch and sent Steve out to put them at the edge of the fire and scoop coals on the lid. The coffee he percolated in the pot on the left-hand burner of his kerosene stove. The other burner he used for the hominy. When the biscuits were about ready, he would make gravy from his can of lard and powdered milk. It would be the kind of breakfast that would last all day.

The gravy made, he put out aluminum plates from his cook kit and silverware and called everyone to breakfast. He was disappointed that Annie Tinsley did not offer to help him serve the others. He took his plate outside, then went back for his coffee cup.

Annie Tinsley started to get up, but Steve offered to wait on her, and she let him.

"I wanted to quirt somebody or something, and there you were."

Breakfast over, Annie Tinsley started to collect the plates, and Steve offered to help by stacking them and the silverware in the big Dutch. Together, they carried it all down to the river for a good rinse before washing them in the bucket at the pump.

Bearman pretended to be unmoved by her disregard, but when he heard their laughter drift up from the river, he poured out the remains of his coffee and went to the corral to feed the mules and the two horses penned there. Dollar-Five trailed Steve and Annie Tinsley up from the river and went to stand by Bearman. She nudged his shoulder twice but got no response. She neighed loudly and shook her mane.

"Not now." Bearman stroked her jaw absentmindedly.

Annie Tinsley spent the rest of the morning with the brothers. After a while of listening to their argumentative stories, she expressed an interest in their Ford. Steve invited her to join him on the front seat while Brother leaned over the back.

"Is it hard to drive?" she asked.

"Oh no," Steve said. "Once you know how."

"Yeah, once you know how to not run through fences." Brother chuckled.

"Shut up."

"Can we take it up the road over the top of that next ridge?"

Annie Tinsley asked.

"You bet."

They did that, and at the top, Annie Tinsley asked Steve to stop. She got out and stood in the road, gazing ahead, then back. She walked a few yards, staring at the rough surface of the road and occasionally kicking at smaller rocks as if looking for something she had dropped. The brothers watched her, then exchanged a questioning look. After several minutes, she came back to the car. She went to Steve's door and said, "Let me drive back."

Brother shook his head, but Steve wanted to know if she was sure she could handle the Ford. They had not had it for very long. She told him she was sure, if he would change the gears.

He would.

Annie Tinsley was heavy on the gas and uneven on the steering wheel so that the car caromed from berm to berm. They came down off the ridge, dust clouds following, gears grinding when Annie Tinsley was slow to depress or too sudden to let up on the clutch. All three were laughing. As they came into the camp, Steve jerked the transmission out of gear, but Annie Tinsley mistook the clutch for the brake pedal, and they almost took out one corner of the ramada and came close to going over the high bank into the river before they slid to a stop amid screams and laughter.

"Dadgum," Yoakum said, sitting under the ramada. He had drawn his Colt's as if he intended to shoot the Ford.

Bearman, already on his feet, turned away and walked past the hut and down to the river. He picked up a piece of cane as long as a pencil and began to splinter it apart as he stood there. The Rio Grande was as low and clear as he had ever seen it. The sunlight created a glare off the rippled surface in front of him and reflected the blue, almost indigo, sky upriver. The river cane swayed with a breeze, the tassels turning from golden into gray. Three children appeared from the brush across the river, one of them carrying a two-gallon bucket for water. He waved, and they waved back. On the bank in front of him were several tokens for *la Mujer del Rio.*

Bearman saw the familiar scene and at the same time saw nothing. He understood what Annie Tinsley was doing. He understood that she was postponing that inevitable moment when she would have to say goodbye to him and the others, which together had made up a kind of family. At the same time, he was jealous of the minutes they did not spend together. He had resolved to see her home that evening, but until then, he had missed her presence, her smiles and laughter, her emerging self. *Is this how it would be?*

Then she spoke from behind him. "What are you doing, Mr. Bearman?"

He dropped the shredded piece of cane and turned to her. Dollar-Five came out of the willows and checked the river before going back into the shade. Bearman suspected the mare liked the children who crossed the river with help to leave their simple gifts. He could hear the voices of the brothers and Wally Yoakum up in the camp, but he did not answer her. He just looked at her until she asked him again, "What are you doing?"

"Having fun?" he asked, more stiffly than he intended. She could see he was doing nothing.

"Steve and Phineas are good boys. Being with them meant a lot to them, and I had to have some time away from you to stop wanting to stay."

"All right."

"You know you are a hero to them. They would do anything for you."

Bearman smiled at that. He felt his shoulders loosen.

"They said they would take my things home for me in their Ford. I told them I would ride Tyler home."

She was now standing in front of Bearman, an arm's length away. Her face had that mysterious look: serious but neither sad nor angry.

"I think I want to go up on the mesa-that-is-not-a-mesa again," she said. "Will you take me up there this afternoon?"

"Yes. We'll ride our horses," Bearman said, a return to fullness that he knew would not last.

"I see the children left something," Annie Tinsley said. "Do you think they will sing for me when I'm upriver?"

"I think the desert itself would sing for you."

They held each other's gaze for a minute or so, long enough to be alone in the world. Then they went down to the river's edge, collected the gifts, and went back up the rise.

Yoakum and the brothers were under the ramada, the brothers sitting side by side on Steve's cot, facing Yoakum. Yoakum was telling a story and still holding his Colt's in his right hand, which he used to make a point, causing the brothers to sway away from the barrel each time he did so. But there were no interruptions or rabbit trails because Yoakum was telling a ghost story.

"It was my own fault to be coming back so late in the first place, you see?" He pointed with his pistol, and Brother leaned against Steve. "I had been by that cave a hundred times in the daylight and more than once in the twilight, and I wasn't expecting anything. A man looking at his footing on familiar ground doesn't expect to walk smack dab into a tree limb, does he?" He gestured with the gun again, causing Steve to lean away and Brother to duck.

"But something sure enough made me look into that black hole where a thousand years ago wandering savages had made a home. Something moved right there." Yoakum pointed with the gun, as if seeing the movement, and Steve flinched.

Brother raised his hand, and before getting permission, he asked, "Was it a panther? I'm sorry! I'm sorry."

Yoakum glared. "It was white, and it stood up like a man. It was dressed like a savage, but that wasn't all. There was a little girl standing beside him. She kind of knelt down and stood up again with something shiny in her hands. By golly, it was gold. The man give me the *come closer* wave of his hand, and the gold shone in that dark place like it was on fire. Then I looked at that little girl, and her face was the face of an owl. I drew my Colt's—"

The brothers tumbled off the cot, afraid of what was coming next, but Yoakum just laughed and holstered his pistol.

"True story," he said.

Brother asked, "What happened after you drew your gun?"

"I had a gun in my hand."

"What about the people?"

"Gone. There was nothing in that cave but dark."

Steve asked, "Did you go back in the daytime?"

"Why would I do that?"

"For the gold," Brother said.

"Son, that wasn't no leprechaun I saw in that cave. That gold would be poisoned, sure."

"What do you think, Mr. Bearman?"

"I think Mr. Yoakum was carrying more than groceries that trip, but you can go see for yourself. That cave is about two and a half miles downriver on the Texas side."

"Want to go?" Steve asked Brother.

"Right now," Brother said, and they went to their Ford for their canteens and matches since Steve had lost their flashlight.

Ready to go, Steve asked Annie Tinsley if she wanted to come along. She thanked him and used packing her things as an excuse not to.

"Just follow the river, but don't cross it," Yoakum said as they passed. He laughed.

Annie Tinsley walked over to him and put her hand on his shoulder. She was facing the other way. Yoakum felt a strike of pure sadness that had nothing to do with the present. He sighed and shook his head as if acknowledging a hopeless situation.

"Dear Wally," she said.

For an hour or so, Annie Tinsley stayed in the hut doing more sorting than packing because there was nothing to put her things in but a few crates that had held cans of baked beans. For a while, she just sat breathing in the fragrance of a man's camp. *His* camp.

By the middle of the day, after a brief luncheon of potted meat and crackers, Annie Tinsley changed into her riding habit and they started up the trail. The ride up on the mesa-that-was-not-a-mesa touched every bruise in Bearman's arms and hips and thighs, but Annie Tinsley was riding her horse behind him and that made a beautiful afternoon even more so. Dollar-Five liked the ridge but never wandered up there alone. Tyler moved up the trail like he was being made to, which he was.

At the top, they found their ledge and dismounted. Dollar-Five was free to move as she wanted. Annie Tinsley ground-hitched Tyler, and she and Bearman went to the ledge to sit down. Bearman sat to begin with but was too sore to find comfort on the hard limestone. He stood but did not like looking down at her, either. His physical pains deepened his sense of impending separation.

"Hurt?" Annie Tinsley asked him.

"Pretty much." He laughed shortly.

"Shall I stand also?"

"From now on, part of you always will. If you let it," he added. "No need at present."

"Am I so different from when we first met?"

"Not to me. You've always been just yourself to me."

"I used to be afraid of my thoughts and impulses—or not afraid so much as ashamed of what others would think. There have been so many times I haven't commented on something that amused, charmed, or angered me for fear of being singled out and ridiculed."

"And now?"

She put her hands on her hips and glared at him furiously. She looked over her shoulder to locate Dollar-Five, then whispered, "*Sho now*!" Bearman laughed in earnest but softly.

"Like that, when you're afraid, huh?" he said.

She laughed too, then broke off abruptly and looked down. "It's going to be hard, isn't it—once word gets around?"

"It already has gotten around, and you did wonderfully. I thought Henry was going to give you the deed to his ranch before he left."

"Because you were there, and Wally, and the brothers."

"Don't let our absence in the future be a weakness. We didn't do anything but watch the wonderful woman you are."

She looked down at the compliment. Bearman studied the drift of the horses as they browsed among the stunted creosote brush. Then Annie Tinsley moved and spread her riding skirt so that it covered part of the ledge beside her. "Do you think you can sit beside me on the edge of my skirt? It would be softer than bare rock. I want to tell you something without looking at you."

He sat. They were hip to hip and shoulder to shoulder. The brims of their hats touched briefly.

"After the baby was born and the rest, I let fear take over. The feeling was like when you are so afraid in the dark that you dare not move, can hardly breathe. I wasn't just afraid for myself, don't think that. I was afraid for this little human being I had brought into the world. I imagined all kinds of terrible things. Then I thought about you."

"Ma'am."

She bumped his shoulder at his stubbornness in calling her that. He gritted his teeth.

"Sorry," she said quickly.

"Forgiven."

"All right." She continued. "I began to realize that I was holding my breath for you. As the days went on, I began to despair that you wouldn't know. That you would never come, and the fear got worse until I was out of my head with it. Why should you come? Why should you care?"

"I'll tell you a secret," Bearman said quietly, moved by her confidence. "When I heard about you, I couldn't think of anything else but to get to you."

"Thank you for telling me that," Annie Tinsley said; then, after a pause, "I was dying, wasn't I?"

"Part of you was. Part of you was being born."

"How do you know that?"

"At first you were helpless as your baby; then you were petulant as a young colt; now you are a full woman. It was easy to see you becoming someone who could ride into a village under gunfire."

"I was terrified and furious at the same time."

"It took some nerve, but you were a lifesaver."

"Did my change happen because of the danger?"

"Partly."

"What else, then?" she said, wanting to hear him say it.

Bearman shook his head and stared across the desert toward Maravillas Canyon.

"Can't you say it?"

"Better not."

She tilted her head against his shoulder, and the brim of her hat flattened against the crown. Bearman hurt, but he did not move. For several minutes they remained silent on that ledge in the soft breeze with the sound of a covey of bobwhite quail as it hurried from shade to shade on the flat below them. Farther out along the river, white-winged doves called from the cane thickets. Annie Tinsley was resting her tired heart. Bearman was looking into the future. Neither one looked at the other.

Presently, Bearman said, "Morton will not let your return be easy. When he was here, he didn't seem to realize how close to death you were."

"I don't want to talk about Morton. He has never realized anything about me."

"Then don't talk about him, but forewarned is forearmed. I want you to hear his arguments in my voice before you face him. If you holler *Sho now!* he won't have any understanding. He'll think you're crazy for sure."

"I may be crazy, Mr. Bearman."

He ignored that. "Morton will try every trick he knows to break down this new self. His arguments will be blunt and harmless if you remember who you are now. He will claim, with the change in your behavior, that your mind has been permanently affected. It has been, but in a new, good way. He will say your actions have been unseemly to the point he would be ashamed to go into Alpine with you. He will accuse you of being immoral, wrong, and bad. Most of all, he will accuse you of being a terrible example for your daughter. He will hit you with all of these arguments and perhaps, worst, he will go about his business in condemning silence.

"You will have to face all of these slings and arrows and probably have no resolution because, by his standards, you have no defense. Everything he accuses you of will be true, but only for the woman you used to be, in the setting where you were raised. The sad thing is, he will feel that now he can hurt you and justify his own inability to make you happy."

She straightened up. "How do you know these things?" she asked again.

He laughed. "I only know what you teach me. I react to you as I would any other force of nature, and that makes me seem smart, when actually, I am often quite dull. I know enough to wear a hat under this sun."

She blew out her breath in denial of his last compliment.

"I remember I started to say *howdy* when I first saw you, but after that one glance, I changed to *hello*. You taught me that, so to speak. Even then."

"Maybe," she said, pensive.

"That's what I think."

"Wally said you had made up your mind to quit thinking."

"We decided it would be a good idea."

"So, what should I do?"

"Don't argue. Don't try to justify yourself. Don't apologize. Don't weaken. Raise up that little girl in the way she should go, so that she can spit in the face of the devil."

"I think I can do that. Is it all right if I think?"

"Anytime, all the time."

She lifted her face to his, and he turned his head and looked at her. Her lashes were wet. She was being brave.

XXIV

Near Big Canyon and Maravillas, April 1945

4/25/1945 Leave-takings.

J Bearman

Among millions of rocks, this one, this one.

"Ma'am"

In the late afternoon of the day Annie Tinsley was leaving Bearman's camp, high cirrus clouds drifted across the sky and caught the colors of a day trending toward sundown. A mild cold front was passing through the canyons and mountains of the Big Bend. In the open, the sun lessened the effect of the cold wind, but in the shadow of the ramada, the wind gave Bearman and Yoakum and Annie Tinsley a light chill.

For those three, the day meant rest. They were feeling the effects of their Mexico episode, especially Bearman. After their noon meal, Annie Tinsley listened for a while as Bearman and Yoakum talked about events in the Big Bend. Then she excused herself and walked down to the river. She sat on the ledge where her clothes had dried and felt the warmth of the ancient rock. Wrapping her arms around her legs, she listened to the river and the songs of the birds who lived along its banks. She looked for the ducks, but they were not on that part of the river. "*Upriver*," she said to herself.

It was impossible for her not to weigh the events of the past few days against what would be waiting when she returned to her home. She tried to imagine what Morton would say, how he would act, and she remembered Bearman's predictions about her return. She tried to look past her doubts, but more than anything else, it made her sad, as the unsatisfied hunger of the heart always does bring on sadness. She would have to guard her emotions.

Then she thought of the mystery of her child, and her imagination began to place the baby in the major events of her own life, leading up to this past week in the spring of 1945, and she felt an excitement at the prospect. She hoped that as a woman, her little girl would meet a man like John Bearman.

When she thought about him, he appeared quietly beside her. He declined to sit, still too sore, but told her she did not have to get up until she was ready. They talked about everything except how they felt about each other. It wasn't time yet. That sort of talk was best after sundown.

"It's pretty quiet across the river," Annie Tinsley said after a while, her own voice quiet.

In response, Bearman looked across the river. From his position, he saw only a wall of brush. "Last night, when I couldn't sleep, I thought about what it must be like to have that kind of cruelty and brutality where you live, without any assurance of protection or recourse."

"That poor girl," Annie Tinsley said, referring to Pulaski's daughter. "I will never forget the look of terror on her face."

Bearman shifted his gaze upriver and sighed. "Daughters," he said.

"What is that supposed to mean?"

"It means I can't imagine what it will be like, raising your own little girl to womanhood."

Annie Tinsley looked up at Bearman until he met her eyes. "Want to find out?" she said.

"Ma'am."

The brothers had spent another day exploring caves along the river.

They came back along the bank through high grass, excited at finding several arrowheads and a length of string woven from the edges of yucca leaves. They claimed they needed to get back to town and helped carry Annie Tinsley's belongings to the Ford under her supervision. Steve invited her along, but she again declined, wishing instead to ride Tyler home.

"I want you to ride home with me and say goodnight at my doorstep."

Leave-takings in the desert tended to be brief. She offered her chair to Yoakum as a gift for helping her over her breakdown, but he told her he would be going "outside" for a while and she might as well keep it, so they put it in the trunk of the Ford, the hatch of which would not close.

"I told you it wouldn't fit," Brother said.

"It'll be fine," Steve said.

"It'll be fine until it falls out."

"You want to walk to Mrs. Tinsley's place?"

"No."

"Then shut up."

"You shut up."

Bearman, Yoakum, and Annie Tinsley were standing together nearby. "They don't want to leave," Yoakum whispered to Bearman. Annie Tinsley heard him. She looked at him without speaking, and Yoakum knew she wanted to stay as well.

She hugged Steve and Brother and told them she hoped to see them again someday. They had a job building stone guardrails over culverts on the road going into the Chisos Mountains. The CCC camp there had closed down, and the area had become a national park the year before.

They shook hands with Bearman. Brother said, "If you ever need us, give us a call. There's no telling where we'll be, but we'll come on the double if you need us. General delivery in Alpine or Marathon." He sniffed and turned away.

Steve said, "Maybe we'll come anyway, Mr. Bearman. Me and Brother saw three or four more caves out there. We'll bring our own food."

Yoakum shook their hands and said he thought they were good boys, if they could ever learn to sit still. Annie Tinsley knew he was fond of the pair.

Steve said, "Thanks for not shooting us."

"Maybe next time," Yoakum replied.

Then they were gone, rattling on the grade up over the ridge and humming away into silence. Yoakum decided to build a fire against the chill of the coming night. Bearman lit his pipe and sat on the edge of his cot smoking. Annie Tinsley took his chair now. She was having trouble getting her breath. She was anxious, fearful, and heartbroken, alternately sighing and wiping her eyes.

They sat in the twilight without talking, for what was there left to say? It was so quiet they heard a beaver splash below in the river, a calf bawling, dogs barking, and always goats from the wax camps. The sky had cleared after sundown, but the moon would be late.

Finally, after a prolonged silence, Annie Tinsley said in a weak voice that she was ready to go. With tightened jaws, the men pretended they did not hear her. She stood up and said it again in a firmer voice that Bearman was glad to hear.

Yoakum stood up and went around the fire to wrap her in his arms, where he held her tightly. "My Marisa would have loved you so."

Annie Tinsley shed tears and told him not to live alone anymore, but to find his daughter. He nodded, unable to speak for a minute, then said, "It's been fun. If a certain man ever needs shootin', come get me."

"I will," she said, but she knew she would probably never see him again.

Bearman brought the horses down, let them blow and tightened the cinches. He gathered the lines on Dollar-Five while Annie Tinsley mounted Tyler. He started up the road, then realized she was not following. He turned in the saddle and saw her in the wavering firelight sitting on her horse and staring at everything in Bearman's camp, as if she would later be asked to draw a picture of it. Then she saw him waiting, blew Yoakum a last kiss, and rode up to join Bearman on the dark road home.

They spoke now and then, but not really about anything in particular: a bright planet, various near and far animal sounds, the ever-changing nature of the river.

"What do you think Wally will do?" she asked.

"He should get out of that canyon. I believe he keeps waiting for Marisa to come back, and being around you, he knows that's not going to happen. He also knows I won't be funded a partner, good as he would be."

"I hope he finds his daughter. He needs someone to love."

Annie Tinsley rode closer to Bearman the farther they went. Now and then, when her courage faltered, she would lean from the saddle and rest her hand on Bearman's arm. She would ride that way until she could recall his scent without being next to him. She asked him what he was going to do the next day and did he think he would feel well enough to do it. She wanted to know where he had grown up and if the story he had told her about the little lost girl when he was trying to get her to drink was true. Sometimes she hummed a familiar piece of music and challenged Bearman to name it. One of the tunes was "Musette's Waltz." When he did not say anything, Annie Tinsley said, "Well?"

"You rode into that village singing that song for a reason. You wanted me to understand something in case it all went bad, didn't you?"

Annie Tinsley laughed softly. *How well he knows me.*

But regardless of how long the road to the Tinsley place was, they eventually saw the dark outline of the windmill and then the buildings themselves, with a lit lantern shining from the kitchen window. They came slowly into the yard. A rooster woke up and greeted them with its shrill crowing.

"Morton knows we're here," Annie Tinsley said, and they both swung down.

She watched while Bearman unsaddled Tyler and turned him into the corral. She did not look at the house but was glad no one came out. She wondered if Esperanza was there, and her baby.

When Tyler was taken care of, they stood by the water trough as tongue-tied and awkward as school children until Annie Tinsley said, "Do you really believe your contract may soon be up?"

"In a way, I hope so," Bearman said. "The foot-and-mouth quarantine has been rough on everybody. On the other hand, it may just be getting started. If American ranchers want to build a herd, they might try to beat the quarantine to do so."

"It's been rough on you," she said.

"And you, too."

"But you may still be here."

"I might."

They were silent. Dollar-Five was looking for the rooster in the willow tree.

"So, this isn't really goodbye," she said.

"It's real enough."

"I can't come to see you? What if I have a relapse?"

"Ma'am."

"Won't you at least say my name one time?"

"It hasn't been about that."

"Of course it has."

She turned away, choking on the very real pain she felt. Bearman stood helplessly by, remembering their adventures together, their sparring. He went to her and put his arms around her shoulders. She clung to him and sobbed twice before sniffing and turning her cheek against his chest. She took a deep, shuddering breath.

Bearman said softly, wanting to be understood, "I can't call you by your first name because I care too much and shouldn't. I can't call you by your married name because I can't stand you being tied to a man too weak to fight for you and with you. Do you understand?"

She said, "The thought that you live just downriver and I can't . . . is harder for me than all the things you said I would face." She was still, then. "But as long as I know you are somewhere in the world, I will be all right."

"Do you believe that?"

"Let me."

Bearman said, "I told you I had once before seen you. It was in a certain beautiful October sunset. There will be other October sunsets and seeing them is seeing you. That is how I will be all right."

"That's not much to live on."

"You will be seeing the same sunset."

She broke the embrace and placed the palms of her hands on his chest. "Can I come over sometime and go up on the mesa-that-is-not-a-mesa? Can I listen to your arias and—?"

"Ma'am," Bearman said, his throat tight.

She laughed shortly, being brave, and he was glad.

She said, "You can be the hardest man I have ever met."

He reached into his trousers pocket and took out a small object that Annie Tinsley could barely see against the lighter shade of his palm. She thought at first it was a coin, but it was a small rock shaped by nature almost perfectly like a valentine heart. "I found this on the bank of the river the first year I was here. I want you to have it."

She took it in her hand and held it in further realization of the rarity of this man. For a moment, she wondered if he had taken her own special rock, but when she reached into her pocket, it was still there, as if waiting. She pulled it out of her skirt pocket and said, "I thought of you when I found this jewel that day you discovered me unhorsed. This rock has always reminded me of you. It kept me alive until you came to get me. I want you to have it."

Bearman took the familiar rock, rubbed his thumb across the face of it several times, then said, "Millions and millions of rocks, and then this one."

"And this one."

There was a sound from the house—a door closing. Annie Tinsley turned that way, listening. "I better go," she said.

"Be brave. You have nothing to apologize for."

"Will you say my name one time?"

Bearman snicked at Dollar-Five, and the mare came to his shoulder. He put his left foot in the stirrup and swung over into the saddle. Looking up at him, Annie Tinsley saw his form framed by a sky breathing with stars.

All the things we could have said.

XXV

Museum of the Big Bend, Alpine, September 1952

Sul Ross University is sponsoring a symposium Tuesday afternoon and evening on the ongoing effects of foot-and-mouth disease on the ranchers of Southwest Texas and Northern Mexico. One of the keynote speakers is the River Rider, Mr. John Bearman. During the quarantine, his office was to patrol the Rio Grande floodplain in search of infected cattle. He is noted for successfully ending the smuggling of infected animals along that stretch of river. . . .

A reception follows.

***Alpine Avalanche,* September 15, 1952**

Not particularly uncomfortable but restless, John Bearman told the symposium crowd of his experiences in a general way, leaving out many details of the people and the difficulties he had faced. What his audience, mostly ranchers, government men, and academics, wanted to hear, he told them. What they did not need to hear, he kept to himself.

He did not tell of his aimless ride through the spring night after he left Annie Tinsley seven years before; nor did he share with them the weight of the brooding silence in his camp while he waited for Yoakum to admit his old friend was going "outside."

"Guess she ain't coming back," Yoakum said a week later, either speaking of Annie Tinsley or Marisa, or both. "Reckon I'll drift."

"Sure."

He did not tell of the loneliness he felt after his friends and Annie Tinsley had gone. For several days, he had sat watching the river road, half hoping to see that skittish horse of hers bringing her up and over the rise to his little rock house.

He had told her not to come.

After a quiet day of patrolling the river breaks and flats, he would often sit on his bunk searching for things she had touched, wondering about her and her baby. Dollar-Five would step halfway into his little rock house, close enough to sniff and blow in his face.

Marcos Pulaski came across the river several times. "*La Mujer del Rio* is gone, eh?" Pulaski asked the first time. They had long talks and remembered the trouble. The Ornelos ranch had been seized by the government. Many, but not all, of his riders were arrested. The remainder had scattered. The ranch had been cleansed of infected cattle and goats. Lenny Carmichael, the missing agent at Black Gap, was found, along with his stolen herd, and arrested. Marcos would be taking his family soon to his home village in Zacatecas.

Bearman asked if the agent had heard anything about Wally Yoakum. Pulaski had not.

In the years that followed, Bearman took long, solitary rides across the Flats toward Maravillas Canyon on patrol but made sure to go no farther than the place along the river where he and Annie Tinsley had met and talked. It was not a trysting place. They had no trysting place. High water had taken the log Annie Tinsley rested on that day. The red color faded from her scarf. His reports from that area were sketchy at best.

He had not heard of, nor from, the brothers. *Why would I?*

He eventually sold the mules, whose ownership had reverted to him, but kept the wagon and bought a second-hand truck. Dollar-Five did not like the truck. She was left behind when he went to town. He built her a stable in the corral, and she liked that. Sometimes she followed him when he walked up the trail to the mesa-that-was-not-a-mesa, but other times she remained at the hut, watching his figure grow small against the rise. He thought of it as *Annie's Mesa*.

Tension along the border increased among the poor and hapless due to official corruption, the slaughter practice, and the spread of false information. Bearman talked about those things, though his station was mostly quiet. Cattle were no longer herded over the pass in the *Sierritas*.

In the second winter, Yoakum's box fell apart, and Bearman used the pieces to start a fire in the woodstove. The peaches girl had rubbed off by then. He rode Dollar-Five across the river in cold weather to buy firewood and fodder and visited the wax camps. Umberto told him they had to go farther for less and might have to leave the valley. One family already had. As cruel as Ornelos had been, they had never known want.

At night, Bearman would occasionally play his collection of arias from *La Bohème*, hearing, as Marcos Pulaski had suggested, "*another woman's voice*." Hers. When winter browned the desert that first year, he put the recordings away. His dream began to stop following him in the daytime.

The children who had sung for Annie Tinsley grew up. He seldom saw them but was sometimes invited to *quinceañeras* and weddings.

On lazy afternoons, he would now and then have arguments with an absent Wally Yoakum, of whom he did not hear as time went by. Absent Wally said he was ashamed of him, that he should saddle up that spoiled brat of a horse and go see her. Dadgum, anyway.

But he did not go.

Bearman pondered what to do if and when his mission along the river ended. By 1948, his friend Josh Garrison had sold off most of his cattle and was letting Angora goats eat up the forage that was left. Mohair continued to bring top dollar. Should Bearman stay along the river, try to get a job from one of the ranchers now raising Angora goats, or leave the ridge for a life outside the border valley?

He stayed, just because she did, but he never saw her.

Those who knew him slightly did not mention her or her husband, even after the wreck on Highway 90 out of Alpine that killed her husband in 1950, but he found out. It was assumed Morton Tinsley, with his poor depth perception, thought he could beat the eighteen-wheeler through the intersection. He couldn't. It was big news for a while, mostly conjecture, then it wasn't, like Bearman's connection to Annie Tinsley years before.

He waited, but the days and nights remained empty.

At the symposium, Bearman did not speak of these things and others too personal to give away, and afterward, at the reception, he was courteous but restrained, nodding rather than answering, until a young girl, with perfect brown hair and eyes, appeared beside him, boldly put her hand in his and asked softly, "Are you John? Mama says you have her heart."

"Annie."

Historical Note

Except for the facts that there were River Riders and a serious foot-and-mouth outbreak in Mexico, following an equally serious one in the Southwest during the late 1940s and '50s, this novel is a work of fiction. The historical quarantine lasted from 1943 to 1956. River Riders often lived in tents, often with their families, and coordinated with Mexican officials and veterinarians.

The curious might consider investigating the following to learn more:

Dudley Dobie. *Adventures in the Canyon, Mountain, and Desert Country of the Big Bend of Texas and Mexico*. Published by the author, 1951.

Joe Graham. "Tradition and the Candelilla Wax Industry." In *Some Still Do: Essays on Texas Customs*, edited by Francis Edward Abernethy. Publications of the Texas Folklore Society Number 39. Encino Press, 1975.

Barney Nelson, ed. *God's Country or Devil's Playground: The Best Nature Writing from the Big Bend of Texas*. University of Texas Press, 2002.

Larry McMurtry. *Horseman Pass By*. Harper, 1961.

U.S. Department of Agriculture. "Foot-and-Mouth Disease and a Collaborative Response from the U. S. and Mexico." National Agriculture Library. www.nal.usda.gov

About the Author

David Fleming, a fourth-generation Texan, was raised on a farm near San Marcos, where he attended the public schools. He graduated from Texas State with a Bachelors in Liberal Arts and an MFA in Creative Writing. He taught English and Creative Writing in Seguin High School for thirty-five years and was a pastor at New Hope Baptist Church, San Marcos, for twenty-five years. Fleming is the author of two previous TCU Press titles, *Summertime* and *Border Crossings*. He and his family enjoy the Big Bend and have been floating the Lower Canyons for the past forty years.

www.ingramcontent.com/pod-product-compliance
Lightning Source LLC
LaVergne TN
LVHW091120080826
845145LV00008B/1986

9780875659480